Wyatt

A Walker Brothers Novel

Seven Sons Ranch in Three Rivers Romance™
Book 5

Liz Isaacson

ISBN-13: 978-1-63876-366-6

1

A groan hissed from Wyatt Walker's mouth as he tried to sit up. He got his legs over the side of the bed and paused, taking a long, deep breath. If he didn't stretch before he stood up, it would be a very bad day.

And today was already a very bad day, so he didn't need his back acting up on him. Because today, he needed to be strong for Marcy, as she was burying her father in just a few hours.

His heart hurt as he stretched his right arm up and over his head, reaching toward the wall until his fingertips pressed against it. Breathing in and out, he held the stretch, finally releasing it. He repeated the motion on the other side, and then twisted side to side as much as he was able.

With the pins in his spine, he didn't have great range of mobility, but he did what he could. The last surgery was nearly five months old, but he'd endured major back surgery, and that didn't heal overnight, despite his pleas to the Lord.

"Help me today," he prayed as he got to his feet. "Help Marcy be strong." He already knew Marcy Payne was a strong woman. One of the strongest he'd ever met. But he also knew she had a soft side, and she suffered behind a mask of confidence. She'd let that down in front of him several times over the past year, and the memories from last week, when he'd found her sobbing in her father's house after he'd passed away, moved through his mind as he showered.

They'd communicated a little bit since then, but she'd been surrounded by family members, and she'd had a million things to do to prepare for the funeral. Once Martin Payne had been diagnosed with colon cancer, he'd started planning everything. But having the floral arrangements chosen didn't mean they'd be ready without phone calls and follow-up.

Wyatt had stayed away from Marcy's house, her father's place, and the hangar on the west side of town. If Marcy wanted him to come visit, bring food, or anything else, she'd call or text. She always had in the past.

Once out of the shower, he stood in front of the mirror and shaved, keeping the edges of his beard trim and neat. He brushed his teeth and got dressed slowly, making sure all the right pieces were in the exact right place.

Black slacks. White shirt. A burgundy, navy, and

white tie knotted precisely at his collar. The navy blue colon cancer pin to show his support. He'd just pulled a pair of black, shiny church shoes from his closet when someone knocked on his bedroom door.

"Yeah, Micah," he said, as he knew his brother's knock by now. Micah had moved to the ranch and Three Rivers just before Wyatt's surgery, and he was Wyatt's best friend.

"Just checking on you," he said, entering the room. "Looks like you're ready."

Micah was too, right down to the red and white paisley tie around his throat. "I'm ready," Wyatt said, inhaling the scent of coffee and sausage floating down the hall from the kitchen.

"How's the back today?" Micah asked, his keen eyes missing nothing.

So he saw the slight limp in Wyatt's step, though it evened out after only two strides. "Not bad," Wyatt said anyway. "I just want to make it through this day."

"Momma would say you need a hearty breakfast to do that," Jeremiah said, leaning into the doorway. "We've got eggs, sausage, and coffee out here."

"Yep." Wyatt smiled at Jeremiah, who welcomed everyone to the ranch, made them whatever food they wanted, and got them to stay awhile. At least that was how Wyatt had felt when he'd come to Seven Sons last year.

"How are you today?" he asked, following Wyatt

down the hall. Wyatt swallowed a sigh, because he knew his brothers meant well. But there had been a reason he hadn't told them about his injuries for almost eight months. At the same time, he was glad he didn't have to try to hide his bad days anymore.

"I'm okay," he said, turning back once he'd reached the kitchen.

"Really?" Jeremiah asked, moving past him to pick up a plate. "Because it's okay to not be okay."

Wyatt glanced at Whitney, who lay on the couch, her phone up in front of her face. She'd had a scare about three weeks ago with her pregnancy, and Jeremiah didn't let her do more than walk a few steps at a time.

"If you keep badgering me," Wyatt said as he took the plate from Jeremiah. "It'll be a double-funeral we go to in a couple of hours—and not mine." He cocked his eyebrows at his brother, who only laughed at him.

"I hear you," Jeremiah said. "I just want to make sure you're doing all right."

"I am right now," Wyatt said, but he wasn't sure what would happen when he saw Marcy. She had a couple of cousins in town, and Wyatt assumed her brother would come from back east. He couldn't remember where her brother lived, but it was a big city on the Eastern Seaboard, where he worked as a corporate attorney.

The Payne's were a Three Rivers generational family, and Wyatt expected the whole town to be at the funeral.

He wanted to see Marcy today, make sure she knew he was there and available to her.

She knows that, he told himself as he put food on his plate and took it to the kitchen table.

He had the very real feeling he wouldn't be able to spend much time with her today, at least not the way he wanted to.

Tomorrow, everyone else would go back to their regular lives. They'd get up with their own problems and go about their business. Every once in a while, they might think of Martin Payne and the daughter he left behind, but the thoughts would be fleeting and momentary. Nothing would come from them.

Wyatt didn't want Marcy to be alone tomorrow, either, and he already had an alarm set on his phone to call her tomorrow morning to check in.

The back door opened, and Liam, Callie, and their daughter Denise came inside. "See?" Liam said to the three-year-old. "I told you Uncle Jeremiah would have breakfast."

The little girl had tight, dark curls, and they bounced as she ran toward Jeremiah, who scooped her up into his arms. They both laughed, and he asked her what she wanted.

"Toast," she said, and though there was no toast on the counter, Jeremiah set about making her what she wanted.

"Dressed already?" Liam asked, glancing around. "Looks like we're the only ones not ready for the funeral."

"We have time," Callie said. "I just hope Vicki doesn't go into labor today."

Wyatt looked up from his plate, glancing between Liam and Callie. "It's that time already?"

"She's due in four days," Liam said. "So yes, any time now."

"Hopefully not today," Callie said again, and her nerves radiated off of her in every direction.

Wyatt didn't want to sit around the house, and a viewing for Martin had been scheduled for that morning. Though he'd gone last night at the funeral home, he cleaned up his breakfast dishes and said, "I'm headed out."

"Already?" Jeremiah asked, still nursing his coffee while he held Denise on his knee as she ate bits of toast.

"Already." Wyatt took his keys out of the kitchen drawer where he kept his stuff and met Micah's eye. "You want to come with me?"

"Sure thing." Micah downed the last of his coffee while Wyatt ignored the concerned looks on his family's faces. He didn't need their pity. Didn't even want it.

The moment he walked out the front door, the weight of all those eyes lifted from his shoulders, and he felt like he could breathe normally. At least for a minute. Micah joined him on the porch, the front door closing loudly behind them.

The oak tree looked forlorn without all the Christmas decorations it had worn so festively for the past six weeks. Jeremiah loved their Christmas traditions, but he wanted the ranch to "get back to normal" after the holidays too. All of the ranch hands and brothers had worked for the better part of a day to get all the ornaments off the front fence, all the tinsel out of the tree—though the Good Lord had sent plenty of wind last week to help finish that job— and all the decorations snugly in their boxes and in the storage shed out back.

"Where do you want to go?" Micah asked, his keys jangling in his hand as he went down the front steps. He didn't pause and look behind him to see if Wyatt needed help, and he appreciated that. Sometimes the way Rhett or Liam wanted to steady him by holding onto his elbow made him feel infantile. And he didn't need to deal with that on top of everything else.

Wyatt pocketed his own keys and followed Micah to his truck, as it wasn't worth the argument with his youngest brother over who drove. Wyatt would get to go where he wanted no matter whose truck they were in or who sat behind the wheel.

"The bakery," he said, using the runners on the side of the truck to get himself into the vehicle. He sighed as he settled into the seat and pulled his seat belt into place. "And that new hot chocolate shack."

Micah fired up the truck and got the heater blowing, the heated seats warming, and the radio volume adjusted.

"Sorry," he said, grinning. "I like the music loud."

"You always have." Wyatt's head hurt, and he should've taken some painkillers before leaving the house.

He thought about asking Micah to run back inside and grab some, but he didn't. Micah was good at letting Wyatt take care of himself, but if he went back inside, everyone would know why.

"Will you open that glove box and see if I have any pills in there?" Micah nodded toward Wyatt's side of the truck. He turned onto the lane and headed toward the highway. Wyatt did as he asked, thrilled when he found the little bottle of ibuprofen.

"Can I have some too?"

"Of course."

Wyatt shook a few pills into his hand and swallowed them dry. "How many do you want?"

"Three."

Wyatt counted them out and handed them to Micah, who drank from a half-full water bottle to take his pills.

"This is a terrible thing," Micah said.

"It sure is." Wyatt didn't usually mince words, and he wouldn't today either. He let Micah drive him to the bakery, through the lane to get caramel hot chocolate, and to the church where the viewing and funeral would be held.

He didn't see Marcy as he went through the line for the viewing, but he shook her brother's hand and moved into the chapel. They saved seats for everyone in the family, and Wyatt's heart leapt and jumped and rejoiced when the Payne family finally walked in.

Marcy wore a floor-length black dress, enough makeup

to hide the fact that she'd been crying, and a bright white rose on her wrist. She held her head high and her brother's hand, and she didn't even glance at Wyatt as she walked past him.

He wanted to reach for her. He wanted to reach *out* to her. He kept his hands at his sides and sat with everyone else. He wept through the songs, the talks, the advice from Pastor Daniels. He wished he could be the Savior in that moment, and take upon himself all of their sorrows, their grief, their pain.

He watched Marcy more than anyone, and she wiped her eyes several times and bowed her head once. She leaned against her brother, and Wyatt wished it was him. He had so many wishes when it came to Marcy Payne, and hardly any of them had come true.

The funeral ended, and after employing his patience once again, Wyatt left the chapel with his brothers and their wives, their children, and everyone else in Three Rivers.

"Are you going to the cemetery?" Micah asked.

"Yes," Wyatt said, deciding on the spot. He shed his jacket as he left the church, as he ran hot almost all the time, and the sun was out, albeit a weak, early-January light and warmth from above. "I can go alone," he said. "If you want to go back to the ranch with someone."

Liam and Callie were going that way, as were Jeremiah and Whitney, and all their ranch hands. Someone would have a seat if Micah wanted it.

Micah said, "I'll come."

Relief filled Wyatt, as he didn't really want to go alone. He didn't function at his best while alone, but he could do it. He'd usually traveled with other cowboys, a trainer, and his manager while he ran the rodeo circuit, but he sometimes had to go by himself. He could stand near the back of the crowd at a cemetery.

Marcy's brother dedicated the gravesite, and four planes flew over the cemetery. Wyatt looked up at the crop-dusters, a sense of peace filling him. Martin had dedicated his life to flying and dusting the fields, farms, and ranches surrounding Three Rivers, and the fly-by was a nice tribute to him.

He didn't dare talk to Marcy at the cemetery, and he and Micah left as soon as the family started putting their corsages and boutonnieres on the casket. He wept openly on the way back to the truck, his heart so full.

"You okay?" Micah asked as they got in the truck.

"Fine," he said, wiping at his eyes. "Thank you, Micah."

"Of course." They drove back to the ranch in silence, and Wyatt beelined for his bedroom the moment they stepped inside the homestead. He just wanted to be alone.

No, what he really wanted was for Marcy to call him. He knew she was having a late lunch at her house after the ceremony at the cemetery, but he didn't want to go. He didn't want to comfort her in front of everyone. He wasn't even sure she wanted him to comfort her.

Wyatt

Frustration filled him over the situation, and he shed all of his fancy clothes and lay down in bed. Maybe a nap would clear his head. Maybe then he'd know what to do about the beautiful blonde who'd crawled into his heart the moment he'd met her, over a year ago.

2

Marcy Payne hated the way her vision blurred. She hadn't been able to see properly all day. Her head felt too hot while the rest of her body was definitely too cold. Her skin cracked when she smiled, but she wasn't sure if that was from the excess makeup or the salty tears she'd cried. And cried, and cried.

But she'd made it through the funeral phone calls. Most of the decisions had been made while Daddy was still alive, but there had been a lot of emails, phone calls, and texts that had needed to happen once he'd passed. Flights booked. Dresses bought. Flowers delivered.

She took in the dozen or so vases sitting on her kitchen counter, her eyes moving to the one filled with red, white, and pink roses. That one had come from Wyatt Walker, and she'd cried a quart from the simple sight of her favorite flowers and Wyatt's scrawled, cowboy handwriting on the card.

I'm here if you need me, sugar. Love, Wyatt.

Out of all the cards that had come with the condolences over the past week, Marcy had kept only Wyatt's.

She had not reached out to him. She wasn't sure why she hadn't, only that she had enough balls in the air, and she couldn't stand the idea of him falling to the ground and cracking. She'd broken up with him once before— maybe twice, if her telling him she couldn't have a relationship while she dealt with her father's health counted.

He'd stayed away for a while, eventually coming back every few weeks. And over the summer, their romance had really blossomed.

"That's it," Bryan said, drawing Marcy's attention away from the roses. He closed the front door and looked at Marcy.

She smiled, the gesture wobbling on her face. "Thanks, Bry." Drawing in a deep breath, she surveyed the house. The sink was full of dirty dishes, and the dishwasher was filled with clean ones. She should've served lunch on paper plates, but she hadn't been able to. This was her father, and he deserved more than paper plates for the last meal memorializing him.

"Are you going to take off?" she asked. Daddy's death and funeral had come at a terrible time for him, as he was involved in a huge, important case in Washington D.C.

where he lived and practiced law for one of the biggest firms in the country.

"Unfortunately, I have to," he said, walking toward her. He had the same sandy hair as their father, the same dark green eyes. Marcy had inherited more of their mother's lighter blonde hair, which she enhanced with Golden Sunshine dye every couple of months. She also had blue eyes instead of green, and her father had often said how much he loved seeing her after their mother died, because then he could see a piece of her too.

Her chest constricted, but she held back the sob. She didn't want her brother to go. Then she'd be all alone in Three Rivers. No parents. No siblings.

Your cousins are here, she told herself, and that did bring some consolation.

Bryan wrapped her in a hug, and she clung to him. "I love you, sis," he said. "Please let me know what I can do."

"I will," she said. She'd turned over Daddy's estate to the lawyers, as he had quite a few things to go through. The house. The land. The business. The airplanes. Marcy had known about the estate planning lawyer, and she'd notified Nick Marlow as soon as all the family had been made aware of Daddy's death.

Bryan exhaled, bent to pick up his bag, and went out the front door too. Marcy flinched with the finality of the click and turned to survey her house again. It was a mess, which wasn't that different from when she lived there alone. She could pile up coffee cups and soda cans on an end table until there wasn't a spare inch before she'd finally haul a trash bag into the living room and clean it up.

Her thoughts again turned to Wyatt, who'd come out to the hangar several times to sit with her while she worked. But sitting was hard for him, and he'd gone around picking up trash and discarded mechanic rags, setting the washing machine, and making her heart glad.

She had to go through Daddy's house. Meet with the lawyers. Go visit the cemetery and make sure the headstone she'd ordered was correct. Not only that, but she hadn't been in the air since Daddy had died, and the work at Payne's Pest-free had been piling up. And up, and up.

She had to fly tomorrow, as people were sympathetic for a time. After that, they just wanted what they'd paid for. Marcy wanted to fly anyway, as the only place where she'd ever felt perfectly in place and at peace was in the cockpit of an airplane, soaring over the good state of Texas.

Her black maxi dress floated around her legs and feet as she started cleaning up. Exhaustion pulled through her, but she didn't want to be here alone. She couldn't stand the thought of going down the hall and sleeping in her bedroom alone.

Before Daddy had died, she'd craved being able to come home and go to bed alone. She'd spent the better part of the last year going straight to his house after work and staying with him until he fell asleep. Heck, sometimes she fell asleep at his house too, and she'd spent more than one night on his couch.

Her tears started afresh as she emptied the dishwasher and reloaded it, put a detergent pod in the compartment, and tried to start it. The buttons didn't light up, and she opened the door and slammed it closed again. "Just start," she said, jabbing at the buttons without looking at them. The machine did not start, and her irritation grew. She didn't have time for this. There was laundry to do, and a hamster to feed, and garbage. And, and, and.

Someone knocked on the door, but Marcy didn't want another casserole. Food didn't fix anything. She didn't have room for more flowers. They did nothing to fill the hole that now existed in her soul.

She held very still, hoping whoever had come to the door would assume she was asleep or away, and they would leave.

"Marcy," she heard, and her heartbeat buzzed through her bloodstream. That was Wyatt's voice. "Open the door, sugar. I know you're here."

How could he possibly know? Her car was at her father's house, and she'd been riding with Bryan for the past week.

She took a couple of steps toward the door, and then paused. She didn't want to see Wyatt with streaked makeup on her face. Her house an absolute mess. What a wreck she'd become since her father's death.

He already knows, she told herself as he knocked

again. He'd been the one to find her at her father's house, with her deceased dad on the couch. She hadn't been able to do anything after Daddy's last breath, and without Wyatt, she wondered if she'd still be in that living room, crying on the floor.

Marcy walked over to the front door and opened it. Sure enough, tall, dark, beautiful Wyatt Walker stood there. She'd seen him at the funeral, wearing his white shirt and tie, as well as his brand of cowboy hat. His actual brand, as he was one of the most-winning cowboys to ever enter the rodeo circuit, and he had sponsors from here to Calgary, even now that he was retired.

The man was made of gold, from his broad shoulders and hard muscles, to the pure concern in his eyes.

Concern for her.

Marcy wasn't sure what she'd done to attract this man's eye, as he could literally have anyone he wanted.

"Hey," he said, obviously nervous. It was laughable that *she* made *him* anxious when he was the celebrity bull rider, when he was the one with international sponsors, when his face appeared in TV commercials, when he was the one with a western wear clothing line.

She glanced up at his cowboy hat, wishing she hadn't broken up with him before the hats had hit the market. "Hey," she finally managed to say.

"Can I come in?"

"I'm tired, Wyatt." She leaned into the door as if she needed to prove it to him.

"Me too," he said. "Tired of waiting for you to call me." He took a step forward. "Please. Thirty minutes. I had a feeling I should come see you, and I couldn't ignore that."

She was tired of pushing him away, and she didn't want to be alone. Besides, who was she to tell him his prompting to come see her was wrong? So she backed up and let him step past her and into the house.

"Thanks." He paused and surveyed the scene before him, and Marcy wondered what he saw. "How are you holding up?"

Marcy didn't want to answer that question, so she just exhaled and went back into the kitchen. She didn't want to entertain anyone right now. She told herself that Wyatt had come out to the hangar several times and simply stayed with her. They didn't have to talk all the time.

"I miss you," he said next, and Marcy's anger sparked.

She glared at him and snatched up the trash bag. She could put napkins and envelopes and half-eaten sandwiches in a bag while he watched. He made no move to clean up, and Marcy poured her last remaining energy into picking up the house.

She moved a jacket someone had left, and she stubbed her toe against the coffee table. She cried out and more tears—more blasted tears—flowed down her face.

"Marcy," Wyatt said, but she didn't look at him. She finished in the living room and turned to the dining room.

He moved out of the way as she started picking up lemonade cans and sweet tea packets from the table.

The trash made a clunking sound as she set it on the ground. She moved into the kitchen and started running the hot water. She could wash the remaining dishes while he watched, though she hadn't planned to do that.

"Marcy," he said again. "Will you just stop for a second?"

"No," she said. "I have to go to work in the morning, and I don't have a maid."

Wyatt probably did, though she knew he lived with his brothers and only had his bedroom to keep clean.

"What do you want me to do?" he asked.

Marcy dropped the silverware she held in her hand, and it made a horrible clanging sound against the plates there. "Why are you here?" She turned toward him, her despair spiraling out of control. She hated this feeling, and she wished he hadn't come. Why couldn't he just leave her alone?

"I want to offer you support," he said. "I know you—"

"Support?" Marcy shook her head, the idea almost laughable. "No, Wyatt, you're not here to support me. You're here for *you*. You're here because you want to ask me to dinner. You want me to be your girlfriend."

He glowered at her and folded his arms. "I do want all of that, but that's not why I'm here."

"Right." She turned back to the sink and plunged her hands into the water. But it was far too hot now that it had been running for a while, and she yelped as she pulled her hands back. Wyatt arrived at her side a moment later, and Marcy couldn't help crying.

"It's okay," he said, handing her a towel. He turned off the water and curled her into his chest. "It's going to be okay."

Marcy opened her mouth to argue, because she could not see how a world without either of her parents in it was ever going to be okay. But all she could do was suck at the air as she started to sob. And sob, and sob.

Wyatt held her close and tight, and she let him, because she needed someone to do it. Bryan had left. Her cousins had families and lives to get back to. The huge turnout from the people living in Three Rivers had comforted her, but they'd all move on with their regular lives too.

Marcy didn't have a regular life anymore. Not one she recognized, at least.

Wyatt began to hum, and his bass voice soothed her. "Come on, sugar," he said. "It's time for bed."

Marcy wasn't sure how long they'd been standing in her kitchen, the sink full of dirty dishes sitting in hot water, but she knew it wasn't time for bed. But she let Wyatt lead her down the hall to her bedroom. She was aware of him opening a couple of drawers and then handing her a pair of pajamas.

He left the room, and she somehow changed. He

knocked before re-entering the room, and he held a glass of water and a couple of pills. "Painkillers," he said.

Marcy didn't want them. "They can't get rid of this pain," she whispered.

"I know, baby. Take them anyway."

She did, and she crawled under the covers. Wyatt laid down with her, a groan pulling through his throat as he did. She curled into his chest and listened to his heart beating. He breathed deeply, and she tried to match her breathing to his.

Finally—*finally*—she drew a breath full of peace and calm, both things she hadn't felt in twelve long months. "Thank you, Wyatt," she murmured just before she fell into unconsciousness.

———

When she woke, she was alone, and panic pulled through her sharply. She sat up with a gasp, searching the darkness for some clue as to where she was.

"It's okay," Wyatt said again, and Marcy looked toward the sound of his voice. He sat in the recliner in her bedroom. "You're safe, Marce."

Marce.

She loved the nickname he used for her, and she sighed as she swung her feet over the side of the bed. "What time is it?"

"Late," he said. "I didn't want to leave you alone."

Reaching over, she fumbled for a moment before snapping on the lamp on her nightstand. Their eyes met, and pure gratitude streamed through Marcy. Everyone else had left her. Wyatt had not.

"Will you be okay now?" he asked. He looked as exhausted as she felt. She wanted him to stay, but she wanted him to get the rest he needed too.

"I'll be okay," she said.

Wyatt got up, pain moving across his face, and stepped over to her. He swept his lips along her hairline and said, "I'll bring breakfast to the hangar in the morning. I won't stay. I know you'll be really busy." With that, he walked out of her bedroom, leaving Marcy to wonder why she'd tried to push him away. Again.

She also needed a plan for tomorrow morning, because she still wasn't sure she was ready for a real relationship with Wyatt Walker. At least not the kind he obviously wanted. She needed to figure out how to live in this new world first. She needed to keep her crop dusters running. She had all the cleaning and estate sorting to do.

She wondered if she actually had room for Wyatt in her life right now, and she certainly didn't think so.

So she'd just tell him tomorrow. With everything else already weighing on her conscious, she couldn't have her poor treatment of a good man adding to it.

3

Wyatt pulled up to the hangar bright and early the next morning. Marcy's car was already there, and the sausage and egg sandwiches he'd brought weren't going to stay hot forever. But he didn't get out of his truck, instead taking a few moments to survey the land and to see if he could see through any of the windows.

He couldn't, as the wind out here on the west side of town could take dirt and blast it against a building, creating a film that was impossible to get off and hard to see through.

His back didn't protest today as he got out of the truck, probably from his long afternoon nap yesterday. It was due to that nap that he'd been able to sit up in Marcy's bedroom while she slept too.

His heart hurt for the woman, and he honestly had no idea what she was going through. He'd spent most of his

23

vigil over Marcy praying for clarity, for guidance, for the best way to help her. His conscience—and the Lord—wouldn't let him leave until Marcy had woken up, and then he'd driven home under the darkest of Texas skies.

"Knock, knock," he said as he opened the door that led into the hangar. Marcy wasn't there that he could see, and the light in her office wasn't on. Wyatt sighed, because if he'd let her, she'd go right back to avoiding him.

"Maybe you should let her," he muttered to himself. He had to get out to Three Rivers Ranch, as he'd taken plenty of time off from the horses at Bowman's Breeds since his surgery. He didn't need the money, but he sure did love spending his time with horses and people who loved horses.

Ethan and Brynn were both rodeo champions, and maybe Wyatt liked that he still had a tie to the world he'd loved. He didn't want to go back to the circuit, but sometimes, he did miss it.

He'd belonged there, and Wyatt was still trying to find his way in the regular world.

He walked toward her office and went inside to set the food on her desk. He'd told her he'd come this morning, and he was a little surprised she wasn't there. A bright pink note had been stuck to the computer monitor, and Wyatt reached for it when he saw his name on it.

I had to fly, Marcy had written. *I'm so behind on my fields. Thank you for coming last night, and thanks for breakfast.*

She'd squeezed the last few words on the side of the note, and Wyatt couldn't help smiling as he turned the paper over to see if she'd written any more. On the back of the note, she'd drawn a heart and left the letter M.

Wyatt's heart skipped a beat, which was utterly ridiculous, he knew. But that heart was almost like her opening the door and saying, "Please come back into my life, Wyatt. I sure do like you."

He grabbed the pen on her desk and laid the bag of food down so he could write on the top. *Sorry I missed you. Please call me with anything you need. Anything.*

Mimicking her, he drew a heart and left a W, noting that his first initial was hers inverted. Wyatt had always been a romantic at heart, and his chest warmed at the thought of having a real relationship with Marcy.

He left the hangar then, because if she was already in the air, she wouldn't come down for hours. He continued to Three Rivers Ranch, finally pulling up to the stables where he'd been working for almost a year about an hour later.

This ranch held as much life as Seven Sons, and Wyatt sometimes thought more. It was a much bigger operation than the one Jeremiah ran, and it had two homesteads, with fourteen cowboys who lived full-time on the ranch. Three full families, all of them with children. Wyatt supposed that with Jeremiah and Whitney due to have a baby that summer, and Liam and Callie getting their foster kids, Seven Sons would be caught up with Three Rivers soon enough.

Not that it was a race.

"Morning, Wyatt," someone said, and he pulled himself out of his thoughts as Kenny walked by.

By the time he said, "Morning," the other cowboy was out of earshot.

"There you are," another man said, and Wyatt turned toward the familiar voice.

A smile bloomed on his face as he reached for Bennett Patterson's hand. "Hey, Ben." They shook hands briefly and Wyatt pulled the other man into a quick hug. "How was your New Year?"

"Oh, you know," Bennett said, sighing.

Wyatt did know, because Bennett was struggling with a lot of the same things Wyatt was. Loneliness. Wondering if the reality he lived in was all he was going to get in his life. Not being satisfied with that. Wanting more. Wanting a wife and family.

"Yeah," he said. "Where are you today?"

"Beau and I are riding out to the north cabin. We won't be back until the weekend."

"So I guess you can't do lunch today." Wyatt grinned at his friend.

"We'll let you buy on Saturday," Bennett said with a smile as he glanced up at Wyatt's hat. "And hey, thanks for the cowboy hat. My brothers were so jealous."

"You're welcome," Wyatt said easily. "If they want, I can get them—"

"Oh, no," Bennett said. "You're not getting everyone in my family one of your hats. This is my only claim to fame, Wyatt."

"Oh, jeez," Wyatt said, pushing his hat forward. "I'm not famous."

"You totally are, in the right circles." Bennett started walking as Wyatt did. "I mean, look at that woman." He lowered his voice and kept his head turned away from the woman working with the two thoroughbreds in the front circle. "She hasn't taken her eyes from you since you got out of your truck."

"You didn't even see me get out of my truck." Wyatt watched the woman—her name was Tara Baylor—and she did seem to glance over at him and Bennett a lot.

"But she did." Bennett chuckled. "She totally thinks you're famous."

"Okay," Wyatt said with plenty of warning in his voice. "That's enough from you. Go out to the north cabin and work up your appetite for fajitas on Saturday."

Bennett laughed, and Wyatt smiled as he turned and headed toward the ranch. "I'll tell Beau."

"Sounds good." Wyatt touched the brim of his cowboy hat and faced the entrance barn to Bowman Breeds. The first time he'd come here, he'd been impressed by the professional atmosphere of the breeding stables. Brynn

Bowman had a passion for horses that included making sure their health remained the number one priority.

She sold the horses she raised and trained to cowboys and cowgirls for competition in the rodeo, and her bull riding husband, Ethan had moved over from his work on the ranch to his wife's operation. He trained horses for bronc riding, and they'd both been thrilled to take on Wyatt to train roping horses and calves, for that matter.

Wyatt had competed in a lot of rodeo events, including the bull riding that had won him millions. He liked bronc riding too, but neither of those could feasibly be done with his back. So the last few years of his career had been dedicated to roping, both calf roping and team roping, and he loved the feel of a length in his hand, the wind kicking up the dust as they got the animals set in the gates.

He could practically taste the energy from a crowd, and a keen sense of missing wound through him as he thought about his days in the rodeo.

"Hi, Wyatt," Tara said, and Wyatt switched his attention to her.

He put a smile on his face. "Morning, ma'am." He wasn't so blind that he didn't see her soften and sigh, but he didn't want to go out with Tara. Ever since he'd moved to Three Rivers and Seven Sons Ranch, the only woman he wanted was Marcy Payne.

He lifted his hand in a wave and ducked into the barn that served as the administration and front offices of

Bowman Breeds. A woman named Jenn ran the front desk, and she barely glanced at Wyatt as he stepped behind the desk to get out his timecard.

"My brother loved his hat," Jenn said. "You made me a real hero."

Wyatt chuckled, because he was tired of being told thank you for the cowboy hats. The NPRA and Wiseman Western Wear had given him whatever he'd asked for, and Wyatt had sent in a request for three hundred cowboy hats. He'd given one to everyone he knew, for them, their brothers, their fathers, whoever. And he still had twenty-five of them stored in the attic at the homestead.

"I'm glad," he said to Jenn. He tucked his timecard back into its pouch and added, "I guess I'm out in the gates today."

"I'll let Brynn know," she said. "Oh, wait. I have a note here for you."

"A note?"

"Yeah, I guess Squire dropped it off for Jeremiah."

Wyatt's hopes crashed to the earth, and he couldn't believe he'd actually thought it might be from Marcy. She'd never called Bowman's Breeds and left him a note before, because she had his cell phone number.

"Thanks." He took the card with Jeremiah's name on it and left through the back door. Fences ran along both sides, creating a sort of alleyway to the next barn. Then the horse stables beyond that. There were breeding pens, and a maternity wing at Bowman's Breeds, as well as a stud sector that Wyatt hardly ever visited.

And then pastures and training facilities as far as the eye could see. Brynn and Ethan had started small and expanded the operation as they had time, help, and money. The first week Wyatt had worked here, he'd offered to donate to their operation monetarily, as he'd just been so impressed with it.

So many training and breeding facilities didn't even treat the animals properly, and it warmed Wyatt's soul to find one that did. If he could help their cause, he would.

Brynn had initially declined his offer, but over the past year, she'd been working on buying more land from the ranch so they could put in more cattle training grounds. Most people didn't know or even consider how much the rodeo relied on livestock. And that livestock needed to be raised and trained with respect, and then honored when they performed—just like Wyatt was.

He hadn't been to work since he'd found Marcy in her father's living room, and he expected to find a mountain of tasks to be completed. Other cowboys tended to his horses and cattle while he was away, but no one took care of his animals the way he did.

The morning passed as he cleaned stalls and troughs and gave his cows and horses special treats. "Yeah, I missed you guys," he said, giving an extra butterscotch candy to Maleficent, a pure black horse who would win championships for her rider one day. She was tall and broad, and Wyatt had been training her to do calf roping and steer wrestling. She never balked, and she could hold the rope no matter how badly he'd thrown it.

The scent of hamburgers filled the air, and he looked east, where the main homestead on the ranch sat. Squire and Kelly Ackerman lived there, and Wyatt had eaten at their table, along with dozens of other cowboys and cowgirls, dozens of times over the past twelve months. And it seemed like today, he could again.

With everyone clean and fed and happy in their stalls, Wyatt washed his hands and joined a couple of other cowboys as they walked over to the homestead. He laughed and talked, but they were just motions he went through. He didn't feel like he was part of the festivities, because he still had so much turmoil inside him.

Didn't these people know there had been a funeral yesterday? Did they know his back had started to ache, and that if he sat down, he might not be able to get back up?

Everyone had problems, he knew that. His phone buzzed in his back pocket, and he couldn't help getting his hopes up. He ignored the device, though, and went to stand at the end of the table where Ethan Greene sat with his wife, Brynn, and their two boys—both of whom were wearing Wyatt's hats.

"Wyatt!" one of them said.

"Hey, Josiah," he said. "Hey, Bosses."

"Wyatt." Brynn stood up and drew him into a hug. He

couldn't lie and say that didn't feel nice. He did feel like he belonged to Brynn and Ethan, and that was something, he supposed. Ethan stood and clapped Wyatt on the shoulder as he hugged him too.

"How's Marcy?" Ethan asked, going right for the jugular.

Thankfully, before Wyatt had to answer, Will, their other son, said, "You shoulda seen me ridin' this horse, Wyatt. He was wild, and I kept 'im right against the rail."

Wyatt chuckled and looked at the boy, who was probably only eight or nine years old. "Yeah? What's his name?"

"Haven't named 'im yet," the boy drawled. "Daddy says we have to wait and see his personality."

"Smart." Wyatt exchanged a glance with Ethan, who was grinning and seemed so proud of his son.

To keep the emotion from choking him, Wyatt took a bite of his hamburger while Ethan started to talk about the phone call he'd gotten that morning.

"We have buyers coming this whole week," he said. "You'll be in, Wyatt?"

"Every day," he said.

"How's your back?" Brynn asked.

"Fine, ma'am." Wyatt didn't want to talk about his back. When he'd first told Ethan and Brynn about his surgery, they'd said he could have as long as he needed to recover. And he'd taken it. He had no problem texting them when he woke up in the morning if he couldn't make it to the ranch.

"Now that everyone is getting back to training, they want horses," Ethan said. "And I told them we've had Wyatt Walker with us for a year, training up roping horses."

Wyatt smiled and popped a couple of chips in his mouth, sure he wouldn't have to respond to that. What was he supposed to say anyway?

"I set up a demo tomorrow at ten," Ethan said. "Does that work?"

"Yep." Wyatt took another bite of his burger.

"The horses will be ready?"

Wyatt looked at Ethan and nodded, still chewing.

"The calves?"

"Yes." He looked at Brynn. "Does he not know what *yep* means? I said I'd be here and that the demo at ten would work."

Brynn started giggling, but Ethan's eyes sharpened. "Wyatt, I've been bragging you up. You'll ride, right?"

"Yes," he said with as much enunciation as he could. "I'll demo the horses and the calves. I'll be in the saddle." He realized all at once what was really going on. "Oh, no. You've invited more than just potential buyers, haven't you?"

"Ethan," Brynn said sharply, and it sounded like this was news to her too.

"Just a couple of people," Ethan said. "Babe, if we

want Bowman's Breeds to be the premier breeding stable and livestock provider, we need some press coverage."

"Press coverage," she repeated as if she didn't know what the words meant. But Wyatt did, and he'd need to press his jeans tonight and buy a new shirt on the way home too. He'd probably need to do some wrist exercises, as he hadn't done his signature cowboy hat wave in a while.

He was tired just thinking about performing for the cameras again. He'd spent so much of his life doing it, and he needed more time to gather his chi together. "You should've told me weeks ago," he said. "I know stuff like this doesn't happen with one phone call."

"You were dealing with a lot," Ethan said. "I wasn't even sure you'd be back."

"So what were you going to do if he wasn't?" Brynn asked in a somewhat shrill voice.

"It doesn't matter," Ethan said. "He's back, and the horses and calves are ready." He grinned around at everyone, his sons included.

Wyatt didn't return the smile and finished his hamburger instead, taking way too big of a bite. But he needed to be done with lunch so he could get back to the training grounds and make sure his animals really were ready for tomorrow's demo.

As he saddled Maleficent, he told her about the people coming to see her tomorrow. "And you have to do real good," he said. "Even if you don't want to leave me." He didn't want her to get bought and go with someone else, but she deserved to show the world what she could do.

And besides, Wyatt was used to the good things in his life ending. At least that was what he told himself.

By the time he finished with the horses and calves, bought a new shirt for the demo, and made it back to Seven Sons, he remembered to check his phone. Marcy had not called or texted, and he wondered if he should count her as one of the good things in his life he didn't have anymore.

"You'd probably be happier," he muttered, though his heartbeat started thrashing against his ribs, protesting that they would most definitely *not* be happier without Marcy in their lives.

As if summoned by his pounding heart, his phone rang, and her name sat on the screen.

4

Marcy had thought she could make it through today without crying.

She'd been wrong.

But these tears were not tears of sadness, loss, or misery. Oh, no. These tears were borne from anger. Pure, unadulterated fury.

And why wasn't Wyatt answering? He'd said she could call about anything, and she had a doozy.

"Miss Payne?" a man behind her asked, and she held up one hand in a universal sign of *I need a moment, please.*

She'd already asked for a few minutes to make a phone call and get some air. Catch her breath. She couldn't actually remember what she'd said to the estate lawyer.

"Hey," Wyatt finally said, his voice a little breathless. Maybe she'd interrupted him. "What's goin' on, sugar?"

"Wyatt," she said, something about his voice calming

her. But she didn't want to be calmed right now. Well, she did, but only so he wouldn't hear the tears in her voice.

"Yes," he said. "This is Wyatt Walker, at your service, ma'am." He really drawled out the words in that cowboy Texas drawl that would've made Marcy laugh a year ago.

Today, it still made her smile.

"I have something I need to talk to you about," she said. "Are you home already?"

"Just pulled up."

Marcy lifted her hand to her mouth and bit her thumbnail. She hadn't chewed her nails since she was a teenager and was learning how to fly airplanes. They'd made her nervous at first, thus the nail-chewing.

And what she had to talk to Wyatt about was as equally as unsettling as learning to fly an airplane when she was fourteen years old.

"Are you going to spit it out, Marce? Or am I supposed to guess?" He chuckled, sobering quickly. "Are you in trouble? Do you need me to come get you somewhere?"

"Yes," she blurted out. "I'm in trouble, and I need you to come get me."

"I'm on my way." She could actually hear his truck's engine roar as he stepped on the accelerator. "Tell me where."

Oh, how she loved that he could and would come whenever she called. He'd always been so good to her in that regard, and she once again wondered what about her was special to him.

"I'm downtown," she said. "The law offices of Marlow and Brandow."

"Law offices? Marcy, maybe you should tell me what's going on."

She turned around and found the shadowy figure of Nick Marlow lurking just inside the doors. He'd handled her father's estate, and he'd started going through all of the paperwork to get things sorted out.

She'd had four messages from him before she'd landed for her first refueling, and she'd called him back only to arrange their late-afternoon meeting. At least she'd finished her dusting for the day before the bomb had been dropped on her.

"Nick Marlow is my father's estate planner," she said. "He's been going through the initial will and stuff."

"Okay." Wyatt dragged the word out, clearly not getting it. And why would he? Marcy had sat in the meeting, and she still didn't understand.

In fact, Mr. Marlow had explained it four times, and then leaned toward her and said, "Miss Payne, what it means is you have to be married in order to inherit the crop-dusting business."

She'd started hyperventilating at that point, claimed she needed a minute to get some air, and fled the room.

She couldn't tell him this over the phone. Why he'd been the one she'd first thought of to call, she wasn't sure. She should've called Bryan, or one of her cousins.

But she'd called Wyatt.

"I'm on my way," he said. "You're okay to wait?"

She eyed Mr. Marlow through the glass. "I'll be here." She hung up, something in the back of her mind telling her that she'd called him, because she hoped he could offer a solution to her brand-new, colossal-sized problem.

She knew the solution—a proposal. And the only man in Marcy's life was Wyatt Walker.

This is so stupid, she thought as she went to open the door.

It was locked, which surprised her, and Mr. Marlow had to open it. "We're closed now, Miss Payne."

She shivered in the January evening. The sun had set while she'd been on the phone with Wyatt, and a new brand of helplessness filled her. "Don't I need to come in and sign something?"

He held the door open for her. "There's nothing for you to sign today."

"Even so I can list the house for sale?"

"Well, that's true. You can sign the release papers on the personal property and assets."

"I can email them to Bryan to get his signature." She stepped inside, out of the wind. "He's in the middle of a big case in D.C., and I'll be handling everything." The weight of the world rested on her shoulders, and it felt so heavy. Somehow, she could still walk, and she followed Mr. Marlow down the hall to the conference room she'd run from twenty minutes ago.

"As soon as he signs," Mr. Marlow said. "You can do

whatever you need to with the personal assets. The house. The belongings. The land. All of that."

Marcy pursed her lips, everything in her drawing tight. "And the business...to get that, I have to be married."

"I'm sorry, Miss Payne," he said, and his expression actually looked sorrowful. "I did try to tell him that was an antiquated thing, and that he would regret it."

"Well, he's dead now, so how could he regret it?" Marcy snapped. She immediately regretted the words, and she sighed.

Mr. Marlow didn't react at all. He probably had angry clients yelling at him all the time. "And you should know he did that for the business ten years ago. I think he hoped it would encourage you to get out of the cockpit and into the dating scene."

Marcy said nothing, because the words piling up in her head were not nice. She'd loved her father with everything inside her, and she didn't want to be angry with him now, of all times. But honestly, how in the world would she have been able to get married ten years ago?

At twenty-six, she'd just finished airplane mechanics at the trade school in Amarillo. She'd been working on all their planes since, and Daddy had started training her on the business side of things a few years later.

The condition that she be married was *ludicrous*. Absolutely *ridiculous*.

And then Mama had died, and Marcy and Daddy had bonded over that. Never once had he said he'd put in his will that in order for Payne's Pest-free to pass to her, she'd need to be married. Why did it matter anyway?

"Anyway." Mr. Marlow cleared his throat. "You have six months, so if you have a boyfriend, you might want to talk to him about it."

Heat filled Marcy's face, and she hastily scrawled her name on the paper to release the personal assets. Mr. Marlow made a copy for her and she said she'd send it to Bryan that night. As she hustled out of the office building, another round of frustration and tears went with her.

Wyatt had not arrived yet, but Marcy wasn't going to wait inside for another moment. She tugged her coat tighter around her and looked up in the sky. If she was out at the hangar, she'd be able to see every star in the sky for miles and miles.

But here, in downtown Three Rivers, at barely six o'clock, plenty of businesses were open, and light spilled up into the sky, masking the stars.

Several minutes later, Wyatt pulled up in his big, black truck. Marcy stepped toward the vehicle before he'd eased it all the way to a stop, because her whole body was shaking with the cold.

"Have you been waiting on the sidewalk this whole time?" he asked. "I've got your seat warmers going." He reached for the knobs on the dash, and a moment later, a blast of heated air hit her.

She calmed instantly, partly because of the heat. But

mostly because Wyatt had arrived, and Wyatt would take care of her.

Just the fact that she thought that surprised her. The fact that it was true was not surprising. Wyatt possessed such a calm demeanor that Marcy didn't think there was anything the man couldn't do.

"Thank you," she said, because she suddenly found she couldn't tell him about the stipulation in Daddy's will.

"Where to?" he asked, both hands on the wheel, ready to take her wherever she wanted to go. "And is your car here?"

"Yes," she said. "Can we just go to dinner? Then you can bring me back here, and I'll get my car."

"Sure," he said, still looking at her.

"Pizza?"

"A woman after my heart," he said with a grin. He eased back onto the road and hummed along with the radio as it played softly between them.

Marcy chewed on the words he'd just said. *A woman after my heart.*

She was after something, but it didn't have to be his heart.

Yes, it does, she told herself. She couldn't just use Wyatt for his last name. Marcy had been fighting something for so long, and she was so tired. She couldn't argue with herself over this too.

She'd never given much thought to getting married. Many women did, she knew that. But she'd been wearing coveralls since the age of six, and she'd dreamt of flying over fields while other girls probably fantasized over what their wedding dress would look like.

Wyatt let her stew in silence during the quick drive to the pizza parlor. They went inside together, and Wyatt ordered a pizza they'd shared in the past. He knew what soda she liked, and he knew she'd want a side salad—no red onions—with her meat and cheese.

Marcy let him take care of all of it, because a siren had started to wail in her mind, and she couldn't think very far past it.

Wyatt picked up their tray and led them to a booth in the corner, away from the door and anyone else in the restaurant. He sat down, took everything off the tray, and set it on another table before he sat across from her.

"Okay, Marcy," he said. "Something's going on, and you better spit it out so we can talk about it."

Marcy looked into Wyatt's dark gray, beautiful eyes. He hadn't shaved that day, obviously, because he almost had a full face of hair. He ticked so many boxes for Marcy, and she couldn't get herself to speak.

Wyatt reached for his glass of cola and drank without a straw, his gaze never leaving hers.

"Okay," she said, reaching for her own soda glass. "This is going to be so crazy. Like, I can't even believe it myself."

"Do tell," he said, his eyes glittering, almost like this was a game he wanted to win.

Marcy tried to smile, but she couldn't pull it off.

"So it's bad news," Wyatt said.

Marcy nodded.

"Maybe I could guess," he said. "I mean, you were at the lawyer's office, and I'm guessing there's a problem with the will."

"Sort of," she said, seizing onto his words. "The personal assets are fine." Before tonight, Marcy had never used the word *assets* before. "It's the business that's going to be tied up for a while."

Six months.

And then she'd lose Payne's Pest-free—if she wasn't married.

"Oh? Why's that?"

Marcy took a long drink of her soda, relishing the burn of the carbonation as it slid down her throat. She set the glass down, willing the words to order themselves properly. "I'm going to lose the crop-dusting business," she said.

Wyatt's whole demeanor changed, almost as if he himself had lost something precious to him. "You are? Why?"

"I have to be married to keep it," she said.

His eyebrows flew toward the ceiling. "Married?"

A teen girl arrived with their pizza, chirping out, "Pepperoni, black olives, mushrooms, sausage, and green pepper." She put down two plates and set the pizza up on the stand in the middle of the table. "Side salad. Everything good?"

Neither Wyatt nor Marcy spoke, and the girl took a few seconds before she walked away.

Marcy glanced around and looked back at Wyatt again. "Married. Daddy put it in the estate that the dusting business goes to me, but only if I'm married. If I am at the time of his death, great. I get the business immediately. No problem. If not, I have six months to get the job done, or poof. Everything I've worked for during my entire life is gone."

"Gone where?" Wyatt asked, sitting very, very still. His mouth barely moved when he spoke.

"The estate will sell it," she said, a sob forming in her chest and working its way up her throat. "I've worked there for twenty years," she said. "I went to college to get a business degree and I went to trade school to be the mechanic." She shook her head, her hair brushing her face.

She finally reached for the serving spatula and put two pieces of pizza on her plate. "What am I going to do?"

Wyatt took the spatula from her and put three slices of pizza on his plate. "What are you going to do? You're going to marry me."

Marcy choked, though she knew he'd say that. She'd actually been hoping he'd offer. "Wyatt, be serious."

"I am being serious," he said. "This isn't a problem at all. I'll marry you tomorrow." He took a bite of his pizza and watched her.

"Wyatt, it's not that simple."

"Why not?" he asked, leaning forward. "Although, I

will say that I learned from my brothers that you need to apply for a marriage license in the state of Texas, and that takes three days to go through. So I can't really marry you tomorrow—unless you want to go to Vegas." He actually raised his eyebrows as if she'd say, *Sure! Let's go to Las Vegas and get married.*

She couldn't believe this was her life. She didn't recognize it at all, from a world without her parents in it to one where she had to get married to keep the family business that she loved.

"We're not going to Vegas," she said through a narrow throat. "And I can't marry you."

"So you'll lose the business?" he asked. "Marce, this is a technicality."

"No," she said. "It's not."

"Why not?"

"I have to be married for a year," she said, dropping the final bomb. She watched him, and he definitely flinched when he realized what that meant. "Yeah," she said. "Just...yeah."

5

Wyatt kept thinking that his stomach would settle down if he took another bite of pizza. Another bite. Then another, while Marcy continued to talk.

"Get married within six months," she said. "And stay married for at least a year, or I lose it all."

He couldn't let that happen, and he saw an opportunity here that made him feel like a real jerk.

"A year is a long time," he said. "For a fake marriage." But he'd still do it. Heck, he'd been shadowing Marcy for over a year already.

Marcy stabbed at her salad, clearly unsure of what to say.

"Marcy," he said, pushing his pizza away. It had not settled his stomach at all. "We could do this. I don't want you to lose Payne's."

"I don't want to ask you do this," she whispered,

keeping her head down. Her pretty blonde hair formed a thin curtain between them, and Wyatt wanted to lift her chin and reassure her that everything would be fine.

"I'm offering," he said.

"Is that a proposal?" she asked, and Wyatt was surprised by the slight teasing quality in her voice.

"I mean, we should talk about this," he said. "Make a plan we're both comfortable with. But I'm totally fine with a pretend pledge." *For now*, he thought. He leaned forward and kept his voice low when he said, "Marcy, my brothers have done this exact thing. Four times. Each of them have done a sort of fake marriage, and they've made it work."

Marcy coughed, her eyes bright and wild now. "Made it work?"

Wyatt realized too late what he'd said. "I'm just saying, we can do this." His phone rang, but he ignored it. "Why did you call me?"

"What?"

"When you found out about the stipulation in the will. Why did you call me? You have cousins you could've brainstormed with over pizza." He leaned back in the booth, a measure of anger simmering in his veins. He was tired of playing games with Marcy, and he thought he'd been ultra-patient with her.

Marcy remained quiet for several long seconds. She seemed to be angry as well, and Wyatt would take that over distant or silent. "I called you, because you always know what to do," she said, her voice shaking. "You make me feel safe, and I don't know. I wanted to talk to you."

"I don't always know what to do," he said, starting a prayer in his heart that he *would* know what to do in this situation. He knew what he wanted to do, but he also wanted to do what God wanted him to. What was right.

"To me, you do," Marcy said. "But I've been a mess for a while now."

"You're not a mess."

She gave a short laugh. "I kind of am, Wyatt."

"A beautiful mess," he said.

Marcy shook her head, but a small smile sat on her mouth. "Maybe we should think about this," she said.

"Okay," he said, his mind already whirring. But not about whether he should do this or not. But *how* he should do it. He'd known enough women to know they liked the romance of things, and every female he'd ever met who'd been married had an engagement story.

He could do that for Marcy. He could throw the biggest wedding Three Rivers had ever seen and not even miss the money. He could help her with the hangar, the business, clearing out her father's house, all of it.

All she had to do was say yes.

"I've got a demo tomorrow," he said. "But after that, I could meet you at your dad's place to start going through things."

"Sure," Marcy said, and Wyatt counted that as a huge step in the right direction. He didn't have to ask her to marry him tomorrow, even if he wanted to. Even if he didn't have a giant crush on the woman, he could give her a year of his life to make sure she got her planes. He knew how much she loved those planes, and he couldn't let her lose them.

So he'd find a way to convince her that marrying him was the lesser of two unideal situations.

Surely she'd see reason and say yes to his pretend proposal. *Please help her see*, he prayed, glad when she asked him about the demo so they could talk about something else for a few minutes.

"Oh, Ethan's going to turn this into a sideshow," Wyatt said. "It's going to be terrible."

Marcy giggled, a sound Wyatt hadn't heard her make in a while. "You like the sideshow."

"I do not," he said, gaping at her.

"Wyatt, you so do," she said. "I've seen you transform from this sort of quiet cowboy to a superstar rodeo king in less than a second."

"That doesn't mean I like it," he said, puffing out his chest. "It means I had a very good manager who taught me how to charm the crowd."

"And you *like* charming the crowd," she said.

"I prefer no crowd at all," he said.

"Sure," she said, her tone dry and sarcastic. "Tell me more about this manager."

"Oh, Jim was a bear," Wyatt said. "An absolute bear."

That got Marcy to laugh, and Wyatt sure did like that.

He went on to tell her about the man who'd made sure Wyatt got entered into all the best rodeos, with the right events that would take his career to the next level. And then the next. And then the next.

Jim had been a good friend, and Wyatt missed the man as he memorialized him for Marcy.

After driving her to her car and then heading back to the ranch, Wyatt let his mind wander. It was the moments of subconscious thought that would help him come up with a great way to ask Marcy to be his pretend wife.

"A pretend pledge," he muttered to himself as he walked into the homestead. He could do that, because he knew it would become real soon enough, and he really wanted a shot at genuine, true love with Marcy.

––––––––

WYATT STOOD at the ironing board, his mind focusing on making sure his blue jeans looked pristine. In the back of his subconscious, he thought about the date he'd had with Marcy last night. Yes, in his mind, he'd categorized their dinner at the pizza parlor as a date. He'd picked her up and dropped her off. He'd paid. They'd talked, and she'd even laughed and teased him.

"You're ironing your jeans?" Jeremiah paused as he came into the kitchen. "Why?"

"I'm doing a demo today," Wyatt said. "Trust me, the jeans need to be ironed."

Jeremiah started laughing, the sound starting low and increasing over several seconds. Wyatt smiled, because he was aware ironing denim was ridiculous.

"No wonder you were the most popular cowboy in the rodeo," Jeremiah said as he moved into the kitchen to pour a cup of coffee.

"Hey," Wyatt said, though he couldn't deny what Jeremiah had said. "I know how to look like I know what I'm doing."

"Wyatt, I've seen you on a horse. You know *exactly* what you're doing, pressed jeans or not."

"Maybe," Wyatt said. He hadn't been on a horse much in the past five months, and while he'd done a little bit yesterday, he certainly wasn't where he'd been while he'd ridden on the circuit.

Jeremiah put cream and sugar and chocolate syrup in the coffee, which meant it was for his wife. A flash of jealousy moved through Wyatt, and he almost blurted out that he might marry Marcy to make sure she got to keep the crop-dusting business.

At the last moment, he sucked back the words, making a gasping sound that Jeremiah definitely heard. He let a couple of seconds pass while he stirred the coffee too much. "You okay?"

Wyatt finished with the pantleg and set the iron upright. "Jeremiah," he said slowly. "Why did you...I mean, why did you and Whitney get married?"

Shock entered his brother's face, and Wyatt watched him closely. "You know why."

"Because I said you were broken." Wyatt nodded, sharp regret lancing through him. "How did you get Whitney to go along with you?"

"Wyatt," Jeremiah said. "What's going on?"

His phone bleeped out the alarm that he needed to get going, but Wyatt simply slid his finger across the screen to silence it. "This is a secret," he said. "Can you keep a secret?"

"Wyatt, come on," he said. "I'm the best secret-keeper in the family."

Wyatt shook his head, chuckling. "You're better than the twins, that's for sure."

"And Rhett. That man can't keep anything to himself."

"True." Wyatt stepped into his jeans and buttoned them up. "Okay, but I just need you to listen for a minute. Literally, a minute. I can't be late today."

"I have a minute," Jeremiah said, still stirring Whitney's coffee.

"Marcy found out yesterday that she can't inherit Payne's unless she's married. For a year."

Jeremiah was already nodding. "And you want to marry her so she can keep her family business."

"Yes," Wyatt said, though there were other reasons. He didn't need to get into those right now. There wasn't time, for one. And for a second, he wasn't even sure what they all were.

"And she's resistant?"

"I think she doesn't want to ask me to do it."

"Oh, this is an easy one," Jeremiah said, stepping toward Wyatt. He patted Wyatt's chest and said, "*You* ask *her*." He grinned, stepped past Wyatt, and went down the hall.

Like it was so simple.

Wyatt drove out to Three Rivers and Bowman's Breeds, his new shirt tucked in perfectly, and his bull riding championship belt buckle gleaming like the stars. He pulled up, noticing all the extra cars and trucks in the parking stalls in front of the stables. His nerves pounced, but he smoothed them back.

He'd felt like this so many times before, and all he had to do was put on that charming smile, hold out a couple of words for an extra beat, and show everyone exactly what he could do.

"Morning, Jenn," he said.

"Wyatt," she said as if she was surprised he'd come in that day. "Ethan wanted me to let him know the moment you arrived."

"I bet he did." Wyatt grinned. "I'm headed out there now."

"Okay." She lifted her phone anyway, but Wyatt didn't wait around to listen to her call Ethan. The man needed to settle down.

Wyatt found him out in the gates, where he'd worked

yesterday. He was setting up folding chairs—a lot of folding chairs. "Morning, Ethan," he said.

"Hey, Wyatt." He looked and sounded relieved. "People are already here. Brynn's taking them on a tour."

"Sounds good," Wyatt said. "I'll go get the animals ready." He turned but Ethan called him back.

"You look great, Wyatt."

"I know what I'm doing," he said, giving Ethan a quick salute before he walked away. He went into the stables where the horses were kept, and he walked down the row, handing out candy to the four horses he'd been working with.

"All right, guys," he said. "Today's your big day. There are a lot of people here to watch you, and it's time to show them how great you are." He paused in front of Harley, and then Maleficent. He didn't want any of his horses to be bought that day, because that meant they'd leave the stables. Leave him.

He turned and went across the path to the barn where the calves were kept. Most people probably thought they looked the same, but to Wyatt, he knew each one of them. He only needed four for the roping demo today, but he'd probably go a couple of rounds.

He opened the huge back doors and let the calves out, telling them to get a snack and he'd be back for them. He returned to the stables and started getting the horses ready, leading two at a time out the ring where he'd warm them up.

He got them all hooked up, and he walked with them, muttering to them about Marcy and the situation that had come up last night. "And I think I'm going to ask her to marry me," Wyatt said. "Then she'll know she's not a burden. That I want to do this."

And boy, did he want to marry her.

Do you love her?

The moment he thought of the question, he knew he didn't. But even more importantly, he knew he could, if she'd just open her heart and let him in.

His phone rang, and he checked it. His mother. Again. She'd called last night while he'd been on his date with Marcy. He hadn't answered the phone then, and he hadn't called her back yet. Glancing around, he decided he had a couple of minutes to talk.

"Hey, Momma," he said.

"Wyatt, my son," she said, and though she and Daddy had been living in Grand Cayman for a few years now, she hadn't lost her Texan accent.

"What's up? I'm doing a demo for the horses I've been training in a couple of minutes."

"I'm just reaching out to all the boys," she said. "To see what you think."

"About what?"

"Daddy and I want to come back to Texas."

Warmth filled Wyatt from head to toe. "That would be great, Momma. I can't imagine anyone saying they wouldn't want you to be closer." Maybe Skyler, but he was away at college and didn't have a whole lot to do with the family right now anyway. Micah had retreated for a couple of years too—maybe five or six—but even he'd come to Seven Sons.

"I'm having a hard time convincing Daddy," Momma said, letting the words hang there.

"Oh, so you're really calling for a favor," Wyatt said, connecting all the dots.

"A little," she said. "Maybe you could text him or something and tell him how much you miss him."

"Sure," Wyatt said, though he wasn't an overly sentimental guy. He had talked to his father a lot while in the rodeo circuit, but he said everything he needed to say with his hat. And somehow, when Wyatt missed his daddy the most, his father knew it. And then Daddy would show up unannounced to watch Wyatt ride. So maybe he could text him and say he missed him. Not only that, but that he wanted his dad there for his wedding....

"I have to go," he said. "I'll call him later." The call ended, and Wyatt started leading his horses over to the gate. Maleficent would've gone without a rope or reins, as she loved to train and work. With fifteen minutes to go before the demo was scheduled to begin, Wyatt had everything ready.

He went out into the crowd and started talking to people, taking pictures, and giving details about the horses. He didn't make direct eye contact with Ethan or Brynn, but he could tell they were pleased with a quick scan.

They'd severely underestimated him. Wyatt had been working reporters and crowds for almost two decades, and this demo was one of the least high-profile things he'd done.

"Are we ready?" Ethan asked right at ten o'clock, and Wyatt nodded. He took the length of rope from his boss and headed toward the gates while Ethan welcomed everyone and got them settled down.

"Wyatt's going to be riding Maleficent first," Ethan called. "She's a two-year-old mare that's been here for six months, training under Wyatt's care." He nodded toward Wyatt, who mounted Maleficent and bent down to pat the horse's neck.

"All right, girl," he said. "Let's show them how it's done." His heart beat rapidly in his chest, as he absolutely loved being in the saddle. There was nothing better than the rush of running out of the gate, of throwing that rope, leaping from the horse, and tying the calf.

He looked over, and Stuart had the calf in the gate. "Ready?" he said to him.

"Yep."

"Hit the bell," Wyatt said, his heart practically in his throat. Every eye was trained on him, and he could see and feel them all.

Then the bell rang, and the world narrowed. Time slowed.

The calf shot out of the gate. Wyatt held Maleficent back, because the horse couldn't bolt at the same time as the calf. He knew exactly when Maleficent could go, and the horse did too.

They moved together, man and horse, and Wyatt threw the rope a moment later. The calf went down; Wyatt slid from the saddle; Maleficent balked and pulled back like a pro. A moment later, the calf's legs were tied, and Wyatt threw his hands into the air.

He sucked in a breath as the applause filled the training arena. He grinned like he'd just done a championship run, and he swiped his cowboy hat from his head and lifted it into the air, wondering if this crowd would know how to cheer with him.

He bobbed the hat up and down, using only his wrist, like he was waving his cowboy hat to the crowd, thanking them for the energy they brought.

At least that was what the reporters had assigned to his actions. Wyatt had started the wrist movement that waved his hat to the cameras as a tribute to his father. His father, who'd taught him everything about riding, about horses, about the rodeo, about living a good, righteous life.

The crowd exploded, whooping as they lifted their right arms into the air and did the wrist-wave back to him.

Pure joy streamed through Wyatt as he laughed, replaced his hat on his head, and looked to the large digital clock on the fence post. Not bad. Not quite championship time, but respectable.

He turned back to Maleficent, who'd done an amazing job. Wyatt reminded himself that the spectators weren't there to watch him. They were there to see how well he trained livestock.

And he'd done a great job with Maleficent, but really, the horse was simply an amazing creature.

He stroked her nose and pressed his face to hers before releasing the rope and saying, "That was awesome, Maleficent. Good job."

He rode the high of the demo, leaving the ranch as soon as he could after charming everyone, staying for lunch, and signing autographs.

By the time he pulled up to the jeweler in downtown Three Rivers, he was exhausted and ready for a nap. But first, he had a diamond to buy.

6

Marcy soared over the fields on the southwest side of Three Rivers. Shiloh Ridge Ranch was some of the most beautiful land in Texas, in Marcy's opinion. She got a view very few people did, and she loved seeing the fields in all of their stages.

Bear Glover had a lot of trees to deal with in the hillier part of the Three Rivers area, and he cut down as few as possible. She liked seeing the fields as bare dirt, when she sprayed them with fertilizer and a pre-spring pesticide that would make sure their fields were ready for planting.

She got the job done and headed back to the hangar to get the next batch of fertilizer she needed. She'd actually be flying over Seven Sons today, and she couldn't help the way her heart beat out a few extra thumps.

But she'd enjoyed eating dinner with Wyatt last night. Too much, probably. He was so cool, and so casual, and

Marcy wondered what it would take to rile him up. Surely he was passionate about *something*. The man had won multiple rodeo championships, but he wasn't anything like the cowboys Marcy had dated before.

He wasn't loud. He wasn't constantly bragging. He was down-to-Earth and—"Normal," Marcy whispered to the clouds in the sky.

She touched down, landing a plane one of the things that brought her the most joy. She taxied to the end of the dirt road, wondering what in the world her father had been thinking when he'd put conditions on her ability to inherit this business.

And he'd never once mentioned it to her. He'd never badgered her about finding a man and getting married. He'd never asked when she could produce some grandbabies. Nothing.

She checked her email as she sat in the cockpit of the plane as the propellers powered down. Bryan had sent back the signed consent papers, and Marcy forwarded them to Mr. Marlow at the law firm.

Wyatt had agreed to meet her at her father's house that night to help her begin the process of going through everything, and Marcy was tired just thinking about it. She knew how much stuff her father had accumulated in the seventy-two years of his life. And after Mama had died, her father hadn't thrown away anything.

So many memories to go through. So many decisions to make.

Wyatt

I'd come help if I could, Bryan had said in his email. *If you want to hire someone, let me know, and I'll help pay for it.*

Part of Marcy did want to hire someone to come go through everything, while at the same time, she didn't want anyone touching her father's things without her there to make sure nothing important got thrown away.

She refueled the plane and filled the tanks of fertilizer. She thought about Wyatt as she took off. Pictured what his demo would look like as she made a wide turn and headed south. Fantasized about holding his hand and kissing him as she picked out familiar landmarks and set her sights on his ranch.

Dinner hadn't lasted long last night, and even with Marcy's exhaustion, she'd laid awake for at least an hour. Wyatt hadn't run from the pizza parlor when she'd mentioned the condition that prevented her from doing what she'd already been doing for a year now. He hadn't laughed at her.

In fact, he'd offered to marry her.

He'd also asked her why she'd called him, and Marcy hadn't been able to tell him the whole truth.

She'd called him, because he was the only man in her life, and she'd been hoping he'd offer to marry her. A hitch in her lungs made breathing difficult. How could she go through with this?

She liked Wyatt, sure. But she didn't love him, and she was pretty sure he wasn't in love with her. How people got

63

married when they were in love existed outside Marcy's understanding. She'd never had grandiose plans for her life that included a husband, and a thread of guilt for tying down Wyatt for a year turned into a rope and then a set of heavy chains.

She finished dusting their ranch and flew back to the hangar, a constant stream of *you can't do this, you can't do this*, looping through her mind.

But if she didn't....

She looked at the dark green hangar, remembering the day she'd painted it with her mother and father. It had taken way longer than a day, and her father had had the bright idea to do the job in June, the sun beating down on Marcy's shoulders and back.

She'd gotten sunburned that week, and it had been so bad, she'd blistered and had to stay home for a few days.

And they were terrible days, with nothing to do and no one to occupy her time. If there was one thing Marcy liked, it was being busy. Too much down time made her nervous, and she hated feeling one breath away from a panic attack.

She pulled into the hangar and climbed down from the plane to close the door behind her. She had more work to do, but not in the air. She didn't like the office work nearly as much as lifting into the sky and viewing the picturesque town of Three Rivers from above. She often wondered if God was looking down on her the way she could peer down on the town from an airplane.

And if He was, what was He thinking? Marcy hadn't involved the Lord too much in her life until this past year, and even then, she felt like she'd only done it because she was going through something hard. When things got easy again, she'd stop talking to Him, stop asking Him for help, stop wondering where her parents were and if she'd ever see them again.

A sigh moved through her body and out of her mouth as she walked into the office. Her stomach growled at the scent of food, but her feet froze to the grease-stained cement.

"Hello?" she asked, peering around the doorframe and into the office. No one was there, but Wyatt had been while she'd been up in the air. She knew, because a white bag sat on her desk that she had not put there. And the delicious scent of teriyaki sauce and sweet potatoes filled the air, and Wyatt knew exactly how to get in her good graces. Vegetable tempura and egg rolls.

Sure enough, when she opened the bag, she found what she always ordered from China Isle. She smiled and sat, pulling her phone from the breast pocket of her coveralls. *Thank you for lunch,* she tapped out, though it was almost three o'clock.

No problem, sugar. Are we still meeting at your dad's tonight?

Yes. 6?

I'll be there.

Marcy tipped her head back and closed her eyes. "I

know I've been asking a lot lately, but could You maybe help me know what to do with Wyatt Walker?"

The heavens didn't open and light didn't stream down. Marcy didn't need a loud answer. Just a push in the right direction would be enough.

Marcy had been at her father's for an hour by the time six o'clock rolled around. She'd brought home two big boxes from the shop, and she'd labeled one with *Keep* and one with *Give Away or Sell*.

Then she'd sat down on the couch and stared at the built-in bookshelves surrounding the TV. Just going through her father's library would take hours, and Marcy didn't have the heart to throw away a single volume.

The doorbell rang, and she leapt to her feet. She couldn't tell Wyatt she'd been staring for almost an hour, with nothing to show for it. No decisions made. Nothing.

"Hey," she said when she opened the door. But it wasn't Wyatt standing on the front porch. "Alyssa. Savannah. What are you guys doing here?"

Her cousins stepped into the house and hugged her, a three-way union that brought joy to Marcy's heart. "We knew you'd be here tonight," Alyssa said. "And we thought we'd stop by."

"We didn't want you to be alone," Savannah added, pulling her dark ponytail out and resetting it. "Oh, you brought boxes."

"Yeah." Marcy glanced at them and closed the door, wondering what would happen when Wyatt showed up.

She couldn't just kick her cousins out, and she didn't even want to. They'd been a big help over the past year, and she loved them like sisters. "I haven't been able to get started, though."

She could admit it to them, because they already knew her faults. She was still trying to hide as many from Wyatt as possible.

"Oh, honey." Alyssa put her arm around Marcy's waist and drew her to her side. "What are you going to do with the house and everything?"

"Bryan and I decided it would be best to sell it," Marcy said. "I have a house, and it's bigger and newer and nicer than this. I don't need it. Bryan's not coming back." Her throat closed for a moment, but she breathed and steadied her emotions. "So we just need to go through it all and get the house ready to sell."

"So an estate sale." Savannah picked up one of the pillows from the couch.

Marcy blinked, and she could see her father lying there, his head on that pillow as he took his last breath.

She couldn't get enough air, and she hurried into the kitchen and opened the fridge, though she had no idea what she was looking for. "How's Aunt Opal?" she asked, glad her voice sounded somewhat normal.

Aunt Opal was her mother's sister, and Alyssa and Savannah were her daughters. After Mama's death, the cousins had stayed close, but Aunt Opal had drifted away from her sister's husband and kids.

"She's doing okay," Alyssa said.

"She is not," Savannah said, always the more blunt of the two sisters. "She's terribly sad, and she doesn't know how to come over here and offer to help."

"She's welcome anytime," Marcy said, straightening from the fridge with a bottle of water clutched in her hand. The fridge hadn't been cleaned out since Daddy had died, and there was plenty to throw away there. Perhaps that was where she could start. Old, rotting food. She wouldn't have an emotional connection to that.

"I told her that," Savannah said. "She doesn't want to impose."

"My father was a closet hoarder," Marcy said. "She's welcome to come do whatever she wants." The enormity of the job before her threatened to drag her underwater and hold her down until she stopped struggling.

"I'll tell her," Alyssa said. She drew in a deep breath and looked around the house. "Where should we start?"

"I'm going to clean out the fridge," Marcy said. She uncapped her water and took a drink.

"Good idea," Alyssa said. "We'll got through the pantry. Maybe he'll have unopened things we can donate to the Food Bank." She pushed up her sweater sleeves and stepped into the kitchen with Marcy.

"And, uh, Wyatt Walker is coming to help," Marcy said, glancing at the clock. It wasn't six yet, and she hadn't even thought to check the time earlier.

"Wyatt Walker?" Alyssa and Savannah said in unison,

as if they'd rehearsed it before coming over. They exchanged a glance, and Savannah said, *"The* Wyatt Walker? The rodeo king?"

Marcy nodded, pure apprehension pulling through. "We're sort of...friends."

They were a lot more than friends, despite Marcy breaking up with him in the hospital over five months ago. They'd shared several kisses, and none of them testified of friendship. The temperature in the kitchen skyrocketed, and Marcy pulled open the fridge again.

"You're friends with Wyatt Walker." Savannah wasn't asking this time. "When did this happen?"

"Last year," Marcy said, her head buried in the depths of the fridge. She pulled out a half-empty bottle of mayo and one of ranch dressing. "I'm throwing all of this away."

Alyssa bent and pulled a trash bag from under the sink. "Good idea." She met Marcy's eye, pure kindness in hers. "And good for you for the whole...Wyatt thing."

Marcy smiled and started throwing condiments and plastic containers of leftovers into the garbage bag. "The Wyatt thing" summed up her current relationship with Wyatt, actually. And that made her heart twist in its spot in her chest.

She realized in that moment that she wanted more than "the Wyatt thing." She may have called him last night because he was her only option, but she did like him. She'd always liked him. She liked him so much, she'd broken up with him and held him at arm's length so she wouldn't hurt him by trying to have a relationship when she wasn't ready for such things.

The doorbell rang again, and Marcy spun toward it. "That'll be him. And he'll probably have food. I should've texted him you two were here."

"Oh, we can leave," Alyssa said. "We just didn't want you to be alone, and now you won't be."

"Speak for yourself," Savannah said. "I want to see what's going on with her and Wyatt."

"Savvy," Alyssa warned.

"What?" Savannah laughed. "Look at her. She's bright red and frozen to the spot."

Marcy felt her cousin's eyes on her, but she couldn't make herself move, nor could she help what her face looked like.

"I don't think they're just friends," Savannah said with a giggle.

"Yeah, no kidding," Alyssa said.

The doorbell rang again, and very clearly, Wyatt said, "Marcy, it's Wyatt, sugar."

"Sugar," Savannah teased, and Marcy blinked her gaze away from the door and toward her cousins. "I'll get it," Savannah said, taking one step toward the front door.

That got Marcy to thaw, and she darted in front of her cousin. "No way."

Savannah's dark eyes sparkled, and she said, "Marcy, you like this man."

"Yes," she whispered. "I do."

"Marce?" he called. "You okay in there?"

"You better get the door," Savannah said, grinning. "Or he's coming through it."

"I think it's great she likes him," Alyssa said as Marcy walked through the living room. "She hasn't dated anyone in so long."

Marcy cringed at the words, though they were true. Savannah said something in return, but Marcy was too far away to hear what. She inhaled and opened the door to find the tall, dark, delicious rodeo king standing on the front porch.

Pure worry lived in his eyes. "There you are," he said, lowering his phone. "I was just going to call you."

"My cousins are here."

"I saw the extra car," he said, hooking his thumb over his shoulder to the driveway. "Good thing I didn't plan an elaborate proposal, right?"

7

Wyatt glanced over Marcy's shoulder and saw the cousins. They hardly seemed like they belonged together, what with Marcy's blonde hair and her cousins with their dark strands.

He watched Marcy blink at him, obviously stunned by the word *proposal*. Wyatt wanted to chuckle and draw her into a kiss. But he couldn't do that with an audience. He knew how to charm the cousins, sure. But it wasn't with a public display of affection for Marcy.

In fact, Wyatt liked to keep those things behind closed doors, and he had the wild thought to pull Marcy onto the porch, close the door, and kiss her there.

Slow down, cowboy, he told himself.

He did lean closer to her and whisper, "I have a ring, Marcy. Have you thought more about marrying me?"

That question certainly wasn't going slow, nor did it

put the brakes on his rapid heartbeat. And when Marcy nodded, Wyatt's most vital organ nearly sprinted out of his body.

She stepped back to give him room to enter the house, saying in a very loud voice, "My cousins were just leaving."

"Were they?" Wyatt entered the house, his gaze trained on the two brunettes hovering on the edge of the kitchen. He walked toward them, his celebrity smile curving his mouth. "I'm Wyatt Walker. I saw you at the funeral, of course, but I don't think we've formally met."

One of them sighed and the other giggled. Wyatt shook both of their hands while Marcy introduced them as Alyssa and Savannah.

"Looks like we're starting in the kitchen," he said, picking up a box of crackers and looking at it. "I brought some crates. We can load up the unopened stuff in the back of my truck. I can take it to the Food Bank on my way to the ranch tomorrow."

The diamond ring in his pocket felt like it was a lead brick, and he was so glad he'd noticed the other car in the driveway before getting down on both knees on the porch. After all, it was hard work for him to get down and up, and the last thing he needed was to embarrass himself. Or Marcy.

"I think we have time to load up the crates," Savannah said. "Right, Liss?"

"Sure," her sister said, and the two of them scampered

out of the house. Wyatt waited until the front door clicked closed, and then he looked at Marcy.

She giggled too, but it wasn't nervous or girly. "Sorry about them. I didn't know they were coming."

"I don't care if they stay." Wyatt scanned the room and saw hours and hours of work. Days. Weeks. Maybe even a month. At least Marcy had brought some boxes home, and she'd even labeled them.

"I do," Marcy said. "We have some things to talk about."

That they did, and Wyatt pushed his patient button while her cousins returned, and they all went through the cupboards to get the items the Food Bank would take. He loaded them into the back of his truck and stood in the dark driveway with Marcy as her cousins loaded up and backed into the street.

He followed her into the house, and the door had barely clicked closed when she said, "You bought a ring?"

"Yeah," he said. "You want to see it?"

She turned to face him, and Wyatt could tell she wanted to see it. He dug in his pocket and pulled the ring out. "I was going to do this super romantic thing. There were flowers involved and chocolate cake, because we both love that. But then, I don't know. I thought maybe I wouldn't even tell you about the ring tonight." Then he'd seen her, and Wyatt's brain seemed to misfire whenever Marcy was in the room.

"It was the first thing you said," Marcy teased.

"You make me nervous," Wyatt admitted.

A brand-new glint entered the blonde's eyes. "I do?" She took a step toward him. "Why's that, Wyatt? Don't you know *you're* the celebrity here?"

"I'm just a regular man," he said. "Who happens to know how to ride a horse and throw a rope." He swallowed, his mouth so dry as his gaze dropped to her lips.

She tiptoed her fingertips up his shirt, touching each one of his buttons. "I've thought about you all day," she said.

"Ditto." Heck, the woman had followed him into his dreams during his afternoon nap.

"I have a dilemma," she said, their faces so close, all Wyatt had to do was lean forward four inches and he could kiss her. "I want to keep Payne's. And I don't want to lose you."

"Sugar, marrying me would make me yours." And oh, how he wanted to be hers. And he wanted her to be his. Only his. "You wouldn't lose me. In fact, you wouldn't be able to get rid of me for a year." He grinned down at her, his hand finally lifting to rest on her hip. "I don't think it's a secret that I like you, Marce. I have for a long time now."

She nodded. "And I like you."

He opened his fist to reveal the ring. "So let's get married." He'd made a mistake last night by mentioning that maybe they could fall in love. So while he wanted to say it again right now, he bit back the words.

"We need to make some decisions," Marcy said,

staring at the huge diamond in his palm. "Before I'll wear that ring."

He wanted her to say yes *and* wear the ring. "Okay," he said. "Let's make them then."

She looked up at him, her blue eyes brighter than he'd seen them in a while. "There's so many things." She blinked, shuttering off some of her playfulness and all of her emotions. "What are you thinking about?"

"Kissin' you," he said.

"Wyatt," she said, smiling. "Be serious."

"Oh, I'm serious."

"I meant, what do you need to talk about?"

Wyatt tried to focus, mentally commanding his hormones to calm down. "Well, the first thing my momma will ask is when we're getting married."

"Has to be by July first," she said. "I got that email today."

"What do you want?" he asked. Wyatt would do everything in his power to give her what she wanted, but he wasn't going to say that. He'd already revealed too much by saying he was thinking about kissing her.

"I'm not a fussy person," she said.

"But I'm the rodeo king," he said, using her words. The media's words. "And my marriage will be a big thing."

"June then," she said.

"June," he said, pulling out his phone. "Saturday? Friday night? Sunday?"

"Friday night," she said. "It doesn't need to be a big thing. Certainly not a whole day."

Wyatt could just see his sponsors turning this into a very big thing, but he didn't say anything. "June sixteenth is a Friday," he said.

"Let's do the second," she said. "Get it over with."

Wyatt flinched at the words. "Okay." He made an event on his calendar that literally said *Marry Marcy* and set it on June second. "What else?"

"I've been thinking about where we'll live," she said.

"I don't have a place of my own," he said. "But I can get one, or I can live with you." The very idea had his pulse and his nerves and every ounce of testosterone in his body vibrating like a horse ready to explode out of a gate.

Marcy stayed silent. She turned and went back into the kitchen, Wyatt following like a puppy dog. "Talk to me," he said.

"I was just thinking it might be nice for us to get married really soon." She lifted her eyes to his, finally. "And move in here together. We can go through the house together, and I don't know." She shrugged. "It might not be so painful for me that way."

"You want to live here?" Wyatt couldn't believe that. The house was fine as far as houses went. But she'd been raised in this house, and he couldn't believe she wanted to start their life together here.

It's not a true start to a true life together, he thought, and the words stung him. Pricking and piercing over and over again until Wyatt shoved them out of his head.

"It was just an idea," Marcy said, reaching into the fridge for something else.

"How soon is 'really soon'?" His brothers had gotten married without their parents, but Wyatt wanted his family there, especially his mother. He'd always been more of a Momma's boy than the other brothers, and he used to feel bad about it.

Not only that, but Liam and Callie were about to have a baby. Wyatt couldn't send a family text and be like, *Surprise! I'm getting married this weekend!*

"I don't know," Marcy said, tossing a head of lettuce in the trashcan. "But the sooner we get married, the sooner the countdown clock starts."

Wyatt pressed his eyes closed in a long blink. "Marcy, I just have to ask. I don't want to upset you or freak you out. But I just have to ask."

She stilled in her cleaning, and Wyatt gathered all the courage he had. This was so much harder than tying himself to a bull and letting it try to buck him off.

"Do you think we could, you know, have a real relationship through all of this?"

Marcy looked resigned, almost like she'd been expecting the question. "Yes," she whispered.

Wyatt's hope took shape as it ballooned in his chest. "So maybe we won't have a countdown clock."

She swallowed and breathed in deep before she said,

"I just feel bad. I feel like I'm making you do something you don't want to do."

"Marcy," he said, disbelieving what he'd just heard. "I've had a major crush on you for over a year. Trust me when I say I'm not doing anything I don't want to do." He ducked his head, the brim of his cowboy hat hiding her face from his view. "And I've kissed you a lot, sugar. You seem to like me well enough."

"It's not that," she said. "I just...I don't want to use you. I don't want to marry you, because you're the only man I know. Literally, Wyatt. The *only* one." She blew out a frustrated breath. "But as I was flying today, I just knew I couldn't give up Payne's either. And I feel stuck."

He stepped around the trashcan, pushing it out of the way with his foot so he could take Marcy into his arms. "But if we like each other, and you actually think we could take this pretend pledge and make it real one day—that's what I think, Marce. I think we would be so good together, and not just for a year." He touched his nose to her forehead and took a deep breath of her skin. She smelled soft and powdery, with always a touch of grease and metal beneath that. And he loved it.

"But forever," he whispered. "I don't love you...yet." He looked at her. "Tell me you don't love me yet."

"I don't love you yet."

"But you could."

She nodded, tears gathering in her eyes. "I think I could, yes."

"I like it when you say yes," he whispered, pressing his lips to her temple, then her cheek. "So sugar, don't think so hard about stuff, okay? We can work out more things. I know we need to. But will you marry me? Yes or no?"

Marcy nodded, her cheek brushing his. "Yes," she said, and that became the single best word in the English language.

"I'm going to kiss you now," Wyatt whispered, and he gave her a couple of seconds to protest. She didn't.

He touched his lips to hers, a firecracker exploding down his throat as he kissed her. She kissed him back, and Wyatt wondered how he'd survived on a daily basis without kissing this woman. Without her, nothing was possible.

With her, nothing was impossible, and Wyatt kissed her until he remembered they weren't quite married...yet.

8

Liam sat straight up in bed, his senses firing at him all at once.

"That's your phone," Callie said, her voice on the edge of sleep still.

"It's the baby," he said, scrambling to throw the blankets off his legs so he could get up. He reached for his phone at the same time, trying to get to the call before it went to voicemail.

"It is?" Callie asked, a measure of panic in her voice now. "How do you know?"

"It's either that or an emergency," he said, though he considered bringing home a newborn baby a total and complete emergency. He felt ill-equipped for a tiny human who needed everything provided for them.

Sure, he and Callie had been taking care of Denise, the three-year-old foster child that had been placed with them, for a couple of months now. Callie had fallen right into the role of motherhood like she was born for it.

Liam had struggled a little bit. He loved the girl with all of his heart, and he'd spent lots of time with her on the ranch, showing her the chickens, the horses, the pigs, and the goats. He'd taken her horseback riding with him, and swimming at the community center. She'd fallen asleep in his arms at the New Year's Eve fireworks, and he'd had a hard time deciding which to watch more—her sleeping soundly or the bright pops of light in the night sky.

But he had no idea what he was doing. He'd been praying since the day they'd picked her up that he'd be guided and led to say and do the right things. He and Callie had gotten a file on Denise, and she'd been through a lot in her short life already.

Liam wanted to make sure she never had to go without food and proper care again, period.

"Hello?" he asked, finally swiping on the call.

"Is this Liam Walker?"

"Yes, ma'am," he said, his heart thumping in such a strange way. He hadn't recognized the number, so it wasn't a family member, nor was it Vicki, the birth mother they'd gotten to know since taking in Denise and preparing for this new baby.

"This is Sheralyn Thomas from the maternity center at the Amarillo Medical Center. Vicki Forrest has asked me to call you."

Liam snapped his fingers and waved his hand, and the bed rustled as Callie got up. "Is she in labor?" he asked.

"Yes, sir. She said y'all could come anytime. The baby will likely be born within a couple of hours."

Liam stood up, ready to fly the hour and fifteen minutes to Amarillo. "We'll be there as soon as we can," he said. "Thank you." He hung up and tossed the phone on the bed. "She's in the hospital."

"I'm getting dressed," Callie said.

Liam stretched to reach for his phone again, realizing he shouldn't have just tossed it away. "I'll call Rhett." His oldest brother had agreed to take Denise at a moment's notice so Liam and Callie could go to the hospital in Amarillo when Vicki called. "Two hours," he added.

"That was the agreement," Callie said, darting into the bathroom.

The line rang at Rhett's for a long time, and Liam remembered his brother put his phone on do-not-disturb after ten p.m. It was definitely way past that.

He hung up and dialed again, only waiting for the phone lines to connect before hanging up again. It would ring this third time, as Rhett had the emergency system engaged. Any time the same number called within ten minutes, the phone would ring.

"Liam?" Rhett answered a moment later, clearly still pulling himself into consciousness.

"We have to bring Denise now," he said as Callie came out of the bathroom. She motioned that she was going to leave, and Liam nodded. She was probably going to get Denise ready to go. "Vicki is having the baby."

"Oh, sure," Rhett said. "We're ready. I'll get Evvy up." Evelyn and Rhett were the obvious choice for babysitting, as they had a nine-month-old baby of their own, and Evelyn didn't work outside the home anymore. Heck, Rhett barely did more than take his dog out and throw her ball, come ride horses at the ranch, and consult on a very few, select veterinary forensic cases anymore.

"Thanks," Liam said. "Probably fifteen minutes."

"We're up," he said. "Come on in when you get here."

"Will do." Liam set his phone on the nightstand and hurried to pull on a pair of jeans and a T-shirt. His wallet from the bathroom counter went in his back pocket and his jacket was in the kitchen.

He'd just stepped into the hall when Callie came out of the bedroom down the hall, Denise asleep on her shoulder. "I'm going to put her in the truck," she whispered.

"I'll grab my jacket and meet you out there," he said.

"And get the baby bag from the bedroom," she said.

He retraced his steps to pick up the bag Callie had packed weeks ago. It had everything she could think of that a newborn might need to come home from the hospital. He'd put the car seat in the back of the truck last week as well, and they had a bassinet already waiting in the corner of their bedroom.

Liam paused for a moment and looked at it, the soft while lace actually calming him. "Bless us all that this will go smoothly," he whispered, hoping the Lord didn't need to be called three times in order to get a message.

Evelyn met Callie on the front porch, and the transfer of a sleeping three-year-old little girl happened seamlessly. Rhett grabbed Liam in a tight hug, for which Liam was grateful. He felt like he had to be the strong one for Callie, who had started weeping on the drive from the Shining Star to the house on Quail Creek Road, where Rhett and Evelyn lived.

But he felt frayed, like he would fall apart at the seams before he got to Amarillo.

"You got this," Rhett said, and Liam nodded.

"I'll call you when we know," he said, Vicki had not wanted to find out the sex of the baby. She'd been in and out of drug treatment facilities, and Callie and Liam weren't even sure if the baby would be healthy.

They'd been praying, of course. Everyone in the family had been.

"I'll call Momma as soon as it's a decent hour," Rhett said. "And everyone else."

"But no one's coming to the hospital," he reminded Rhett. Vicki hadn't wanted a show, and with the Walkers, even going to a movie became a production. Liam remembered when Rhett's son was born, and the nurses had had to ask the family to calm down or go outside.

Callie had laid down the law and said that only she and Liam would be going to the hospital. And even then, they couldn't go in the room where Vicki had the baby.

They'd have to wait outside until the nurse brought them the infant.

Liam's stomach boiled as he stepped back and swept his arm around Callie's waist.

"No one's coming," Rhett said. "Keep us updated, and I'm sure Jeremiah will have something at the homestead."

"Simone's been putting things in the freezer for weeks too," Callie said.

"Let's go, sweetheart," Liam said, anxious to be on the road. They loaded back into the truck, but Liam didn't pull out of the driveway. "Let's have a prayer, should we?"

Callie nodded, sniffling. "I can't say it."

"I will." Liam hadn't grabbed his cowboy hat before leaving the house, so he didn't have to swipe it from his head. He simply closed his eyes and took a deep breath. "Dear Lord, please help us to drive safely to the hospital. Bless Vicki to have an easy delivery, if it be Thy will." His voice stalled as his throat closed. He wanted to pray that it would be easy for her to give them her baby, but he knew no part of that would be easy.

"We're so grateful for this opportunity to be parents, and bless us that we can do what's right for Denise and this new baby. Bless the baby that he or she will have few complications, and that we'll know how to take care of them if there are some." He paused again, swallowing to try to steady his voice.

"Amen," he finished, because he'd begged God for everything already. Callie reached over and threaded her fingers through his, squeezing his hand to let him know she would've said everything he had.

They drove through the darkness, along a lonely strip of road no one else was using at three-thirty in the morning.

The hospital was well-lit, a glowing beacon in the much bigger city of Amarillo. Liam parked near the main entrance, and he and Callie managed to get all the way to the maternity department on the fourth floor.

"Bella Forrest?" he asked at the nurse's station there. "I'm not sure if she's had her baby or not." He looked down the hall, but there were only white walls, wooden doors, and windows with curtains drawn over them.

Callie's nerves radiated from her, and Liam kept her close to his side. For some reason, now that he was here, he only felt calm and ready.

A blessing from God, he knew, as every time he'd previously thought about holding a person who weighed less than ten pounds, he'd nearly had an anxiety attack.

"The doctor went in about ten minutes ago," the nurse said after checking something on her computer. "I'm sure it won't be long now."

"So we'll just wait over there," Liam said, indicating the waiting area down the hall.

"Yes," she said. "Sheralyn will bring the baby out when she's ready."

"She?" Liam asked, his heart jumping. "Is the baby a girl?"

"Oh, sorry," the nurse said, smiling. "We don't know that yet. I was just saying when the baby is ready, Sheralyn will bring her out." She shook her head. "See? I did it again. I guess unborn babies where we don't know the sex are just all girls." She gave a quick laugh and went right back to her work.

Liam took Callie down to the waiting room, and they settled in.

Ten minutes became twenty, which became thirty. When an hour had passed, Liam had gotten up to go to the bathroom twice, and he'd bought a soda from the machine that stood guard over all the empty chairs.

"She's coming," Callie said, and Liam looked up from the floor, where he'd been memorizing the pattern in the carpet. She stood, and Liam got to his feet too, mesmerized by the woman coming toward him, a soft smile on her face, and a perfect bundle in her arms.

A perfect, pink-wrapped bundle.

"It's a girl," Liam whispered at the same time Sheralyn asked, "Liam and Callie?"

Callie nodded, as did Liam, and Sheralyn passed the tiny girl to Callie. "It's a girl. She's doing great, as is the mother."

A soft, "Oh," escaped Callie's mouth as she gazed down at the baby girl. She had perfectly pink skin and the cutest little nose. Her eyes were closed, but she grunted as she shifted against Callie.

"Liam, look at her." Tears streamed down Callie's face, and Liam put his arm around her to give her strength.

"She's beautiful," he said.

"What are you going to name her?" Sheralyn asked. "I can get going on the birth certificate and all that."

"Ginger," Liam said. "Ginger Elizabeth Walker."

Callie hummed and swayed with their new baby, and Liam wanted to take a picture so he could remember this moment forever. There was so much love filling him, and so much peace, and he couldn't help gazing at the little girl in all of her newborn glory.

Sheralyn repeated the name, and added, "And Miss Forrest doesn't want to see her again, just so you know. We'll need to keep her in the nursery for at least twenty-four hours, and I've got a room for the two of you, if you'd like to follow me."

"Okay," Liam said, guiding Callie to follow the nurse. She took them to a room that had a couch and a recliner, but not a bed. He knew he wouldn't be able to get Callie to leave the baby for more than a few minutes, and he eyed the couch like it had already robbed him of a good night's sleep.

She sat down, and Liam sat next to her. Sheralyn said she'd bring them something to drink, and she left too.

"I wish my mother could see her," Callie said.

"She did," Liam said. "She knows."

Callie nodded, smiled down at Ginger, and leaned her head back against the couch.

Exhaustion pulled through Liam too, and he sent a quick text to Rhett. It's a girl. We named her Ginger Elizabeth, and they gave us a room because Vicki doesn't want to see her.

How long until we can come? Rhett asked. And I just mean us, with Denise.

Come this afternoon, Liam sent back to him. And let Jeremiah know we won't be home until at least tomorrow.

With his texts sent and his plans made, he said, "Rhett's going to bring Denise for a couple of hours this afternoon."

"Okay."

He'd just started to doze when Sheralyn returned. "Liam? Callie?"

His eyes shot open. "Yeah?"

"We need to talk about Ginger's test results."

9

Skyler woke to a slew of messages on his family text string, instant annoyance soaring through him. His brothers all woke with the sun, but Skyler did not. Which was why he'd muted the family texts and only looked at them when he was good and ready.

He hardly ever contributed anything, but if anyone noticed how quiet he was, they'd never said.

He yawned as he tapped on the phone to see he'd missed eighty-seven messages since last night.

"Eighty-seven?" The level of incredulity in his voice filled his bedroom. He put the phone back down, already overwhelmed with his family.

He loved them, sure. But at times like these, he was glad he was a little bit removed from them. In the shower, he hoped the thoughts of his brothers and all the families they'd started would wash down the drain with the water.

Honestly, it was hard being a Walker. There was a standard his parents expected, and Skyler had already fallen short of that several times. He'd never be as compassionate as Rhett, who looked over all the brothers, texting them individually and checking in constantly. At least he did that for Skyler, and he appreciated it.

Without Rhett, Skyler would feel very little connection to the brothers, and his oldest brother seemed to know it.

He'd never be able to play the role Jeremiah did, as family manager, cook, and the open-arms party planner. There was always room for one more with Jeremiah, especially now that he'd found a woman and was starting a family too.

The twins were great examples of how to avoid letting money and fame go to their heads, but they'd always had each other, and Skyler had given up trying to crack into their relationship. His best friends in the family—besides Rhett—were the younger brothers: Wyatt and Micah, and thankfully, neither of them had gotten married yet.

Skyler couldn't imagine what his life would be like if he were the last Walker to get married. The phone calls and texts he'd have to endure then.

The swirling thoughts of his family maintained him through his morning routine, and Skyler found himself grabbing a protein bar and a bottle of soda on his way out the door, just like he did every day. The thoughts were still with him. His phone felt heavy with all those messages, and Skyler kept looking at the device sitting in the console as he drove over to campus.

He didn't particularly like college, but he wasn't going to quit. He couldn't fail again.

After sliding into a seat in the back of his business finance class, Skyler decided to get the messages read and done with.

He now had over a hundred to sift through, and he wondered how any of his brothers could keep up. They had lives and responsibilities too.

He knew why the moment he tapped on the string. Rhett had texted first, and he'd said Liam and Callie just had a baby girl! They named her Ginger Elizabeth Walker. They'll keep us updated with more details, but they'll be in Amarillo until at least tomorrow.

Skyler's heart skipped and leapt as if it were running through a dewy meadow. He wasn't surprised by the name; it had been discussed to death on the family text. Ginger was Callie's mother's name, and Elizabeth was his great-grandmother's name.

The texts that came after were congratulations and well-wishes, followed by a couple of pictures of the new infant from Liam. Lots of hearts and *aww*-ing after those, and Skyler found himself smiling at his device while his professor talked about something he'd probably need to know to pass the class.

He reached the end of the texts and quickly added a *Congrats, Liam and Callie!* with his own heart emoticon, sent the message, and turned his phone over. Guilt threaded through him that he'd been frustrated with his brothers and their wives. A new baby was a good thing to celebrate, and one of the few reasons Skyler believed the family text should be used to communicate.

And he'd been surly about it.

He wondered if there would come a time when he didn't feel guilty, if that religious upbringing his parents had provided for their family would ever truly fade. The only time Skyler went to church anymore was when he was living at Seven Sons, and he'd been considering not going back to the ranch until his degree was finished. He could stay here in the summer, and take a few classes as he explored all that Amarillo had to offer.

His phone buzzed, which meant he'd gotten a message that wasn't from the brothers. He picked up his phone and saw a message from Mal. They'd been friends for a while, and he'd recently been attending her yoga class after she'd begged him to.

Skyler didn't enjoy yoga, just like he didn't like school, but Mal needed bodies in the class right now, and Skyler couldn't say no to her.

She was full of life and fun, and she liked a lot of the same things Skyler did—seeing the sights, talking about frivolous things, eating at every restaurant in the city.

Saw you smiling at your phone. What's on that thing that's so interesting?

He grinned again, looked around the huge auditorium-classroom for her, and didn't see her high, dark ponytail.

Hey, anything is more interesting than what Jackson is talking about. Skyler glanced up at the instructor. He honestly didn't even know what he was saying. *You'll have to help me catch up later.*

Right, Mal responded. *You'll get Suzie-Sally-Sarah to help you. Or some other blonde.*

Skyler shook his head, his smile widening. *Nope, it's gotta be you, Mal. I haven't been coming to all those yoga classes for nothing.*

Skyler had no romantic interest in Mal. Or Suzie, Sally, or Sarah, all of whom he'd flirted with like this via text or in person. He simply wasn't interested in having a real relationship with a woman at all.

Some people—the twins, Jeremiah, and probably Rhett too—called him a player. Heck, his own friends here at the university did too. He was comfortable in that role, and he didn't mind the negative label. Women knew what they were getting with Skyler Walker, and it wasn't his heart or his time.

Only if you tell me what had you smiling at the phone. If it's another woman, I'm out. She can help you with risk and return.

My brother had his baby this morning.

As soon as Skyler sent the text, he realized how it sounded. A laugh started in the bottom of his stomach, and he knew he wouldn't be able to contain it. And there was nothing funny about risk and return in the financial sector.

I mean, he didn't have a baby. He and his wife are adopting, and the baby was born this morning.

He heard someone giggle to his right, and he knew it was Mal. He had to get out of there. He quickly tapped send on the last message, grabbed his backpack, and headed for the door, a chuckle escaping his mouth as he went.

In the hall, he laughed before the door was all the way closed. The thought of Liam having a baby shouldn't be this funny, and maybe Skyler was stressed. Maybe he felt ashamed for thinking his family was a burden when the texts were worthy and about something he wanted to know.

A moment later, the door opened again, and Mal and her giggles spilled into the hallway too. Skyler started laughing again, and it sure was nice to chase away some of his darker emotions with laugher.

And oh, Skyler was very good at covering up his true feelings with laughter.

"Your brother had a baby," Mal said, still laughing.

"He did," Skyler said. "And I need to call him and see if I can go visit. They're here in the city." That would probably earn him some much-needed family points, but Skyler hated that thought too. No one was keeping score with points. He knew that, but it still felt like he was

Wyatt

playing catch-up, especially with Micah living at Seven Sons now.

"You better get back in there and take notes," he teased as Mal pulled her long, dark hair into a ponytail. She had olive skin and a pair of deep, dark eyes too. She hailed from South of the border, and she was an exotic kind of beautiful Skyler really liked.

Their eyes met as she sobered, and something arced between them that he had never felt with her before. "I can't go back in there," she teased. "I had to climb over four people with all my stuff." She lifted her backpack and her purse, both of which were quite bulky. "As I laughed out loud."

She shook her head, her eyes glittering at him. "No way. You go take the notes."

"I have to call my brother." Skyler was the master at finding excuses, and he tapped Liam's name in the family text string, which was still going strong, and then the phone icon to call him.

"Skyler," Liam said, his voice full of warmth.

"Hey, bro," he said. "Congratulations on the new baby."

Mal dissolved into giggles again, and Skyler couldn't help grinning. "I know Callie said no visitors, but it would just be me, and I'm not loud." *Not like the other brothers*, he wanted to say. But honestly, when the seven of them got together in the same room, Skyler could be just as loud and just as obnoxious. It was almost like a different version

97

of himself emerged around the men he'd grown up with, and he had no control over that side.

"Sure," he said. "How do you feel about bringing us lunch? What's your class schedule like?"

"I can do that," Skyler said, because he didn't need to go to his auditing class. If there was anything more boring than business finance, it was auditing. "Tell me what you want, and when to bring it, and I'll be there."

He looked at Mal and caught her watching him. He smiled, and she returned the gesture. Nothing romantic had ever sparked between them before, and he'd seen her wearing super-tight clothing as she contorted her body during yoga classes. So what had changed?

"I want that roast beef sandwich from that place you took me to last time I was here," Liam said. "And all the salt and vinegar chips I can get."

Skyler chuckled. "Papa Henry's," he said. "Hot or cold?"

"Hot, of course," Liam said as if eating a cold sandwich was ridiculous. And actually, in Skyler's opinion—and Liam's too, apparently—it was.

"And for Callie?"

"She wants the BLT," Liam said. "With a side salad. Ranch dressing."

"I'll get it and bring it over around noon?"

"Thank you, Skyler," Liam said, and he truly sounded grateful. Skyler knew it wasn't an act, and his heart shriveled a little more when he remembered how annoyed he'd been at the family texts.

"See you then," he said, hanging up quickly, before his emotions could overwhelm him too much. Plus, he had an audience.

He looked back at Mal, wondering if maybe he'd just had a moment of weakness with her. "I'm taking them lunch. You wanna play hooky with me and go see my brother, his wife, and their new baby?"

"Oh, playing hooky is what I do best," she said, lifting her backpack to her shoulder. "But I have to get rid of some of this stuff if we're going to the hospital. Drive me home?"

He'd taken her home several times after her evening yoga classes, as she had an unreliable car. "Let's go, Miss Mallery." He grinned, because he knew she hated her full name. He'd teased her in a heavy Texan accent, because he knew it would cover up anything else that had happened between them.

And Skyler needed there to be nothing between them, because he absolutely wasn't going to get seriously involved with anyone while in Amarillo.

Ever, he told himself, glad when everything went back to light-hearted and easy between him and Mal as they walked out to the parking lot.

10

Rhett held his son on his lap as he waited for the rest of the family to arrive at Seven Sons. Jeremiah was already here, of course, as he'd been laboring in the kitchen for a couple of hours now. He whistled while he kneaded dough, and out-right sang as he formed meatballs and slid them into the oven.

His wife, Whitney, appeared from the hallway that led down to the bedrooms, and she smiled at Rhett as she joined him in the living room. "Can I hold him?"

"Sure thing." Rhett passed Conrad to Whitney, who gave the baby a kiss on his cheek before settling him onto her lap. Conrad was used to being passed around, and he continued to babble as he clutched the teething ring Evelyn had bought for him.

Rhett had taken it out of the freezer just before bringing the boy to the ranch, and Conrad loved the thing.

"Where's Evelyn?" Whitney asked.

"She's next door," Rhett said. "Helping Callie get the kids ready."

Callie and Liam had returned from the hospital that day, but Rhett hadn't seen them yet. Simone and Evelyn had been at their family ranch for an hour or two, and everyone was gathering at Seven Sons for dinner.

As if on cue, the back door opened, and Wyatt and Micah came inside, talking. They washed their hands while Micah laughed at something, and they stayed in the kitchen, giving some kind of report to Jeremiah.

Rhett was content to sit in the background and watch. He hadn't known when he'd first bought the ranch that it would become a beacon of light for their family. He'd known it was the right thing to do, but he could not have predicted the events of the past four years.

The front door opened, and eight-year-old Oliver called, "Jeremiah?" He came running down the hall from the door, and Jeremiah went to greet him. Rhett marveled in the change in his younger brother, because when Jeremiah had come to Three Rivers, he'd been filled with resentment and anger.

Rhett knew most of that had been directed inwardly, but at least some of it had projected onto God.

He'd prayed for his brother for a solid year, and he was so happy Jeremiah had found happiness with Whitney.

Jeremiah scooped Oliver into his arms with a smile

and a laugh. Before Rhett could eavesdrop further on them, Liam said, "We're here," and chaos broke out.

Rhett was on his feet faster than lightning, and he paused next to Whitney. "You okay with him?"

"Yes, go," she said, and Rhett did. He hugged Tripp and Ivory first, welcoming them to the ranch. Then he took Denise from Liam and hugged him with the little girl balanced on his hip.

Callie carried the baby, and her sisters had rallied behind her. They all seemed to be glowing, and Rhett hardly recognized the Foster sisters. They'd come so far since that first time he'd met them in the cellar beneath the house, a tornado raging around them.

He'd always known of their strength, and wow, they all possessed an iron will. Evelyn hadn't been an easy one to convince that she needed Rhett in her life, and Callie had resisted Liam just as much.

Rhett gazed down at the beautiful little girl in Callie's arms, and he couldn't believe he'd once had a human that tiny to take care of.

He glanced up, his eyes immediately going to Micah, who stood back by the island, his eyes glued to Simone. Rhett knew there was something going on there, but from the storm on his youngest brother's face, it wasn't something good.

"We have a quick announcement," Liam said, and everyone quieted. "First, we want to say thank you to everyone for the prayers, and a special thanks to Jeremiah for cooking for us tonight."

Everyone clapped, and Jeremiah simply ducked his head.

"Skyler said he wishes he could be here with us," Liam said, but Rhett wondered if that was true. He hadn't texted that particular brother in a while, and Rhett could feel him slipping further and further away. But he didn't know how to reel him back in.

He couldn't imagine not being at this ranch for this celebration. It was exactly where he should be, and where he wanted to be, and he wanted every one of the brothers, their wives, their parents, everyone, with him.

That was heaven to Rhett, and he hoped he'd get to see all of these people there too.

"And last," he said, glancing at Callie and their new baby Ginger. "Ginger was born with some addiction, though it is slight. She's going through a detoxification process, and we have to monitor her heavily for the first several months. She's a little fussy because of it, and we're getting the help we need."

He looked so calm, but Rhett could feel the emotion pouring off of Liam. He grabbed him in a hug, and Liam held him tight. "Love you, brother," Rhett said. "I can help. I'm not doing anything right now."

"I might need you," Liam said.

He worked as an animator, and he'd taken on a four-year project with one of the biggest superhero franchises in the world. And he'd gotten two children in the span of a few months. Rhett couldn't even imagine how much Liam and Callie must be reeling.

More hugs were given out, and Evelyn took Conrad from Whitney and put him in a highchair. He'd gotten a headstart on dinner by the time Jeremiah said, "Okay, we're ready to eat?"

Rhett jostled for a seat close to Conrad, and he watched Micah try to sit next to Simone. She'd actually sat down, and she jumped back to her feet. "Let me help with Denise," she said to Callie, and she picked up the little girl and put her in another highchair.

Micah clenched his teeth and kept his eyes on Simone. When he finally turned away, he wore a look of disappointment and resignation.

Everyone was talking and chattering, and finally Jeremiah said, "Rhett. Call on someone to say the prayer, would you?"

"Oh, right." He'd forgotten that as the oldest brother, he usually did that. "Tripp, would you?"

"Of course." Hats were swiped off heads, and Tripp closed his eyes. Rhett didn't though. He looked around at all these people he loved as Tripp said, "Thank you, Lord, for the blessings we enjoy. Thank you for family. For a good reason to get together to celebrate the birth of this precious baby. Bless Ginger that she will heal quickly, and that Callie and Liam will know exactly what to do for her.

We pray for Thy hand in our lives, always, guiding us and helping us. Amen."

"Amen," filled the homestead, and Rhett lifted up his voice in praise to God too.

"And bless the food," Jeremiah said. "It's barbecue meatball pockets. Come get it."

Rhett made sure he stood next to Micah in line, asking quietly, "What's with you and Simone?"

"Nothing there," Micah practically barked.

"No?"

"She's made that clear," he said, putting three meatball pockets on his plate and moving down to the salad.

"Maybe—"

"No," Micah said. "In fact, she's dating someone else. End of story."

"Oh, okay," Rhett said, though he had not heard that Simone was dating someone else. He'd have to ask Evelyn about that. "You want to go riding tomorrow?"

"Yeah," Micah said. "Jeremiah has his ranch owner's meeting in the morning, so anytime works."

Rhett didn't care if Jeremiah didn't like what time he showed up to ride his horse. But he just said, "I'll come over in the morning then," and left it at that.

"Uh, guys?" someone said, and Rhett looked over to find Wyatt trying to get everyone's attention. The chaos calmed slightly, and he added, "I should've done this before we started getting food, but I have an announcement. A couple of them actually."

He held up his phone, and Rhett's curiosity shot through the sky.

"Momma's on speaker, and I just told her Liam and Callie were home with their kids. Tell 'em, Momma."

"Hello, boys," she said, and Rhett smiled at the sweet sound of his mother's voice. He missed her with a fierceness only the heat of the sun could rival, and he hoped the announcement she was about to make would be the one they'd been discussing for the past few days.

"And wives, and now new grandbabies." Her voice choked for a moment. "Daddy and I are moving to Three Rivers," she finally said.

A roar went up, and smiles exploded onto every face. Rhett knew then just how much his parents were loved, and he couldn't wait for his father and mother to be more involved in Conrad's life. And honestly, Evelyn would love to have them close by too, as she'd lost her mother at a very early age.

Once that started dying down, every eye trained on Wyatt again. Finally Micah asked, "What's the second announcement, Wyatt?"

"Yeah," Jeremiah said. "Spit it out. We're starving."

Wyatt looked at the phone. "You still there, Momma?"

"Right here, sugar."

He looked out at the mass of people, and Rhett knew what it was like to talk to all of them. He loved them, but there were some strong opinions among the Walkers, that was for certain.

"I'm engaged," he said. "To Marcy Payne. We're getting married next month."

A beat of silence passed, then two. Rhett didn't know what to say or do. Of course, he knew Wyatt had liked Marcy for a while now. But marriage?

On the third beat of silence, a general roar went up, with questions flying from one side of the kitchen to the other, congratulations being said, and some people laughing.

Wyatt wore his fake, rodeo smile, and Rhett suspected something was off. This was Wyatt, the man who'd ridden the fiercest horses bareback, and calmed the toughest bulls for eight long seconds.

So why was he treating the family like they were reporters?

He picked up another meatball pocket and bit into it, the sweet and tangy barbecue sauce the perfect pairing with the savory and salty meatball, and the perfectly browned bread with garlic butter brushed on the outside.

Wyatt answered all the questions with the smooth demeanor of someone who'd been behind a microphone before. Who'd performed for a crowd, who'd made complete strangers fall in love with him.

Rhett stepped to his side and said, "Congratulations, Wyatt."

"Thanks, Rhett." Wyatt beamed at him, but Rhett saw something in the depth of those eyes that couldn't lie.

"Stop by for breakfast tomorrow?" he asked, expecting

Wyatt to decline. He had a job a long drive from the ranch, and he'd literally never stopped at Rhett's for breakfast before.

But tonight, he said, "Sure thing."

"Great," Rhett said. "We need to talk."

11

Marcy sat at her father's dining room table, an assortment of papers spread in front of her. Thankfully, they weren't anything to do with the will, or the ridiculous stipulations of her inheritance of Payne's Pest-free.

No, these were checklists and to-do lists for her wedding. Her wedding with Wyatt.

Marcy waited for the familiar nerves and slip of guilt to accompany her at the table, but they didn't come. She paused, wondering what that meant.

She'd been kissing him hello and good-bye for a week now, and she expected him to show up at the house any minute now.

His parents were coming to Three Rivers in three weeks, and they'd be married in four.

Married in a month.

Marcy's vision blurred as she looked at the lists in front of her. Wyatt had said he'd book the venue, but he hadn't confirmed anything quite yet. Marcy had ordered the flowers—check. She'd asked Alyssa to make her a cake —check. She and Wyatt had agreed to forgo announcements, so there were no pictures to take. Whitney, Jeremiah's wife, had agreed to take the photos on their wedding day—check.

They'd be living in this house until it was cleaned up and ready to put on the market, and Marcy should probably at least try to go through one closet today. That was her deal with herself. Keep up with Payne's. Get all the fields dusted she'd committed to. Keep up with the paperwork and the emails and the phone calls.

Then, at night, she'd get to see Wyatt, and they'd do at least one task around her father's house.

She looked up, the house suddenly so empty. A chill ran through her so strongly that she looked around for an open window. There was none. The house where her parents had lived for over fifty years was just empty now that they were gone. Hollow.

She got up and started brewing a pot of coffee in the kitchen. She and Wyatt had gone through the kitchen cupboards, drawers, and pantry. She didn't keep hardly anything to eat here at all, but there was coffee and cream and sugar. Wyatt brought food with him every night, and Marcy ate breakfast and lunch from her own house.

A few dishes, cups, and utensils remained, but the

majority of the items had been boxed up and put in the garage. She and Wyatt would take them to the Salvation Army tomorrow morning, though Alyssa and Savannah had mentioned having a massive estate sale.

That sounded like so much work to Marcy, and when neither of them had brought it up again, she'd let it go too. It was easier to donate the items than try to price them and then watch neighbors and friends buy them.

She faced the living room, with all the books and movies and family pictures. She'd just stepped over to the mantel where her father kept dozens of pictures of her and Bryan, as well as their mother.

She saw their family pictures, taken every October, as Marcy's mom had loved the fall leaves, and there was a very narrow window to them in Texas. She remembered the trip to San Antonio, the vacation to Chicago, one to Washington D.C., and one to Florida. Mom had wanted to go to Hawaii, but she'd never made it there.

Florida was warm and humid, and she'd been like a kid in a candy shop on the white-sand beaches of the Gulf of Mexico.

Tears slipped down her face, but they weren't uncontrollable or even borne from sadness. They were simply her body's response to happy times, and she lovingly touched the top of one picture frame that held their last family picture before her mother had died.

"Marce?" Wyatt asked as he came through the front door. He brought the scent of freshly baked bread with him, and she wiped her face quickly, sniffled, and turned to face him.

"Hey, here comes the king," she said, smiling at him.

He paused, a smile on his face, but not the one that carried its normal wattage. "Okay, never say that again." He chuckled as he went into the kitchen.

She laughed as she followed him. "I thought you liked being called the rodeo king."

"Not by you," he said simply.

Marcy looked at him, but he focused on pulling out breadsticks and then a plastic container that she hoped contained pasta carbonara. And it totally did, because Wyatt knew what she liked. "Not by me? What does that mean?"

He sighed and set another container that had spaghetti and meatballs in it, and a flash of pride moved through her that she would've ordered that for him. "It means, Marcy, that I want you to know the real Wyatt Walker. Not the one who smiles at the cameras and signs autographs."

He looked at her, an intensity on his face she hadn't expected. She'd seen it before, of course, on the Internet videos she'd watched of him riding the bulls and throwing the ropes. He was a champion who charmed thousands by taking off his hat and waving it at them, giving them all the credit for cheering for him. He was a man who knew what he wanted, worked to get it, and achieved things. He was someone who could get in the zone and block out all other distractions. He kissed her like that, and Marcy had never been kissed so thoroughly.

"I know the real Wyatt Walker," she said, her voice a touch too high. "And I sure do like how he brings me the exact pasta dish I love, and that he comes over here to help me with my father's house." Her breath caught in her lungs, but her voice stayed steady. "And I love that he's going to help me keep the business, and that he's hard-working, and kind, and loves his momma, and—"

"Okay," he said. "This is worse." He grinned at her and took her into his arms.

"And for the record," she said, sliding her hands up his chest until they curled around the back of his neck. "I would've known to order you the spaghetti and meatballs. And I started coffee a few minutes ago, because I know you love it fresh and hot. And I keep cream here, because I know you like it."

"So you kinda like me too," he whispered, leaning toward her.

Marcy giggled, tipping her head back to receive his kiss. And she got that bone-melting kiss, where she was the absolute focus of Wyatt's attention. And he was definitely a king to her.

"Okay," she said, pulling away. "I'm starving, and we need to go over a few things for the wedding."

"Right, the wedding." Wyatt wiped his mouth and pulled plastic forks out of the bag. "How do you feel about having puppies for ring bearers?"

Marcy looked at him, and she knew instantly that something was up, because he wouldn't meet her eye. "Puppies?"

"I'm good friends with a former rodeo guy, and he now owns a huge animal rescue and training operation on the east side of town. Lots of space. Big trees. And he said we could have the wedding there, and there would be a lot of room for people."

"And by people, you mean reporters."

"There's gonna be some reporters, yes," he said. "As soon as we lock down the location, I'll have Jim make the formal announcement, and then we can coordinate from there." He took his food to the dining room table and surveyed her lists.

"We're only feeding family, though, right?" she asked.

"Yes," he said. "And Jeremiah said we could do it at the ranch or here or wherever. He says food transports pretty easily. Tripp offered his house, and it's huge."

"Okay." Marcy exhaled as she sat at the table with him. "So we're talking venue and food right now. And we need to discuss refreshments too, if we're going to offer them for wedding guests or restrict everything to family."

"If it's all the same to you," he said. "I think we should have refreshments at the wedding. It's just money."

"And you have plenty of that," Marcy said. She did too, actually. Maybe not enough to refresh the entire town of Three Rivers, as well as those who rode the rodeo circuit. But enough.

"Maybe those little bundt cakes," he said. "And sweet tea and lemonade."

"Oh, now you're just naming all your favorite things," she teased.

"Well, it's my wedding," he said, cutting a meatball in half. "Shouldn't I have all my favorite things?"

"Absolutely," she said, reaching for one of her lists. "I'll just jot that down right here."

"I'll do all the refreshments at Four Paws, and Jeremiah will cook for the family."

Marcy consulted her sheet, noticing how many boxes this one conversation would tick. She started marking them off. Venue—check. Food—check. Refreshments— check. "Things are coming together," she said.

"What's left on that list?" he asked.

"I need a dress," she said with a sigh. She put the paper down and picked up her fork. "I don't have time to look for a wedding dress." She thought of the one down the hall in her parents' bedroom closet. The dress had been haunting her during quiet moments, and she actually looked down the hall.

"We can go tomorrow," he said. "After we drop the stuff off at the Salvation Army."

"You can't see me in the wedding dress, Wyatt," she said. "Not before the wedding."

"Oh, so we're sticking to some traditions too."

"Yes," she said, looking at him. He gazed at her too, and Marcy thought of the conversations they'd had over the past several days. This was real for her, and she wanted to treat it as such. "Weren't you the one who told your brother that yes, the marriage might be a little fake now, but it was definitely going to be real later?"

Wyatt nodded, stirring his spaghetti around. "I did say that. I can't believe I told you I said that, but I did say it."

"I need to meet Rhett," Marcy said. "He seems like the kind of man who can get you to say exactly what's what."

"I do that for you too," he said. "In case you were wondering. And I can't keep a secret from my momma or my manager either."

"So do they know our little union is a little fake?"

"Not yet." He grinned. "But as soon as I call Jim and tell him to reach out to everyone about my marriage, there will be a lot of questions."

"And your mother didn't have any?"

"I mean, I may or may not have told her we'd been dating for a year." He lifted one shoulder in a shrug. "In my mind, we've been dating for a year."

Marcy gaped at him, her heart beating surprise through her bloodstream with every pulse. "You told her that?"

"Maybe," he said. "Don't look like I hit you with a frying pan."

Marcy gathered herself together and shook her hair over her shoulders. "How's the house-hunting going for your parents?"

"Rhett and Tripp are handling it," he said. "They're

the least busy of the brothers, but they're fighting over the location."

"Like, really fighting?"

"As much as Walkers do," Wyatt said. "So arguing, sending texts, looking at half a dozen houses each day. That kind of thing."

"And your mother trusts them to find her a house?"

"Oh, Momma trusts Rhett explicitly. You should hear her talk about him." He looked up toward the ceiling. "We're all surprised God hasn't taken Rhett straight to heaven yet."

Marcy burst out laughing, glad Wyatt did too. "I love him to death, don't get me wrong," he said. "But yeah. Rhett can do no wrong in Momma's eyes."

"You're like that too, though," she said, giving him a look out of the corner of her eye. "I mean, your mother thinks you walk on water too."

"Does she?"

"Doesn't she?" Marcy put a bite of noodles, bacon, and peas in her mouth, her taste buds rejoicing mightily.

"I wouldn't say that," he said. "And I can't wait for you to meet them. She's going to love you. Daddy too."

Marcy could hardly swallow after that. She'd somehow forgotten that she'd have to meet his parents and pull off this sham of a wedding. As they continued eating, Marcy reminded herself that it wasn't one-hundred-percent sham. She liked this gentle giant of a cowboy next to her, and she liked him a whole heckuva lot.

"What about the brothers?" she finally asked, once she'd eaten more carbonara than was probably healthy. "When am I meeting them?"

"How about Sunday after church?" he asked, glancing at her. "It's loud, and messy, and we have babies and kids now. But no one bites all that hard."

"Even Jeremiah?" she asked.

"He's settled right down now that he and Whitney are permanent." Wyatt flashed her a grin and pushed his nearly empty container of spaghetti away. "All right, sugar. What are we doin' tonight?"

Marcy put one more bite of salty, savory pasta in her mouth. "Let's tackle the hall closet," she said, looking at the family pictures along the mantel. She wanted to leave them there for another day, because the memories were happy, and she craved seeing her family in this house even if their spirits had departed.

"Oh-ho," Wyatt said, chuckling. "The hall closet. Should be fun." He got up and took their containers into the kitchen. Marcy just watched him, because he was all of those things she'd said earlier.

And she did like him. As she gazed at him as he cleaned up and poured two cups of coffee, Marcy may or may not have slipped a little further along the path toward loving him.

Maybe, just like he'd said. *Just maybe.*

And while a vein of fear accompanied her thoughts, Marcy got up and joined him in the kitchen. "Thank you,

Wyatt," she said. It could've been for the food. Or for his company. His help over the past year, with everything from taking her father to a doctor's appointment to picking up the blue mechanic rags around the shop.

He looked down at her. "You don't need to thank me." His arm snaked around her waist. "Remember how I'm not doing anything I don't want to do?"

"Except for cleaning out a hall closet," she said.

He touched the tip of his nose to hers. "That's where you're wrong, Marce. I'm right where I want to be, doing exactly what I want to be doing." He straightened, a flicker of discomfort moving through those gorgeous eyes. "Now, let's get 'er done so I can take a nap."

Marcy laughed, and they went down the hall together, opening the closet to find it stuffed—literally stuffed—with towels, bedsheets, board games, and more.

"Oh, boy," Wyatt grumbled under his breath. He pulled on one towel and a mountain of them started raining out of the closet.

"I'll get the boxes," Marcy said, leaving him with the linens. He was definitely doing something he didn't want to do, and Marcy could only hope that it only extended to washcloths and tea towels, and that when he said he wanted to marry her, he was speaking the truth.

12

W yatt stepped onto the back deck, leaving the scent of fried eggs and bacon behind in the homestead. Jeremiah was really taking this dote-on-his-pregnant-wife thing to the extreme. But one thought of Marcy, and Wyatt realized he'd do the exact same thing if she needed him to.

Plus, he liked bacon and eggs and coffee for breakfast. Micah wasn't complaining either, that was for dang sure.

Wyatt lifted his phone to his ear after tapping Jim's name on the screen. His manager would most likely answer within the first couple of rings, as he never went very far from his phone, never slept past five a.m., and loved to hear from his star rodeo client.

"Mornin', Wyatt," he drawled out. "It's bright and early on a Saturday."

"Did I wake you?" he asked, smiling at the fatherly

sound of Jim's voice. Sometimes, Jim was the only friend Wyatt had on the rodeo circuit, and the older man had taken really good care of Wyatt. He'd helped him out of a couple of tight situations, including one with a pair of women that still made Wyatt shiver in fear.

"Not at all," he said. "I just thought you'd sleep past dawn now that you're not training."

"Old habits die hard," Wyatt said, smiling as the sun started to turn the world gold. "Listen, I'm calling because I have an announcement I'd like you to make."

"Lay it on me."

"I'm getting married, and I'd like anyone who wants to show up in Three Rivers, Texas, to come."

A beat of silence passed, and then two. "You're getting married?"

"That's right." Wyatt closed his eyes in a long blink, expecting a deluge of questions. "February twentieth."

"You're getting married in four weeks?"

"That's right."

"How long have you known this woman?"

"Over a year, Jim."

"Is she willing to sign a prenuptial agreement?" he asked. "I know you don't like talking about that, but Wyatt, you have a lot of assets to protect."

"I know that," Wyatt said. He and Jim had had this conversation before, though Wyatt had never really had a serious relationship while on the rodeo circuit. His mind flew back to those days, and in comparison to what he did now, they were definitely simpler. Yes, traveling could be difficult from time to time.

But he had someone paying his bills, telling him what and when to eat, and all he'd done was train or drive—or sleep while someone else drove. His life in the rodeo had been physically exhausting, mentally challenging, but so many of the little pieces were taken care of by someone else.

Wyatt was trying to manage all of those balls now himself, and he constantly felt like he was about to drop them all.

"So she signed one."

"I haven't brought it up yet."

"Wyatt," Jim said, and that was all. He didn't need to say more than that.

Wyatt rolled his shoulders. "I'm going to," he said. "Today, actually. I just need to know what you need from me to make the announcement."

"Okay, cowboy, let's get something straight," Jim said, and Wyatt grinned at the familiar phrase. He'd missed it more than he'd admitted to himself. Jim would say it to him only minutes before every event he did.

Okay, cowboy, let's get something straight: You're the top roper here. Go prove it.

"All right," Wyatt said, chuckling. "What do I need to get straight?"

"I'm not the one going in front of the media with this news."

Horror struck Wyatt right behind his heart. "Well, I'm not. That's why I have you."

"I can call all the right people," Jim said. "And you'll be the one to get up there and break the news to all the cowgirls out there still holding onto the hope that you'll somehow show up at their doorsteps, a diamond in your hand."

Okay, cowboy, let's get something straight: You've drawn the highest ranked bull. Go ride it. Eight seconds.

Wyatt wondered how long it would take to tell the world that he was engaged and about to be married. Couldn't take more than eight seconds. Could it?

"All right," Wyatt said with a great big sigh. "When?"

"You tell me," he said. "The hype over the rookies has died down, and there's a definite lull in the industry right now. This will be huge."

"Let's do it next Saturday," he said.

"In Three Rivers?"

"That's quite a drive for people," he said. "What would be easier? I can fly in somewhere." He had the sudden thought that he should probably show up to the press conference announcing his engagement with his fiancée. Marcy had commitments and work to do, and she might not be able to come along next Saturday.

And she's not just coming along, he told himself. This wasn't a show. It wasn't another rodeo event.

She was going to be his *wife,* and he was entirely too excited about that. At the same time, Marcy had loosened up around him over the past week since she'd said yes to his proposal, and he knew she liked him.

This marriage isn't a charitable event, he thought.

"Why don't you see if you can come to Dallas?" Jim asked. "And I'm going to need all the details. Date, time, place, how you two met. I'm going to need pictures and all of that."

Wyatt's throat narrowed, his task list for the day exploding right before his eyes. "Yeah, sure," he managed to say. He'd played a part for long enough in his life that he sounded natural and like he had all of those things ready for his manager.

"I'll wait for it," he said. "And Wyatt? I just have to know one thing...."

Wyatt tipped his head back and filled the Texas sky with laughter.

"I'm going to take that as a yes," Jim said, chuckling too. "Good for you, Wyatt. I'll wait for your email before I make any phone calls."

The call ended while the last of Wyatt's laughter died out. "Yeah, Jim," he said almost under his breath. "She's blonde."

———

THE NEXT DAY, Wyatt enjoyed church more than he ever had before. His back felt great, number one. Number two, Jeremiah had made his favorite food for dinner—prime rib.

And thirdly, he currently sat on a bench next to Marcy, her hand solidly in his. He'd dreamed of this hour of his life for far too long, and it was as magical as he'd imagined.

He loved the calluses on her hands from where she worked on her airplanes, and he loved the soft peach scent of her perfume, that hint of grease just underneath. He liked the cute little pencil skirt she wore, and the heels, and the bright pink blouse with airplanes on it.

His heart thumped in that odd way it did whenever he was around Marcy, but this time it was because they were sitting just across the aisle from the rest of his family. The Walkers had grown a lot in the past couple of years, and they took up two benches in the little white church in downtown Three Rivers.

Wyatt loved the slower pace of Sunday, and he loved singing praises to the Lord. He hadn't always taken the time he needed to feed his spirit, though, and the rebellious side of him often thought he was smarter than God.

Today, though, he closed his eyes as Pastor Daniels talked about how to better study the scriptures, and he prayed that the Good Lord would help him make sure Marcy was well taken care of. Wyatt wanted to be the one to provide for her every need, but he hadn't thought of anyone but himself for so long, he wasn't sure how.

The sermon ended, and Wyatt's back didn't protest as he stood to sing the last hymn. Marcy's mouth moved, but he couldn't hear her singing at all, and he slipped his arm around her waist. "You're not singing."

"My momma taught me that sometimes it's okay to lip sync." She smiled up at him. "Which is always for me. I can't carry a tune."

Wyatt's eyebrows went up as her eyes twinkled at him. "Is that right? I didn't know that about you."

"Now you do. And I expect to know one of your flaws before lunchtime." She hipped him, clapped along with the song, and moved her mouth, no sound coming out.

A rush of affection for her filled Wyatt, and he pressed his lips to her temple. Even her flaws were awesome, and Wyatt fell a little further in love with her in that moment.

He took time to savor the feeling, because the moment the service ended, his family descended. "Are we heading straight to the ranch?" Rhett asked.

"I need ten minutes with the food," Jeremiah said.

"Ivory has to change her shoes." Tripp started for the exit first, thank goodness. The others followed, Liam's new baby crying and Whitney pressing one hand to her pregnant belly as she followed everyone.

Wyatt watched them all go, and he caught sight of the dumbfounded look on Marcy's face as she stood in the aisle too. "It's going to be fine," he said.

"I hope I don't get married last," Micah said, joining them in the aisle. "Can you imagine?" He shook his head and reseated his cowboy hat. "It's a good thing Skyler says he's never getting married."

"He says that?" Wyatt looked at his youngest brother in surprise.

"All the time," Micah said. "And you've met him. He's not serious about much of anything."

"He's getting good grades in college," Wyatt said.

"Yeah, and taking mostly things like yoga and flower arranging, with one accounting class thrown in."

"He takes yoga?" They started toward the back door, and Wyatt realized he needed to talk to Skyler more often. "Wow, that's a really low low, right?"

"I think he thinks it's a high," Micah said, chuckling. "Comparatively."

"Oh, we've all had our hearts broken," Wyatt said. "Look at Jeremiah. His fiancée left him at the altar, and he got married again."

"Skyler said he's not cut out for it."

Wyatt reached the door and paused to let Micah go first. He kept hold of Marcy's hand as she exited too, and he went right behind her. "Interesting. How are things with you and Simone?"

"There's no me and Simone," Micah said, his voice a little bit false. "We're just friends."

"Yeah, and so were Evelyn and Rhett. And Callie and Liam."

"Yeah, and Simone has a boyfriend." Micah gave Wyatt a piercing glare. "So just drop it."

Marcy's hand in Wyatt's tightened, and he looked at her. "You okay to go straight to the ranch?"

"Do I have a choice?"

"Sure," he said. "Do you want to change or anything?"

"I'd love that."

Wyatt helped her into his truck and drove to her house, the silence between them comforting and welcome. He waited in the truck while Marcy ran inside, the idea of asking her about a prenuptial agreement rolling around his mind. He hadn't brought it up yesterday, because they'd had a great morning together taking a dozen boxes to the Salvation Army and then going to breakfast.

They'd worked through one of the spare bedrooms at her father's house, and then they'd taken a nap together on the couch while a movie played. He'd bought dinner, and they'd eaten together, and he couldn't imagine bringing up the idea that he didn't trust her.

She came back outside wearing a pair of jeans, her combat boots that got his heart racing, and a jacket in green camouflage. Wyatt found her downright desirable with those blonde curls making her clothing choices oh so feminine.

"You look great," he said as she climbed into the truck.

"Thanks." She flashed him a smile, and Wyatt flexed his fingers around the steering wheel. "What's wrong?"

"Nothing."

"We're not moving," she said. "And you're kneading that wheel like it's your next breadstick. Something's wrong."

"I sent everything off to my manager so he could announce the wedding," he said.

"Okay," she said, drawing the word out.

"He wants me to make the announcement in Dallas on Saturday." He looked at her. "I want you to come with me."

Surprise filled her face. "Oh, this Saturday?"

"Yes."

"I can move a couple of fields," she said. "I don't do a whole lot on the weekends."

He smiled at her, his stomach clenching and not only because it was hungry. "There's one more thing."

Marcy nodded and swallowed, the movement drawing Wyatt's attention to that slender throat.

"Jim is insisting you sign a prenuptial agreement." He cleared his throat. "I don't think it's necessary, for the record. I know you're not marrying me for my money."

Marcy had that look again, the one that said he'd hit her upside the head with a frying pan. "You said you wanted to."

"I do," Wyatt said.

"It's a favor for me," she said. "I would never—"

"Marce," he said, because he hated the panic in her voice. "I know all of that. Jim's job is to make sure my assets are protected. He just said it would be wise." He put the truck in reverse, because sitting there talking was way worse than driving while they had the same conversation.

"It's no big deal. He sent me the form. All you do is sign it."

She folded her arms and looked out the passenger window. "Okay."

Wyatt sighed internally, because he didn't want her to think he was frustrated with her. He was simply annoyed at the situation. "You have a lot of assets," he said.

"I know you would never try to take Payne's from me," she said.

"I wouldn't," he said. "And I don't think you'd ever try to take something from me either."

"Do you have this form with you?"

"I need to print it," he said, navigating out of her neighborhood. "If you don't want to, it's fine. I just told Jim I'd mention it, and I did." And foolishness had every organ in his body rioting.

Okay, cowboy, let's get something straight: You like this woman. Don't ruin this.

"Marcy—"

"I'll sign it," she said. "It's smart, and I don't want anything to be hard for you."

"Marcy, it's not about being hard."

"It is if we split up," she said.

He jerked his attention to her then.

"And so I'd like you to sign one too." She clenched her arms across her body and didn't look at him.

Wyatt got on the highway and got the truck going faster. "I'm sorry to bring it up. I shouldn't have."

"It's fine," she said. "You can print at the homestead, right?"

"I'm not having you sign it on the same day you're meeting my whole family." Wyatt shook his head. "It can wait." He glanced at her. "Honestly, Marcy, I don't care about it."

She finally looked at him, and Wyatt wasn't sure what emotions she had swimming in her eyes. He couldn't look at her for long, as he was driving highway speeds and needed to focus on the road.

"I'll do it," she said. "It's fine."

Wyatt may not have had a lot of girlfriends, but he knew when a woman said "it's fine," in that way-too-casual tone, it definitely wasn't fine.

But he had no idea what to do about it, and he sent up another prayer like the one he'd issued during the sermon. *Just a hint*, he pleaded. *Of what to do or say so I don't mess this up.*

An idea entered his mind, and he toyed with it as the miles rolled by under his tires.

13

The silence in the truck suffocated Marcy, but she didn't know what to say. Prenuptial agreement.

Of course, it made sense from Wyatt's point of view. He did have a lot of money and a lot of assets, and he was only marrying her so she could get Payne's Pest-free.

Even as she thought it, she knew she was wrong. Wyatt was doing her a favor, sure. But he was doing it out of the goodness of his heart, and he truly liked her. No man could kiss the way he did and not mean it.

He pulled up to a beautiful, sprawling ranch that screamed wealth from the fences that stretched east and west to the giant house sitting back off the road. The landscaping obviously had someone with a deft hand looking after it, and she felt like the Lord shone the sun differently on this piece of land than any other.

"Wow," she said.

Wyatt put the truck in park behind several others already in the driveway. "Marcy," he said. "We're okay, right? I mean, I'm stupid for bringing it up, but you said you were tone deaf. Maybe I just didn't want you to think you were the only one with flaws."

An instant smile formed on her face, and she giggled as she turned to look at him. "You're not stupid." Looking at him fully now, that compassion rampant in his eyes, and she knew he didn't believe she would do something to hurt him financially, even if they did break up.

And she didn't want to break up.

"Like I said, it's smart." She reached toward him and cradled his face in her palm. He pressed into her touch, and then leaned toward her to kiss her.

"I'm sorry," he murmured.

"You can buy me a ticket to Dallas," she whispered back. "And we're not sharing a hotel room, cowboy. So pull out the money bags to pay for two."

"You wanna make it a weekend while we're there?"

"Definitely." Marcy kissed him again, and she thought a weekend in Dallas would be exactly what the doctor ordered for her weary soul. She pulled away from Wyatt and looked toward the house. "I think they sent a spy."

"That's my nephew, Oliver," Wyatt said. "He's great, and he's probably just excited to tell me about the new horse Orion got." He grinned toward the house. "We should go in, though."

Marcy wanted to meet his brothers and their wives

and families. She did. She spent so much of her time alone, and she knew it was time to stop flying solo on everything. Still, she was comfortable with solo. She knew how solo worked. What it looked like at dinnertime, and what it smelled like in the morning.

Wyatt slid out of the truck, and before Marcy could move, he opened her door and extended his hand toward her. She put her fingers between his, and suddenly everything was going to be okay.

"Uncle Wyatt," the little boy called from the porch, and Wyatt turned toward him as he closed the truck door.

"I know about the horse, buddy," he said. "I was here when Orion paraded him around."

Oliver came flying down the steps, his excitement apparently too much to be contained by the porch. "Will you take me out to see him after we eat? Uncle Jeremiah says he's too tired, and Tripp says I can't ask Liam because of the baby."

He skidded to a stop and looked up at Wyatt expectantly from under the brim of his child-size cowboy hat.

"Sure thing, bud," Wyatt said with a chuckle. He reached for the boy and gave him a quick hug. "This is my fiancée, Marcy Payne. You can be the first to meet her."

Oliver looked at her then, and ridiculously Marcy wanted the little boy to love her as much as he obviously loved Wyatt. "Hey," she said, her experience with children limited. Another flaw, and Wyatt was going to know in a matter of seconds.

"Good afternoon, ma'am." He swept his cowboy hat from his head and bowed.

Delight filled Marcy. "My, what proper Texas manners."

"Can you tell my mom?" he asked, putting his hat back on. "I get a quarter every time I remember my manners."

Marcy laughed then, and they made room between the two of them for Oliver, each of them taking one of his hands, whether they wanted to or not. Marcy looked at Wyatt over the top of the boy's head, and when their eyes met, the familiar and excited crackle of attraction snapped between them.

"You go tell everyone we're here," Wyatt said when they reached the top of the steps. "I have to talk to Marcy alone for a sec."

Oliver skipped inside, leaving the front door wide open behind him, which gave them no privacy.

"Dear Lord," Wyatt said. "I can hear them all already." He looked at her with an apology in his eyes. "I'm sorry about this. Maybe we should've gone out with them a couple at a time."

"No time for that," she said. "You have a million brothers."

He grinned and leaned closer to her. "Just real quick. You know how we have things to work out between us?"

Marcy could fall into a hypnotic state within seconds when Wyatt spoke in that low, sexy voice that was almost a growl. "Yeah."

"I just thought of one: kids."

"Oh."

"Do you want kids?"

"I've got to have someone to pass Payne's onto, right?" She looked up at him, that dazzling rodeo king smile on his face. In that flash of time while he breathed before he spoke, she could see a future with him, with a couple of little boys with those eyes and that smile on their faces.

"I'm going to take that as a yes."

"It's a yes. You?"

"I love kids," he said. "I've got to have someone to show new Tennessee walking horses to, right? Teach them how to throw a rope and how to hold onto a bucking bull."

"What if we have girls?"

"Girls love horses," Wyatt said without missing a beat.

"They don't ride bulls," Marcy said.

"Yet." Wyatt gave her another grin and pressed his cheek right against hers. "I sure am falling in love with you, Miss Payne."

"Why are you lurking out here?" Tripp said. "Come in already. Jeremiah's been holding the prime rib, and I have holes in my chest from the way he's been staring at me like it's my fault y'all are late."

Wyatt turned toward his brother during the short monologue and said, "Oh, come on. We're not late, and we weren't lurking."

Marcy smiled at Tripp as Wyatt took her past him. "Nice to meet you."

"Oh, right." Wyatt paused in the entrance of the house. "One of the twins, Tripp. He's Oliver's dad."

"Nice to meet you too, ma'am."

"I see where he gets the manners." Marcy shook Tripp's hand. "I'd give him a dollar just for being cute."

"And then we'd be broke," Tripp said with a wide grin, gesturing for them to go first down the hall that led to all the noise.

Marcy went with Wyatt, and it could've been her imagination, but it sure felt like he was barely walking by the time they arrived in the living room, the dining room and kitchen expanding beyond that.

The shared space really was huge, so that the fifteen or so people in the room—many of them broad-shouldered, six-foot-tall cowboys—fit easily. Comfortably.

All at once, Marcy realized what kind of luxury Wyatt was used too, and she couldn't believe she'd asked him to live in her father's house.

"Everyone," Wyatt said, and that got most of them to quiet down. The baby fussed still, despite Callie's efforts to soothe her with a pacifier. "This is Marcy Payne, my fiancée. I've given her a quiz on all of you, so she knows your names already." He took a breath. "But Marcy, this is Whitney, Simone, and Evelyn." He nodded to the three women sitting on the huge sectional in the living room. "Micah, Liam, Callie, Rhett, Ivory, Jeremiah, and you met Tripp." He finished with the man she'd already shaken hands with.

"Oh, and Liam and Callie have two kids, Denise and Ginger. And Rhett's got his son, Conrad. And we met Ollie on the porch." Wyatt nodded once, like that was everyone. "Who did I miss?"

"No one," Jeremiah said. "Welcome, Marcy." He actually stepped over to her and gave her a quick hug. "Let's eat."

Just as quickly as the noise had muted, it came roaring back, and Jeremiah somehow succeeded in calming everyone again so they could say grace. He said it himself, and the man didn't waste words. *Dear Lord, thank you for this food, bless us and this food, amen.*

"Some of the prime rib might be a little overdone," he said, stepping over to the stove. "But if that bothers you, just don't eat it. Penny, Winston, and Willow like it at any temperature."

"Those are the dogs," Wyatt murmured, and that got Marcy to smile. Of course Jeremiah would feed his dogs steak. Didn't all cowboy billionaires do the same? As if summoned now that he'd spoken their names, Marcy saw all three dogs outside on the back deck, their noses pressed up against the glass as if they knew their master had prime rib, and they'd get some if they looked forlorn enough.

In the blink of an eye, Wyatt let go of her hand, and she got separated from him almost instantly.

"Nice to see you again, Marcy," Liam said. She'd met with him about dusting the Shining Star Ranch next door.

She nodded and smiled, smiled and nodded at everyone in the room.

She went through the line and got her prime rib—cooked perfectly medium, despite what Jeremiah had claimed—and mashed potatoes, a roll, and roasted vegetables. "This is amazing," she said to Jeremiah. How he could feed this many adults and have everything hot and ready was amazing. And he didn't run out of anything, even as the last person moved through the buffet-style line at the island and went to sit at the dining room table.

"Thank you for agreeing to feed the family for the wedding," she said.

"Oh, I secretly love it," he said with a smile. "I do want to talk to you about the menu and how many people there will be."

"I just have a couple of cousins," she said.

"Don't you have a brother?" He spread butter on both sides of his roll.

"Uh, I need to talk to him and see if he can come." For some reason, she didn't want Bryan to see her marry Wyatt, as if her own flesh and blood would be able to smell the scam from a hundred miles away.

"Aunts, uncles, grandparents?"

"I have some of those, yes," she said.

"I'll get your number today," he said. "And we'll chat." He grinned at her and took his place next to Whitney at the table.

Thankfully, Wyatt had saved her a spot, or Marcy

thought she'd be out on the back deck. "It's one for all at meal time," he said, taking her plate so she could pull her chair out and slide into it.

"I can see that," she said.

"Overwhelmed?"

"A little." She picked up her fork, comfortable at Wyatt's side. Evelyn asked her something about flying, and Marcy loved nothing more than talking about airplanes. Before she knew it, they'd seamlessly integrated her into their lives, and it happened over the course of a single meal.

Marcy hadn't even known how they'd done it. But she would have to learn, because she wanted everyone she met to feel as welcome and as loved as she did by this family.

As she participated in the meaningless chatter about what movies everyone had seen, or what the weather would be like for Valentine's Day, Marcy wanted to be part of this family.

And not just for a year.

Permanently.

"I'm taking Ollie out to see the horses," Wyatt said. "Do you want to come?"

"Sure." Marcy stood up and put her plate in the kitchen sink before going outside with Wyatt and Oliver. The dogs there greeted her enthusiastically, and Wyatt bent down to give them all a healthy pat.

"Winston likes me best," he said. "But don't tell Jeremiah that." He stroked the dog's head again. "Don't you, bud? He likes to sleep on my feet at night." He grinned at the dog like he'd told him a lot of secrets, and Marcy wished canines could talk.

"We have to check on Kessler too," Wyatt said, looking at Oliver. "That's my horse." He looked at her.

"The animals are like members of the family," she said, almost guessing.

"Yep."

"So they're like my airplanes."

"Do you name your planes?" He took her hand in his and let Oliver skip ahead of them.

"I sure do."

"Like what?"

"Better than Kessler," she teased, nudging him with her shoulder.

"Oh, wow," he said, chuckling. "That horse came with that name, I'll have you know. And we won a lot of championships together. He'll probably like you better than me in five seconds flat."

"How do you know if a horse likes you?" Marcy asked.

"You just do." Wyatt didn't explain further, and they walked through one barn to the rest of the ranch, and again, Marcy felt more peace here on this land than she had in the year leading up to her father's death.

"Wow," she said, breathing everything in around her. "This place is stunning."

"Jeremiah works hard," Wyatt said. "This way, Oliver," he said, nodding to the left. They went to the last stable on the lane, and Oliver climbed up on the outside rung while Wyatt went inside to let the horses out.

"That's Kessler," the little boy said when the first horse came out of the door that had been opened. "Wyatt's horse. And that's the new one." He climbed up another rung, leaning out into the pasture as if he could get to know the horse that way.

Kessler was a beautiful black beast, and he seemed to know he was a champion. Wyatt came back outside, and Kessler lifted his head from the grass where he'd been snacking. The horse walked right over to Wyatt, a sense of urgency in his eyes.

"Heya, bud," he said, stroking the horse's neck and nose. "This is Marcy. I'm going to marry her." He beamed at her and looked back at his horse. He handed her a peppermint disc, and she just looked at it.

"What's this for?"

"You give it to the horses," Oliver said. "They like 'em."

Marcy had no idea how to feed a horse, and she pinched the candy between her fingers.

"Not like that," Wyatt said. "Just lay it in your palm, nice and flat."

"He grabs it with his lips," Oliver said. "Uncle Wyatt, do you have any more of those?"

He passed one to Oliver, who unwrapped it and held it up for the other horse. "What's his name?"

"It's a girl," Wyatt said. "And Orion named her after his mother. Christmas Carole."

Marcy's heart softened as she let Kessler suction up the peppermint. He shuffled a couple of steps over to her and pressed his nose into her palm.

"I knew it," Wyatt said. "He likes you better than me."

Marcy shook her head as she laughed. "That's because I gave him a candy."

"And now you know my secrets," Wyatt said, sliding his arm around her waist and pulling her into his body. Marcy sighed, a happy smile on her face.

"I don't think I know all your secrets," she said as she watched Oliver feed a sweet to Christmas Carole.

"Oh, we have to save some things for after the wedding," he whispered, and Marcy snuggled further into him. This man made her feel alive in a way she hadn't felt in a long time. He brought her comfort when she needed it most, and he accepted her just how she was.

Oliver jumped off the fence and moved down it with the new horse.

"Here you go, bud." Wyatt flipped him another piece of candy, and Marcy looked at the man.

"Wyatt," she said, her throat sticky and somewhat clogged. "I'm falling in love with you too."

"I'd hoped you were." He touched his lips to hers, and Marcy could not imagine a better day than the one she'd just experienced. She held Wyatt's face in both of her hands, feeling like she had the world between her palms.

14

Wyatt stood at the barrier keeping him from going past airport security, scanning the crowd of people streaming past. His nerves jumped and bumped and thumped through his bloodstream.

He hadn't seen his parents since last Thanksgiving, when they'd come for a few weeks to visit.

"Where are they?" someone asked.

"Their flight landed twenty minutes ago," someone else said.

Wyatt couldn't keep track of all the voices amid the noise and hustle of the rest of the travelers in the Amarillo airport. The whole Walker crew had made the drive in four separate vehicles to greet their parents, and Wyatt really wanted to hug his mother first.

So badly, in fact, that he'd called it on the family text. *First hug.*

No one had argued with him either, which said they all knew he was the Momma's boy, and if he didn't see his mother in the next five seconds, he felt like he might burst.

"There she is," someone said, and he whipped his attention to the speaker.

"Where?" he asked.

Rhett stood on his tiptoes and pointed. "She's wearing a pink coat."

"She doesn't need a coat."

"Why is she wearing a coat? She came from a tropical island."

Wyatt tuned them all out as he caught sight of his mother. Her footsteps seemed to get slower and slower as she neared, and then finally, she reached him.

"Momma," he said, enveloping her in a tight hug and lifting her right off her feet.

She laughed and hugged him back. "My baby," she said, and warmth moved through Wyatt. But he couldn't really hold her for very long with his back, and he set her down a few moments later.

She wiped her eyes and moved to the next son, which was—of course—Rhett. Wyatt was actually surprised Rhett hadn't played the Oldest Card to get to hug their mother first.

"Oh, my boys," she said with each one. "And my new daughters." She hugged them too, smiling and patting and wiping her tears.

"Daddy," Wyatt said when it was his turn to greet his

father. He admired his father on a deep level, especially his work ethic and the way he treated Momma like royalty. "It's so good to see you."

"It's good to be back in Texas," his father said, and Wyatt could only agree.

"You didn't like the tropics?"

"I like them fine," he said. "For a visit."

Wyatt grinned at him as he fell back a step, and Marcy's hand slipped into his. "Hey, Dad," he said. "This is my fiancée, Marcy Payne."

"It's a pleasure to meet you, sir," she said, her enthusiasm gushing out of her.

"Oh, you're Wyatt's." Daddy grinned at her, and the big, broad-shouldered cowboy who'd made all the other big, broad-shouldered cowboys in the near vicinity took Marcy right into a hug.

Wyatt laughed at her yelp of surprise, and he loved the way her face flushed when Daddy released her. The past three weeks with her had been absolutely amazing. They were *easy*, even as they cleaned out shelves, closets, and bedrooms. Even as they planned refreshments and meals and activities for the wedding.

It felt very real to Wyatt, and he loved training horses at Bowman's Breeds. He loved that his mom and dad would be here for the wedding.

Because he was in love with Marcy Payne.

The general excitement continued until everyone had hugged his mother and father, and then Wyatt took Marcy to meet Momma. He introduced her, and the two women looked at one another for just a moment.

Then Momma said, "Oh, you're perfect for him." She too drew Marcy into a hug, and Marcy seemed more ready for it this time. "I feel like I know you already, for how much this boy talks about you."

"Momma, I'm almost forty years old."

"Oh, you're just a big teddy bear." She swatted his chest and hooked her arm through Marcy's. "Now, tell me about the wedding. What can I do to help?"

"I think we have everything," Marcy said as the group moved toward the baggage claim area. "Right, Wyatt?"

"Most things," he said.

"Well, what do you need?"

Marcy met Wyatt's eye again, and he didn't like the nervous edge there. "I don't quite have a dress yet."

"You don't?" Wyatt asked at the same time his mother stalled.

"No dress. You're getting married in six days." She looked from Marcy to Wyatt and back again. "What are you going to wear?"

"Well...." Marcy ducked her head and tucked her hair behind her ear. "My mother has a wedding dress, but I'm afraid to try it on."

"Marce," Wyatt said, as she hadn't mentioned this at all. True, he hadn't followed up on the wedding dress situation, but then again, Marcy had said she had it handled.

"Would you like me to help you with it?" Momma asked, and to Wyatt's surprise, Marcy nodded.

"I was hoping you would," she said.

Momma patted her arm and started walking again, her head now held high in an air of importance. "Of course I will, dear. You let me get settled tonight, and I'll come over first thing tomorrow morning."

"Momma," Wyatt said, watching the satisfaction roll across Marcy's face. "Marcy flies in the morning."

"Oh, that's right," Momma said. "You fly airplanes."

"That's right, ma'am."

"Don't call me ma'am," Momma said. "I'm far too young for that, despite Wyatt almost being forty years old." She smiled in a way that only Momma could, and added, "You tell me when, dear, and I'll come over and help you with the dress."

"Nice move," Wyatt muttered as the whole lot of them arrived at the baggage claim. Momma and Daddy got their bags, and the entourage moved out to the parking garage. It was decided that they'd go home with Liam and Callie, who had purchased a minivan when they'd gotten their new baby.

"That way, Daddy's hip won't have to exert itself."

"What's wrong with Daddy's hip?" Tripp asked as Daddy said, "Penny, I didn't think we were telling them about the hip."

Wyatt's gaze flew back to his mother, and she had the decency to look ashamed. "Oops. Sorry, Gideon."

"It's nothing," Daddy said with a sigh. "I hurt it hiking, and I had to have surgery."

"You had surgery?" Jeremiah demanded, his voice definitely on the angry side of the line. "Daddy. Why didn't you tell us?"

"It's fine," he said. "Can we go? I'm starving, and I hear you've inherited my mother's cooking genes." He beamed at Jeremiah, who was definitely his favorite, but no one moved. "Really, sons. It's fine. *This* is why I didn't tell anyone."

Wyatt understood on a deep level, because he'd concealed his rodeo injuries from his family for several long months. He might never had told them if not for the major back surgery he couldn't hide.

"All right," he said loudly. "First one back to Seven Sons gets my new work shirt before it hits shelves."

"Oh, it's on," Tripp said, and Rhett herded Evelyn down to his truck with the words, "Let's go, sweetheart."

"I can just buy that," Jeremiah said, but he went to his truck too, telling Micah to hurry up.

Wyatt grinned, glad he could still have some sway in this family of loud, amazing men. He looked at Marcy and found her shaking her head. "You're impossible."

"Impossibly awesome," he said, slinging his arm around her and helping her into his truck. He leaned into the doorway. "Why didn't you tell me about the dress?"

She lifted one shoulder into a shrug. "I felt silly. My

mother's been gone for a while now, but I just can't get myself to open that closet and pull out that dress."

"And you don't want me to see it."

"Right."

"Well, you made my mother's whole year." He smiled at her and leaned in for a kiss. "I think she might love you more than I do."

Marcy sucked in a breath, her eyes flying open. Wyatt hadn't imagined telling her that he loved her in the short-term airport parking garage, but what was done was done.

"Wyatt."

He couldn't stop the grin that spread across his whole face. "I love you, Marcy."

Tears filled her eyes, and her chin quivered. "I love you, too."

Joy like he'd never experienced before exploded through him, especially when she took his face in her hands and kissed him again. He loved the way she held him close, as if he were precious to her, the tender touch of her fingers along his jaw almost as sensual as the kissing itself.

"And we're gettin' married next weekend," he whispered, ducking so his forehead rested against hers. "I'm so happy."

"Me too," she whispered, breathing with him.

Wyatt pulled himself away from her with difficulty, thinking that maybe their wedding next week wouldn't be a pretend pledge after all.

15

Jeremiah had never been happier to have his father working beside him as they drove back to the hay barn, a load successfully put out for the goats in their pasture.

"Thanks for letting us stay at the ranch."

"Of course," Jeremiah said. "When will the house be ready?"

"Thursday."

"Just in time for the wedding," Jeremiah said, dying to talk to someone about it. Wyatt and Marcy sure seemed like they liked each other, but he knew for a fact the woman had broken Wyatt's heart in August.

"Well, we'll be able to get in the house, but we have no furniture, and our stuff from Grand Cayman doesn't arrive for another week."

"I didn't know that," he said. "So you'll stay for a while then."

"No, we're going to Liam's on Tuesday, like we said," he said. "Be there for a few days. Your mother wants as much time with the babies as she can get." Dad smiled, and Jeremiah understood how he felt. He had all kinds of feelings about being a father, and one of the loudest was anxiety. How would he know if he was doing things right? What if he was a terrible father?

"Then we're going to Rhett's until our things come. Momma will order new furniture as soon as she can, I'm sure." Dad sighed like his wife ordering furniture was a burden. "We didn't have much in Cayman. Nothing we'd want to bring back to Texas."

"Where's all your stuff from before?"

"We got rid of all of it," he said. "Which was fine. A lot of it was old." Dad was the perfect man to bump around with in a ranch truck, over dirt roads. He just sat in the passenger seat and watched the scenery go by, and love for him filled Jeremiah.

"Have you been by the place?" he asked. "Or did Rhett send you pictures?" His parents hadn't been in Three Rivers for more than a few hours, but he'd driven separately from Liam and Callie, and they could've easily swung by the little farm Jeremiah and Rhett had found for their parents.

"Haven't been," he said. "I think Rhett sent Momma a link, but I didn't look at it."

"Should we go?" he asked. "I can be done for the rest of the day."

"You've got good men," Dad said. "That's invaluable."

"I do," Jeremiah said as the homestead came into view. "Let me ask Whitney if she wants to come for a ride."

"She's great," Dad said. "I'm glad you found someone new, son."

"Me too." Jeremiah's fingers tightened on the wheel, because his emotions over having Whitney in his life overwhelmed him sometimes.

"And lunch was amazing. Thank you for cooking it."

"Yeah, sure," Jeremiah said. "I like doing it."

"Grandma Lucy did too." Dad smiled. "She'd be so happy to hear you've taken after her."

"Well, we spent plenty of time with her growing up," Jeremiah said. "I was always shelling peas or shucking corn or stirring something on the stove for her. I guess I just felt the spirit of it."

"Did she give you her recipes?"

"Yeah, years ago," Jeremiah said. "That beef stew we had today was hers. The potato rolls too."

"I knew the rolls were," Dad said. "I should think about bringing them up here."

"They'd leave the farm?" Jeremiah chuckled. "I don't think so."

"My mother is pretty stubborn," Dad agreed. "But it might be worth a conversation. I never thought I'd get your mother to leave the beach."

"Why does she love the beach so much?"

"Oh, I don't know." Dad sighed. "Something about how it soothes her soul or something."

"Did you like it there?"

"Yeah, sure," Dad said nonchalantly as they approached the homestead. "Your mother was happy, and I like the sunshine more than the rain."

Jeremiah heard what his father was saying: If Momma was happy, so was he. Jeremiah knew, because he felt a lot the same about Whitney. If she wanted to sleep in, Jeremiah wanted her to. If she wanted hot coffee when she finally got out of bed, Jeremiah wanted to be the one to give it to her.

"Let me call Whitney," he said, reaching for the display in front of him. He tapped, and the low-playing radio stopped as the line rang. He adjusted the volume so he could hear his wife.

"What's up?" she asked.

"Dad and I are going into town to look at the farm," he said. "Do you want to come?"

"Yes," she said before he'd even finished speaking. "I'll be right out."

"Great, we're pulling around the house now." Jeremiah continued down the dirt lane and toward the huge oak tree in the front yard. He drove under the boughs between it and the house and braked. "We can stop at Whitney's store, too," he said to his dad. "And get some of that flavored cream I was telling you about."

"Sounds good."

Whitney came down the steps, and his father got out of the truck. "It's fine, Mister—"

"I'm not riding in the front," Dad said gruffly, opening the back door and climbing into the backseat. "I can see just as good back here."

Jeremiah met Whitney's eye, glad she'd found a moment to slick on some of that red lipstick he liked so well. "Hey, baby." He leaned over and kissed her. "How ya feeling?"

"Good," she said, smiling. "How are the goats?"

"Good," he said. "Daisy Mae is doing well, and she'll be grown up before we know it."

"You and those baby goats." She shook her head as he passed through the gate and headed toward town.

"I like them," he said, not really needing to defend himself. Whitney didn't care if he had goats, pigs, or llamas on the ranch.

"I booked another family," she said. "And a bride for September." She rolled her eyes, and Jeremiah smiled at her.

"You don't have to do the super-hot wedding in the fall if you don't want to," he said.

"But I do want to," she said. "I just wish it wouldn't be five million degrees."

"Any more babies?"

"Yeah," she said. "Two in July."

Jeremiah grinned at her and shook his head. "I still

don't think you're going to be up and able to do that for our baby."

"I've already started picking out props," she said.

"But how?" he asked. "You don't even know if it'll be a boy or girl."

"Rope is gender-neutral," she said, and Jeremiah fell in love with her a little more, if that was even possible.

Several minutes later, he pulled off on a road that led east, almost directly across the highway from Rhett's right turn-off. "Rhett lives down there," he said. "You'll be like five minutes apart, and only fifteen from the ranch."

"And where's Tripp compared to here?" Dad asked.

"He's got a great big place on the east side of town," Jeremiah said. "It's probably ten minutes from here." Jeremiah pulled up to the cheery white brick home with the bright blue door. "Here it is."

The yard had been well-kept, and it had big trees like his father liked. But the best part was the—"Look at that front porch," his dad said, already sliding out of the truck.

"Dad." Jeremiah hurried to get out too. "You don't own this place yet, Dad."

But his father didn't care, and he went right up the front sidewalk and the several steps to the front porch. "I can put a chair right there. Whittling table next to it." He surveyed the space as if he could envision it already. And he probably could.

He looked at Jeremiah, and a new light had entered his eyes. "This is great."

Jeremiah glanced around, though he knew the house was empty. He'd tagged along with Rhett and Tripp as they'd looked at it without any furniture in it, and it seemed plenty big enough for two people. *And a dog*, he reminded himself, as his father had already told Momma that he'd be getting a new dog as soon as they were settled.

"How big is the yard?"

"It's not huge," Jeremiah said. "There's a small corral for maybe one horse."

"I'm gettin' old to be takin' care of a big yard." He tapped the brim of his cowboy hat. "That was one good thing about Cayman. Small yards, with low maintenance."

"I'll come do it, Dad," Jeremiah said. "And any animals you want, we'll keep at the ranch." He smiled at his father and put his hand in Whitney's as she joined them on the porch.

"The neighbors are looking out the window," she said almost under her breath, nodding across the street.

"And we don't need to get arrested today," Jeremiah said. "Let's go, Dad." He was beyond excited his parents had decided to move to Three Rivers, and when his mother had called and asked him his opinion, the first thing he'd said was, "I would love that, Momma. Truly."

He was fairly certain all of the brothers had said the same thing, and his mother didn't waste time when she'd made up her mind.

Back at the homestead, he found Momma with baby Ginger in her arms, both of them sleeping on the couch in the living room. He smiled at them, an overwhelming sense of love filling him.

"Thank you, God," he whispered, because he'd never thought he'd have a life like this. He still remembered keenly the day Rhett had come back to the ranch and said he was married, and the inexplicable anger that had taken over his mind and body.

Now, he felt only joy and peace when he thought of marriage and family, and he couldn't wait for his baby to be born so he could try to build the best life for his son or daughter that he could.

He sat next to his mother, who made a small noise. "Love you, Momma," he said, laying his head against her shoulder.

"Love you too, baby," she whispered, and everything in Jeremiah's life made sense for this one moment.

16

Marcy folded the tea towel she'd brought from her house and laced it through the handle on the refrigerator. Her nerves buzzed like the bees Wyatt had shown her on the ranch, as his mother should be arriving any moment.

She still hadn't been able to go into her parents' bedroom closet and get out the dress. For all Marcy knew, it wouldn't fit, or it would be stained or covered in mold and mildew. She wasn't sure which she wanted most—for the dress to be perfect or for it to be a complete failure. What she knew was she still hadn't been able to take down any of the family photos, though she and Wyatt had gone through everything else in the living room.

She'd kept a few boxes of books she knew her father had loved and spent a great deal of time or money to acquire. They were in her spare bedroom in her own house, and Marcy would probably never look at them again. But she couldn't get rid of them either.

They'd cleaned out his movie collection and gotten rid of his impressive collection of National Geographic magazines. She'd sold the couches to a neighbor down the street who had a daughter getting married, and she'd given them the television too.

The living room was a skeleton of what it had once been, and Marcy didn't like the sterility in the house. When Wyatt was with her, she didn't feel as hollow, and neither did the house.

She'd enjoyed their weekend in Dallas a few weeks ago, and she couldn't wait to be married to the man who'd become her best friend.

The doorbell rang, and Marcy startled out of her thoughts. She hurried over to the door and opened it to find both Wyatt and his mother standing there.

"Good morning, Penny," she said. "Wyatt, you're not staying, right?"

He held up both hands in surrender and said, "I'm off to get breakfast by myself, and then I'll see you ladies later at church." He leaned in and kissed Marcy quickly before backing up. "Unless you want me to stay."

"Go on, baby," his mother said as she came in. "It'll be so boring here." She closed the door while Wyatt still wore that hopeful expression on his face, and she patted Marcy's shoulder as she went by. "Don't mind him. He'll be fine."

Marcy turned and followed his mother into the house. She was already dressed for church, but Marcy hadn't mentally committed to going to Sabbath services today. But one look at Wyatt's mother, and Marcy knew she'd be running home to put on a skirt and heels so she could go to church.

"All right," she said. "The dress is back here." She started down the hallway, the sound of Penny's footsteps behind her sounding like the pounding of a hammer. The door to the bedroom stood open, and Marcy had been inside several times. She'd gone through her father's nightstand one day, weeping the entire time. Every little thing held such strong memories from the mint tins he'd kept and stored random amounts of money in to the newspaper clipping of his and Momma's wedding.

Marcy had kept the clipping and the money, but she'd thrown out the tins. She wasn't even sure why her father had kept them, other than to store little bits and bobs in, which she'd also thrown away. After all, she didn't need safety pins or old buttons that didn't match anything.

"This is a lovely house," his mother said.

"Thank you," Marcy said. "Wyatt and I have been going through it bit by bit."

"Yes, he told me all about it last night." She paused and looked earnestly at Marcy. "I'm so sorry about your father."

Marcy's heart shivered, but she managed to nod. "The dress should be back here." She moved over to the door of the closet and opened it. She hadn't made it this far in her purging yet, because she knew the scent of her father's cologne, aftershave, and the synthetic oil that belonged uniquely to Payne's Pest-free.

She backed up after opening the door, but all of those smells assaulted her, awakening her memories in a single breath. Her emotions spiraled, and she didn't even startle when Penny put her hand in Marcy's and squeezed.

They stood there, the two of them, holding hands as she faced this closet full of memories. After what felt like a long time, Penny said, "I can tell you loved your father very much." She released Marcy's hand. "May I?"

Marcy could only nod, and Penny stepped forward to start leafing through the clothes in the closet. "I'm sure I can find it," she said, and the sound of hangers scraping along the rod met Marcy's ears.

She sat on the bed, feeling a little numb as Penny continued to look through the closet. She hadn't expected the fresh waves of pain to roll over her, but they did in full force.

"Here it is," Penny said, backing up as she pulled out a garment bag. "This has to be it." She laid the bag on the bed beside Marcy and started to unzip it. "Yep, this is it."

A moment later, the bag had been shed, and Penny was holding up Marcy's wedding dress. She hadn't even realized the tears had gathered in her eyes before they fell, and Penny sat beside her on the bed, letting the dress drape across her lap.

"I wish I could've met them," she said. "Your folks."

Marcy nodded, because she couldn't say anything.

"They must've been very special for you to love them so much. I hope when it's my turn to go, my sons won't be sad, because I've lived a good life."

Marcy looked at her, and so much was said without any words. "I just miss them," she said, swiping at her tears. She'd carefully made up her face too, as if she needed to impress Wyatt's mother.

"I still miss my mother too," she said. "And she died twenty years ago." She gave Marcy a small smile, the kind filled with empathy and a soul that knows. "And you've done an amazing job cleaning out this house as much as you have."

She looked down into her lap, and Marcy followed her gaze. "I think this dress could be lovely," Penny said. "We need to see how it drapes on you, and we might need to do a little updating."

Marcy drew in a long breath, using it to strengthen herself enough to stand up. "All right." With Penny's help, she stepped into the dress and got it zipped up.

"Plenty of room," Penny said, circling her. "Probably too much." She pinched some of the fabric along Marcy's waist. "I can put a pleat right here, and we can take off some of the old lace. It's a little gray, and lace is kind of out right now anyway. Isn't it?"

"I have no idea," Marcy said, her tears returning. "But you think it could work?"

"Why don't you step into the bathroom and look for yourself?" Penny swept her hand toward the bathroom, as if Marcy didn't know where it was.

Marcy looked at her again, her fears subsiding with the older woman's kind smile and encouragement. She took another big breath and walked into her father's bathroom. She hadn't cleaned up this room either, because these were the things her father had touched last.

She gasped as she took in the image of herself in her mother's wedding dress, the bodice tight across her chest, and the straps laying just right over her shoulders. "I need a different bra," she whispered, but she could find one of those in the next six days.

She ran her hands down her torso, and Penny was right. The dress needed to be taken in an inch or so, and the lace definitely told everyone the dress was fifty years old. But Marcy loved it, and as Penny stepped into the bathroom with her, she asked, "Can you do it, Penny, or should I call a tailor?"

"I can do it," she said. "Don't tell me Wyatt hasn't told you about the horrific shirts I used to make for all the boys."

"He's mentioned it," Marcy said. "Something about matching clothes when y'all traveled?"

"I had a lot of kids," Penny said, lifting her chin as if she were being challenged. "If they all wore the same thing, I could find them all in a hot minute."

Marcy smiled and nodded. "That was it."

"I can fix this right up for you," she said. "You need something else to wear underneath it." She touched Marcy's hip, where the outline of her underwear could be seen.

"I can take care of that," she said, facing Wyatt's mother. "Penny? Would you help me get dressed on my wedding day?"

Penny's dark eyes softened, and she reached up and touched her perfectly styled hair. She was dark like her sons, and Marcy could see bits and pieces of Wyatt in her. "I'd love to, my dear." She embraced Marcy, and Marcy hugged her back, closing her eyes in bliss. She may not have any biological parents left in Three Rivers, but Penny felt like a kindred soul, and Marcy wouldn't have to deal with wedding day things alone with her here.

Before she knew it, the week slipped away from her. She dusted all the fields she needed to. She fell a bit behind on paperwork, because she had to shop for new underwear and a pair of shoes to get married in.

And then she woke up on Friday morning and looked up at the ceiling. "I'm getting married today," she whispered to the empty house.

Wyatt's announcement in Dallas had gone well, and he'd been on the phone with his manager for what felt like a long time yesterday. His friend at Four Paws had confirmed that they could get into the buildings where they'd change and stage before the ceremony by ten a.m. for a wedding that would begin at noon on the dot.

Her phone buzzed on the nightstand beside her, and she picked it up to find a text from Wyatt. *Everything good?* he'd asked. *Can't wait to see you today.*

Everything's good, she answered. *I'll see you at noon.* She let the phone fall to her chest, and she stayed in bed for several more minutes, letting her mind roam wherever it wanted. When she finally sat up to get out of bed, she said, "Wish you were here, Momma. You too, Daddy, though it's your fault I'm getting married only two months after you died."

She wanted to ask him what he was thinking, just as she had for the past several weeks since she'd found out about the stipulation.

She showered and double-checked that she had everything, towing her bag down the hall to the living room just as Savannah entered. "Hey." She hugged her cousin, so glad to have some sort of anchor to hold onto.

"Are you ready for this?" Savannah asked.

"Yes," Marcy said, because once they got going there would be no turning back. Not that Marcy would do that at this point. She had to get married in order to keep Payne's. And Wyatt wouldn't likely back out, as he had his whole family here, as well as actual news reporters. The wedding itself was being recorded and shown online on a rodeo website, for crying out loud.

She let Savannah take her bag, and she let her drive her across town to Four Paws. Everything seemed to be happening in a blur, from getting her makeup done, to her hair curled and set just-so on top of her head. Before she knew it, Penny had arrived with the dress and a wide smile.

"I think you're going to love it."

"I'm sure I will," Marcy said, hugging her. "Thank you so much."

"Let's get you dressed." Penny held the straps while Marcy stepped into the dress, and then she zipped it up. The fabric fit like a glove now, and Marcy didn't dare turn to look in the mirror.

"I've got your shoes," Alyssa said, placing them on the floor in front of Marcy. She held her hand to steady her as Marcy stepped into the shoes. "Oh." Her eyes filled with tears and she clapped one hand over her mouth. "You're so beautiful, Marcy."

She embraced her cousin, trying to hold back her own tears. "Thank you for helping me this morning," she said. "Where's Savannah?"

"She went to get something. She'll be back." Alyssa stepped back, wiping her eyes. "Now I'm going to need Nessa to fix me up again."

"I can," the makeup artist said from a couple of chairs down.

Alyssa went that way, returning quickly when Savannah entered the room. She carried a small black gift bag, and Marcy eyed her and then it. "What's that?"

"Something from Liss and I." Savannah thrust the bag toward her. "Open it."

Marcy did, and she pulled a single black glove from a box. "What's this?" She fingered the material, and it almost felt like rubber.

"We know your dad can't be here to walk you down the aisle," Savannah said. "So we had a glove made from something he loved, and Gideon has agreed to wear it. That way, it's like your daddy walking you toward your husband."

"The inner tube," she said, surprise twining with joy inside her. "Is this the inner tube from the front of that airplane?"

Savannah grinned so, so wide. "That it is."

Marcy did cry then, embracing her cousins with everything inside her.

"Come on, dear," Penny said as they stepped apart. "The wedding is going to start in five minutes."

"Let me fix you up real quick," Nessa said, and she deftly removed any evidence of tears from Marcy's face. She handed the glove to Penny who took it and left.

Then she finally turned and faced the mirror. The dress was stunning. It had clearly been cleaned as it gleamed a bright white now that it hadn't in her father's bathroom. The lace along the bodice had all been removed, replaced with a white satin that made the top half of the dress shine like white silver.

The waistline had been bedazzled with beads and gems, and the skirt fell softly to the floor from there.

"I can't believe it," she said, running her hand along

the neckline and up the strap. "It hardly looks like the same dress."

"It's lovely," Alyssa said, and Savannah agreed. "Okay, we're going to go take our seats." They hurried out of the room, leaving Marcy with the hairdresser and the makeup artist. Not five seconds later, someone knocked on the door, and Wyatt's father poked his head into the room.

"I've been sent to get you, young lady." He smiled at her, and Marcy blinked as she saw the image of her own father standing there. And not the frail, sickly man he'd been when God had finally seen fit to take him, but the strong, vibrant man who'd taught Marcy everything she knew about flying and airplanes.

She took Gideon's gloved hand and said, "Let's go. I'm ready."

17

Wyatt walked around the grounds at Four Paws, shaking hands and giving man-hugs, complete with all the back slapping he could stand. It felt like he'd been dressed and ready to get married for at least five hours, though he knew he hadn't even been awake that long.

He was surprised at the sheer number of people who had shown up for his nuptials. Dalton, Whitney's nephew, hadn't strayed more than ten feet from him, and the teen was in pure heaven talking to some of his rodeo idols.

Wyatt was glad to have Dalton along, because he wanted to talk to everyone, and Wyatt definitely had some people at his wedding he'd hoped to never see again. Dalton didn't need to know that, and the boy allowed Wyatt to move to someone else after saying a quick hello.

It wasn't hot by any means, and yet Wyatt had a ring

of sweat along his hatband. "What time is it?" he hissed to Micah, who'd also been hovering on the peripheral, just in case Wyatt needed some help getting out of a situation.

"It's time to head down to the altar," Micah said, and Wyatt put his fake reporter smile on his face as he said hello to just one more person. Cameras had been set up at the back of the swelling crowd, and Wyatt walked right past them to go down the aisle to the front. Every eye felt like a ton of bricks, and they were all watching him.

He cursed himself for setting this all up. Marcy was going to hate it. Absolutely hate it, and his anxiety bounced through his throat like a pulse. He'd gotten dressed in a cabin about fifty yards away, and he knew Marcy had been sequestered in the one right next door. He looked that way and caught sight of the door closing.

"She's on her way," Micah said. "Stay right here. I have to go join the wedding party." He jogged away, leaving Wyatt all alone in front of the whole crowd. His eyes scanned the sea of people in front of him, and they found his mother sitting in the front row.

All at once, his nerves calmed, and the smile on his face felt genuine. He hoped the cameras caught that, because he didn't feel very real right now. He'd be here at the dog sanctuary until two, with the ceremony, refreshments, and dancing with anyone who wanted to come for the two hours.

The family dinner was happening at three, at Seven Sons Ranch. And he and Marcy needed to be on the road by five to make their flight in Amarillo. They weren't leaving for long, but Wyatt had convinced Marcy to rearrange her flying schedule so they could spend four days in sunny, peaceful Cancun.

They'd be arriving fairly late that night, and by the time Wyatt lugged his suitcase to their private cabana— just one room this time—it would be after midnight. He'd have been up for almost eighteen hours, and he was hoping for a very late start tomorrow.

Thankfully, he'd been able to book a private jet through someone Jeremiah knew, so they didn't have any layovers.

The crowd stood up, and Wyatt shook himself out of his honeymoon fantasies. A collective sigh moved through the crowd as Marcy came to stand right between the cameras.

He sucked in a breath at the sight of her, though she was still quite a distance away. Daddy beamed like he was escorting a princess down the aisle.

Because he totally was.

The wedding party flowed around Marcy, and Wyatt grinned as his brothers and their wives came toward him. Skyler had brought a friend from Amarillo whose name Wyatt had forgotten the moment Skyler had said it. And Micah walked with Simone, though they weren't exactly talking to each other at the moment.

Wyatt was going to ask him about it as soon as he returned from Mexico. He'd been so busy for the past several weeks, but Micah hadn't taken a step away from Wyatt at all.

The flash of guilt passed as Rhett arrived and drew Wyatt into a brotherly hug. They all did the same thing, and Wyatt had never been more grateful for his brothers than he was in that moment.

They all circled back to the front row, leaving the view of Marcy walking toward him wide open.

He'd always found her the most beautiful woman he'd ever met, but wearing that dress only tripled that. Whatever his mother had done had worked, and Marcy looked absolutely angelic.

"She's a keeper, son," Daddy said, passing Marcy to Wyatt. "Good luck, you two."

Wyatt nodded to his father, his vocal cords filled with sawdust. He couldn't speak even if he knew what to say. He simply brushed his lips along Marcy's cheek and turned to face the pastor. He didn't know Pastor Daniels all that well, but Marcy had grown up in Three Rivers, and she'd known him for years.

The man said good things on Sunday, Wyatt knew that. He welcomed anyone to their congregation. He organized meals for people, sent out prayer roll reminders, all of it.

Thank you, Lord, Wyatt thought as the man started talking. His hand in Marcy's tightened, and she squeezed back. Thankfully.

This was no pretend pledge. It couldn't be. She'd said

she loved him; he loved her. But they hadn't amended any of their rules or discussed anything further. As far as he knew, he'd still be moving into her father's house come Wednesday morning, and Wyatt wondered what the bed would be like.

Did she really want to sleep in her parents' bedroom?

"Marcy Payne," Pastor Daniels said. "Do you take this cowboy, Wyatt Walker, to be your lawfully and legally wedded husband?"

He blinked, having missed the entire advice portion of the ceremony.

"I do," she said.

Pastor Daniels turned to him, his eyes positively radiant as he looked at Wyatt. "Yeehaw."

Everyone chuckled, and Wyatt joined them. "Do you, Wyatt Walker, take this beautiful woman, Marcy Payne, to be your lawfully and legally wedded wife?"

"I do," he said, his voice just the tiniest bit hoarse.

Several cowboys cheered from the crowd, the same way they would for a rodeo champion.

Wyatt laughed now and looked at Marcy. "Sorry. Maybe this whole spectacle was a bad idea."

"Just hold your horses," Pastor Daniels said, holding up both hands. That played right to the crowd of cowboys and cowgirls, and several more yips and calls went up before they settled into silence again.

"Now that they've both said 'I do,' I can pronounce

them husband and wife." His eyes glittered like lit stars. "You may now kiss your bride, cowboy."

Wyatt's heart sang as he turned toward Marcy and said, "I love you, Marce." He leaned closer so no one else could hear. With his lips right at her ear he said, "And that is not pretend." He kissed her in the next moment. The way Marcy kissed him back, she wasn't pretending either.

And now he was hers; she was his.

He broke the kiss, laughed, and turned to face the crowd. They were already jeering and hollering like he'd just won another grand championship, and he raised his left hand with Marcy's secured in it.

In his right hand, he took off his cowboy hat and waved it at the crowd like he did after every win. This was his tribute to these people who'd taken time from their lives to celebrate his.

He loved them, even if some of them weren't his favorite people.

All the cowboys wearing hats, pulled theirs off and waved them right on back at Wyatt and Marcy, who said, "Wow. You really are a celebrity."

The cheering and whooping increased, and even the women in the crowd waved with their right hands. Wyatt's emotions overwhelmed him, because he was just so grateful. So amazed that what had started out as a way for him to communicate with his father across hundreds of miles had become a way to say *I love you* or *Thank you* to everyone.

So happy, all he could do was smile out at everyone who had taken time out of their Friday to attend this wedding.

"Y'all," someone said over the speaker system. It took several more attempts to get everyone to settle down enough to hear Rhett. "We have chocolate, vanilla, and carrot cakes over on the east side of the seats here. Everyone is welcome to sample them. There's chocolate milk, hot chocolate, and coffee too."

Rhett continued to tell people that the dancing would begin in fifteen minutes, and that they should find their partners now. "Yeehaw!" he practically screeched into the microphone.

Wyatt put his hat back on and held tightly to Marcy's hand as the crowd surged toward them. He shook her brother's hand, and he did let go of his new wife so she could hug Bryan. They got separated for several long minutes while congratulations went around, and thankfully, Rhett got back on the microphone.

"I need the bride and groom over here, please. They'll be doing the first dance, and then we'll welcome everyone to pick a patch of floor and have a twirl."

"Have a twirl?" Wyatt chuckled as he pressed through the people to the open patch of grass that Dustin had roped off for the dance floor. Someone he didn't know moved the ropes so he could step through, and he took Marcy into his arms as effortlessly as breathing.

"I'm so sorry," he whispered as the first strains of a love song filled the air.

"Don't be," she said back. "This is every little girl's dream."

"Is it?" He laughed, glad the smile would be natural for Whitney, who seemed to be everywhere and nowhere every time he looked.

"Wyatt, this is fantastic," she said, pressing her cheek to his. He closed his eyes, because this was like heaven to him. He had fallen right into a dream, and he couldn't wait to be alone with his wife.

The song ended, and Rhett said, "Let's liven this party up a little, shall we?"

"I should've never put him in charge," Wyatt said. The music blared through the speakers, and Rhett had known his exact audience for this wedding. Cowboys flooded the dance floor, because they liked quick-tempo music to swing to.

Wyatt thought he'd probably catch an elbow if he stayed on the dance floor for too long, and he managed to get Marcy out of harm's way and over to the mini-cake table. "Chocolate for you, my wife," he said, grinning at her.

"And chocolate for you," she said as he picked up the same flavor for himself.

Wyatt laughed, as he continued to do for the next hour of dancing and merriment. Then he escaped to the quiet of his truck, where he drove Marcy to her house to change for the family dinner. He changed in her spare bedroom into a pair of jeans and a button-up shirt with the signature two W's on the breast pocket. One of his shirts. The bestseller, in fact.

He looked good in blue, he knew, and he felt his confidence soar when he left the bedroom and found Marcy in a tight pair of black jeans and a sweater.

She melted right into his arms, and Wyatt kissed her. Nothing else needed to be said, because she had a way of saying everything he needed to hear without uttering a word.

And this time, he didn't put the brakes on his kiss before it went too far, because this time, he was married.

18

S imone sat on the couch at Seven Sons, feeling very out of place. Everyone around her was nice, sure. But they all had someone to chat idly with, and she did not. Her sisters had their Walker brother husbands, and Simone felt more left out than she ever had.

Skyler had brought a friend from Amarillo, but if Simone were a betting woman, there should've been a *girl* in front of *friend*. Judging from the way Skyler kept grinning at her, and putting his arm around her, and leaning close and saying something no one else could hear, the two of them were definitely more than friends.

Her name was Fiona, and Simone didn't even know regular humans used that name. She looked away from them, as Skyler and "Fi" weren't helping in the kitchen.

The twins had disappeared out on the ranch when Wyatt had called to say he and Marcy would be a little bit late, and they'd taken all of the kids with them. Callie helped Jeremiah in the kitchen, and Evelyn currently had her eyes closed as she cuddled into Rhett's side.

Simone herself felt like taking a nap, but she couldn't let her guard down. Not for one single second. If she did, Micah would sidle up to her, and she didn't want to talk to him. Linking her arm through his and walking down that impossibly long aisle had been hard enough.

She'd managed to keep him at bay with glares and frowns, but he was wearing her down. Now that he lived here full-time—and that she'd broken up with Jarrod—he'd been trying to wiggle his way back into her life.

But she'd had enough of the on-again, off-again drama. He didn't get to toy with her like a yo-yo, reeling her back in when it was convenient for him, and throwing her for a loop when his ex came calling.

And wow, Stephanie didn't understand the meaning of a break-up.

Simone did, as she'd been through several in her life. More than either of her sisters, who'd almost lived like spinsters until Rhett Walker had bought the ranch next door and moved in.

Truth be told, Simone wanted her fairy-tale Walker wedding too. And Micah seemed to know it.

If only he wasn't so good-looking. So rich. So kind. So good.

If only he didn't look at her with that longing in his

gaze, or text her a funny meme exactly when she needed to see it.

She'd laughed more times while alone in her she-shed than she cared to admit, all because of something Micah had sent her or something he'd said.

He'd gotten really close to kissing her once, and Simone wouldn't have objected. Her boyfriend might have, and thankfully, Jarrod had knocked on the door of her workshop before any lip touching had happened.

So maybe she'd gone cold on Micah a time or two as well. He'd accused her of giving him mixed signals, and Simone had tried to deny it. But in all honestly, he was right.

"Hey."

She looked up from her perfectly manicured nails—a treat she'd given herself for the wedding. By Monday morning, they'd be chipped and broken, as Simone did a lot of sanding, staining, and stitching to make her junkyard pieces into cherished antiques.

Micah had sat beside her, and she hadn't even seen him coming. "Could we...go talk on the front porch? I promise I won't take you far or take up too much of your time." He got up almost the moment he finished talking and walked away.

Simone watched him go, aware that several others were now watching her.

"Well, go on," Evelyn said, her eyes still closed.

"Evvy," Rhett said. "Let them work it out."

Simone didn't know what to do, but the chatter in the kitchen and living room had almost died, so she heard the defining click of the front door as Micah closed it behind him. Indecision raged through her, and another long stare at her fingernails didn't give her the answer she needed.

At one point in her life, she might have prayed to know what to do. But she'd given up the habit about the time she'd realized her pleas to the Lord fell on deaf ears. At least that was how it felt to her.

"He says they're ten minutes out," Jeremiah said, and Simone thought she might as well give Micah ten minutes. They wouldn't be able to talk longer than that anyway. Once Wyatt arrived, dinner would be served, and there would be no time for private talks.

Like a shot, she bolted to her feet and started for the front door. Behind her, she heard Callie ask, "Where's she going?"

Someone responded, but Simone didn't know who. Probably Whitney or Ivory, as they were both curled into the couch too, and had likely heard what Micah had said.

The sun's rays slanted across the porch when Simone reached it, and she too brought the door closed gently behind her. Micah sat in a rocking chair in the sunshine, the slow squeak of the wood almost comforting.

"This seat's open," he said, indicating a second chair. Simone approached him slowly, wanting to jump into his arms at the same time she wanted to tell him to just leave her alone. The internal war was exhausting.

She sat down and folded her hands in her lap. He'd asked her to come talk to him; he could start the discussion.

"Listen," he said, but he didn't follow it up with anything.

Simone lifted her eyes to his face and found him gazing across the porch to the oak tree. He wore one of Wyatt's hats, as had many at the wedding. There were plenty of other cowboys to choose from. Simone didn't know why she was so hung up on this one.

She remembered the time she and Micah had worked on painting her cabin, back behind the homestead at the Shining Star. They'd flirted shamelessly, and Simone had enjoyed herself so much. She hadn't had that much fun since then, and she'd started a relationship with one of the cowboys on their ranch after Micah had left.

He hadn't moved to Three Rivers permanently until last July, and by then, Simone had herself a boyfriend. That didn't prevent them from texting and sharing funny videos and memes with one another. It hadn't stopped him from coming to her workshop and showing her the piece he'd found on the side of the road. It hadn't stopped the flirting or the way they circled each other.

"Will you go to dinner with me?" he asked, his voice soft and full of the tenderness Simone ached for.

Surprise flowed over her. "Dinner?"

"I know you broke up with Jarrod."

Simone started nodding, but she didn't know what to say.

"I like you, Simone," Micah said, and blast him, he knew exactly what to say.

"When's the last time you talked to Stephanie?"

A hiss leaked out of his mouth. "I don't know."

"Yes, you do." She looked at him, but he only held her gaze for a moment before focusing on that stupid oak tree again.

Fine, it wasn't stupid. Simone rather liked the oak at Seven Sons. She'd been jealous of the way the brothers dressed it up at Christmastime, because it made the whole lane look like a scene straight from a Hallmark movie.

Micah's jaw jumped, and Simone's heart fell to her shoes. "Does she still think she can win you back?"

"No," he clipped out. "She knows that's not going to happen."

"So when's the last time you talked to her?"

"*She* sends *me* stuff," Micah said, his dark eyes flying back to Simone's. They glittered with danger, but Simone knew he was all bark and no bite. All the Walkers were, though she had been quite careful around Jeremiah for a couple of years. That man had a loud bark—that Whitney had completely silenced.

"You don't know what it's like," he said.

"And you send me stuff," Simone said. "I know exactly what it's like."

"What do you think I'm doing when I send you stuff?"

184

He stopped rocking in his chair, and Simone stilled hers too so the country silence wouldn't be broken.

"Trying to win me back," she said simply.

A quick smile crossed his face, making him devastatingly handsome instead of just drop-dead gorgeous. "Is it working?"

The grumble of a truck engine filled the air, and Wyatt and Marcy pulled into the driveway. Simone stood up, well-aware that she hadn't said she'd go to dinner with Micah. "Maybe you better send me another cat video," she said over her shoulder as she walked away from him.

When she reached the door, her phone chimed.

Her heart leapt, and she spun back to Micah, who wore a hopeful grin on his face. "Maybe you should check that," he said, getting to his feet too.

Simone pulled her phone from her dress pocket and saw the message was from him. She shook her head, a smile already tugging at the corners of her mouth and she hadn't even opened the text yet.

It was a cat video—one of her favorites. A gray cat stared at something intently, his fangs out. The caption said *smile for the camera*, and about six seconds in, his eye twitched. Simone's funny bone got triggered, and she couldn't help the giggle that spilled from her mouth.

"Please?" Micah whispered, his hand landing lightly on her elbow. "Just dinner. Two hours."

Simone looked up, and he stood so close, the heat from his body mingled with hers. Her mind blanked, because if she just tipped up a little, she could kiss him. And oh, she wanted to kiss him.

The front door opened before she could move or speak, and she got jostled to the side as the whole crew spilled out onto the front porch to welcome the happy newlyweds. Wyatt led Marcy up the steps, his hand securely in hers.

Simone had heard the rumor that Marcy had needed a groom, and fast, or she wouldn't be able to keep her crop-dusting business. But anyone looking at Marcy and Wyatt wouldn't think their marriage was a sham. They glowed like two people in love with one another, and an ache that Simone dulled with ice cream and her never-ending quest for the next amazing antique roared at her.

She wanted happiness like that. She wanted a loving husband who adored her. She wanted the big wedding, with the whole town, the tiny bundt cakes, the cowboy billionaire groom.

She only needed to look to her immediate right to find Micah, who wasn't focused on his brother and Wyatt's new wife.

Their eyes met. "Okay," she said. "I'll go to dinner with you."

19

Marcy sat at the computer in her office, piecing together the new video snippet she'd taken that morning with the others she'd been working on since last fall.

She wanted a year-long birds-eye view of Three Rivers for the new Payne's Pest-free website, and with this morning's flight, the video footage was finally all done.

She'd captured every season at Seven Sons Ranch, and she'd need to get Jeremiah to sign off on using his ranch in the footage. He'd won Ranch of the Year for this year, and Marcy really wanted to capitalize on that.

She could just heard the slogan now: Want Ranch of the Year? Hire Payne's Pest-free to help get you there.

She'd been taking a video editing class for the past several months, and she hadn't breathed a word of her project to anyone, not even Wyatt.

Her husband.

In the quiet moments of her life—now that she had quiet moments again—she couldn't believe she was married.

Four months had passed since she'd said I-do, and Marcy could admit she was blissfully happy. The kind of happy she thought only women in cheesy romance movies got to experience. In fact, that was why she'd stopped watching them during the year of her father's sickness.

She couldn't find anyone like her, and she'd needed to see someone in a tough situation come out the victor.

But there were no heroines with fathers dying from cancer. No women dealing with running their own business, working on airplanes, or trying to juggle five thousand balls, one of which was actually the heart of a very handsome cowboy.

The women in the movies didn't have any true decisions to make. They could go back to the city and live their life as a fancy doctor and be happy. Or stay in the small town and marry the guy and be happy.

Either way, they ended up happy.

And Marcy, at the time, had not been able to see a path toward happiness for herself.

The rumbling of the garage opening gently vibrated the house, and she thought again of Wyatt's idea to find and buy a house of their own. She hadn't been able to move into her father's place, and they'd just gone over there at night for another month to finish clearing it out.

She owned it, and she didn't need to sell it, so she hadn't put it on the market yet.

Wyatt had moved in with her, and Marcy sure did like having his big, broad shoulders in her bed, his cowboy boots by her back door, and his aftershave in her bathroom.

And suddenly, she knew why he wanted them to buy a house together. She was still thinking of everything in this house as hers.

"Hey, sugar," he called.

"In the office," Marcy said over her shoulder. The video wasn't quite ready yet, and she'd be surprised if he came into the office without asking her if he could. She'd banished him from the room altogether, claiming she was working on something she wanted to have perfect before she showed it to anyone.

"Hey," he said again, his voice much closer now. "Can I come in?"

She turned around in her desk chair, and smiled at him. "I think I'm ready to show you, so yes. Come in."

"Ooh," he said. "Intriguing." He grabbed a folding chair and swung it around so it faced the computer. "Let's see what you've got."

"I need to adjust the music," she said. "I just shot this this morning, and the colors might need some fixing too." She clicked once, twice, and the video popped up.

"It's a video?"

"A promotional video," she said. "I've been taking a class on video editing."

"You have?" Wyatt's eyebrows practically disappeared under his cowboy hat. "Why didn't you tell me?"

She shrugged. "I don't know. It was just something for me, I guess." She clicked to start the video, and she knew the first seventy-five percent of the video was flawless.

"Hey, that's Seven Sons," he said.

Marcy just smiled, admiring the work she'd put into this video.

"Oh, I see what's happening here," he said. "You're going through all the seasons."

"In less than a minute," she said, as winter faded into spring. Finally, the summer shots she'd been taking for the past few mornings filled the screen, and yes, the music was too loud. It needed to taper at the end. And she needed to make the sky bluer, as sometimes she lost color while up in the blueness of the atmosphere.

"I need to put the title on the end here," she said.

"I loved the beginning," he said. "Want an award-winning ranch? Genius." His hand found hers and squeezed.

"Do you think Jeremiah will sign off on letting me use the footage of the ranch?" She'd gotten shots of several other ranches too, but Seven Sons was special to her. And it was the only award-winning ranch she currently dusted.

"If he won't, I will," Wyatt said. "Remember how I signed the original contract with Payne's?"

"We should still talk to him about it."

"I'll call him right now." Wyatt pulled out his phone, but Marcy put her hand on his. He looked into her eyes, and she shook her head.

"I'll talk to him," she said, her nerves firing. "You really think it's okay?"

"Sweetheart," he said. "It's perfect. What are you going to do with it?"

"Advertising," she said. "On my website, maybe some through Facebook. That kind of thing."

"I thought your schedule was full."

"Barely," she said. "And if I get more customers, I can hire another pilot. Daddy and I used to both fly before he got sick." Her throat narrowed, but only for a moment. She painted a smile on her face and said, "Should I heat up some of that meatloaf from the other night?"

"I brought home sandwiches," he said, standing up.

She joined him, but he turned back into the doorway of the office, easily taking her into his arms. "I think you're pretty incredible, Marce."

She grinned easily now. "Thanks, Wyatt. I think you're great too."

He touched his mouth to hers in a tender, loving kiss. Oh, how Marcy loved kissing him. And instead of going down the hall to eat dinner, Wyatt led her into her bedroom.

Their bedroom.

Later that night, she lay in his arms while his chest rose and fell in an even pattern. "Wyatt?"

"Hmm?"

"I think we should look at buying a new house."

His muscles tensed for a moment. "Really?"

"Yes," she said, sliding her hand across his chest. "Really."

He twisted to reach for his phone on the nightstand. "I'll call Rhett right now and find out who he used to buy Momma's place."

Marcy should've known Wyatt would take action immediately. That's what Wyatt did. If there was a problem, he solved it. If he had something on his mind, he talked about it. If he got the green light to buy a house, he called a real estate agent.

Naturally.

Marcy smiled to herself as he talked to his brother on the phone, and when the call ended, he said, "Jim texted."

"He's just going to ask you to do that tour again."

"Maybe I should think more about it," he said, keeping his back to her as he sat on the edge of the bed. "I mean, we're settled now. You're flying every day. I'm just working at Bowman's."

"Uh, we have a dinner with your mom every other day."

He chuckled, his thumbs obviously moving across his screen. "He said I can call."

"All right," she said, laying back onto her pillow. "Call him then."

Wyatt stood up and left the bedroom, the words, "Hey, Jim," coming from his mouth before he made it to the hall.

Marcy sighed, because she did not want Wyatt to go on the road to promote his western wear line. The last time Jim had called, he'd proposed a six-week tour all over the South, leaving Marcy in Three Rivers to fly over the same fields day after day.

She didn't like the bitterness in her thoughts, because she loved those fields. She loved flying. Heck, she'd gone straight to Wyatt to ask him to marry her so she could *keep* flying over the same fields day after day.

Last time Jim had asked, Marcy had said they'd just gotten home from their honeymoon, and they needed some time to settle in. But Wyatt was right. They were settled now.

She sighed up at the ceiling, as if it would have any sway over what Wyatt did. But Marcy knew it wouldn't. She barely had any sway over him, and she got up and padded across the hall to the computer.

She'd never come back to finish the music or the titles, and she clicked and dragged and got everything where it needed to be. She saved her project, pushed play to watch it one more time, and clung to the happiness streaming through her the same way the plane flew effortlessly over the fields, maintaining them with precision to make Seven Sons the amazing ranch it was.

Because she had a very real feeling that things were about to change.

"Marce?" Wyatt asked from behind her. "Come listen to what Jim has to say, would you?"

No, she did not want to. She thought she'd dodged this bullet.

You should've known better, she told herself as she got up and followed Wyatt into the kitchen. After all, her husband was a celebrity. A minor one, to a very niche group of people, but still a celebrity.

She'd never have him all to herself.

"She's here, Jim." Wyatt leaned his elbows on the counter as he hovered over the phone, which was on speaker.

Marcy got a bottle of water out of the fridge, though she'd probably only take a sip. She should've been asleep thirty minutes ago, as she had early mornings during the week. The best time to fly was as the sun warmed the earth in the morning, and every sunrise soothed her soul.

"Okay, hey, Marcy," Jim said.

"Hi, Jim," she said. She'd met him in Dallas, at the wedding, and another time when he'd been in the area with one of his cowboys. She liked the man; she did. He was about ten years older than Wyatt, and he possessed a kind face and a warm spirit.

Marcy just didn't want him to take Wyatt from her.

She wasn't sure why. She'd spent many years alone, and she valued her independence. She didn't need a man to keep her warm at night, and she wasn't afraid of the dark. But somehow, over the course of the last six months, she'd gotten very comfortable with Wyatt, and she liked having him around.

"Wrangler would like to do a joint promotion with Wyatt."

Marcy watched Wyatt, and she saw something come alive inside him. He loved being in the spotlight, and Marcy didn't want to deny him that.

"The tour is eight weeks, and we'll be going around Texas, Arkansas, Oklahoma, Kansas, Alabama, Kentucky, and up to Montana."

"Wow," Marcy said.

"Wyatt would be on the road during that time, but he doesn't have something every day."

"What would be the schedule?" he asked.

"Nothing's set," Jim said. "Wrangler just called last week, and they have to know you're in before they can put anything together."

"Who will they send?" Wyatt asked.

"Jake Burrows," Jim said.

Wyatt nodded, so Jake Burrows must be someone he could stand traveling around with for eight weeks. "He's the rookie of the year."

"That's right," Jim said. "And it would be from Labor Day to Thanksgiving."

Marcy pulled in a breath. "But he'll be home for the holidays, right?"

"Yes," Jim said. "I can guarantee that, Marcy."

She looked at Wyatt, who gazed steadily back at her. "We need to talk about it," he said, as if he could read her mind. "When do you need to know?"

"End of the month," Jim said. "Take your time."

"Thanks, Jim." Wyatt hung up and straightened, and Marcy knew what he was going to say before he said it.

"It's just eight weeks," they said together. "And I'll be home for the holidays," he added.

Marcy nodded, but she was somewhat desperate to find a reason he should stay with her. She wasn't sure why. "Let's think about it this week," she said. "And pray about it, and talk on Sunday, after church?"

"Sure, okay." Wyatt couldn't argue with taking time to pray about the decision, but Marcy only felt guilt as she went back down the hallway and into her office.

There was that darn *her* again, and she twisted into Wyatt when he joined her. He pressed a kiss to her jaw, and she murmured, "What about the house?"

"I'll get us something lined up in the morning," he said.

"They're going to ask us what we want."

"They are?"

"Yes," she said with a smile, glad their tiny disagreement over his tour hadn't put too much distance between them. "So you better start thinking about that too, cowboy."

20

Wyatt felt like he was playing a game of "say the first thing that comes to your mind when I ask you this question."

Rhett had recommended a realtor to Wyatt, and only a couple of days had passed since he'd called the woman and set up this meeting. And boy, Marcy had been right. The woman had questions about everything.

"How many bedrooms?"

Wyatt had looked at Marcy. She'd looked at him.

"Four?" he guessed. He couldn't even fathom why he'd need that many bedrooms. All of his family members lived right here in Three Rivers, and they didn't need to plan for guests.

"Baths?"

"Four?" he'd guessed again.

"One level or is two okay?"

"Two?"

How big of a yard do you want?" Melissa wore a pair of thick, black-rimmed glasses, and she looked up with every question. After Marcy or Wyatt had guessed at the answer, she'd tapped on the tablet in front of her and fired off the next insane question.

Yes, he wanted central air conditioning. No, he didn't want anything he had to fix up. He wanted the whole yard landscaped and done. He wanted a pasture for horses, and he couldn't imagine a world where he couldn't walk outside and see Kessler or any other animal he might buy in the future.

Yes, they needed a big garage. They both had cars, and Wyatt's truck was actually a beast. So an over-sized garage would be great.

And a master wing, sure. He wanted privacy if they hosted parties, and if they had any children, any future parties could be contained in another part of the house.

Before Wyatt knew it, he'd realized he did have a lot of things he wanted in a home. He'd never thought about it before, and he'd lived out of a touring trailer for years of his life.

But that isn't where you are anymore, he told himself. He'd done that to make the big bucks so he *didn't* have to do that anymore.

Melissa had been quiet for a few minutes now, and Wyatt reached over and took Marcy's hand in his. She could always calm him, and for some reason, he felt like he was about to get bad news.

Especially when Melissa said, "Hmm, really?" and started tapping furiously.

"There aren't any houses for sale in Three Rivers," he joked, and that brought the middle-aged woman's head up again. She had thick, brown hair that fell in curls to her shoulders. She blinked as if she'd just realized she wasn't alone in her office.

"There are," she said slowly. "But nothing I think you two want."

"Really?" Wyatt asked, leaning forward to look at her tablet. Because of the angle, he couldn't see anything but a black screen. "There aren't any houses with a small pasture and central air conditioning?"

"And a storage shed in the large backyard," Melissa said. "And all one level, with a master wing, and a theater room, with a hot tub pad." She cocked her eyebrows, and Wyatt took a turn blinking.

Marcy started to giggle, but Wyatt asked, "Did we really specify all of that?"

"And an office," Melissa said. "Plus at least four other bedrooms, besides the office."

"Don't forget the large kitchen," Marcy said, still grinning like this was a comedy act.

"How could I?" Melissa gave them both a smile and folded her arms over her tablet. "Here's what I think. I think the two of you should build. There are some great lots—"

"Build?" Wyatt blurted out. "Like, a house?"

"You wouldn't build it yourself, cowboy," Marcy said, bursting into laughter right afterward.

Melissa chuckled too, but Wyatt didn't want to build. He wanted to move into a new place that belonged to him and Marcy, so she'd stop saying everything was hers. And he wanted to do it in the next couple of months so they'd be settled before the tour. And then they could have their first Christmas together in their new house, and everything would be perfect.

So maybe he fantasized a little too much. Maybe he romanticized things when he should be teaching a horse to pull harder the moment the rope left his hand. Maybe he'd laid awake for a night or two, thinking about what a new house for him and Marcy could do and be.

"If you build," Melissa said. "You'd get exactly what you want. And there are some animal lots on the west side of town."

"In Rosewood?" Marcy asked.

"Yes," Melissa said, a measure of surprise in her voice. "You know them?"

"I drive past them on the way to the hangar every morning." She looked at Wyatt. "We should look at the lots and think about building."

He studied her fair features, and she sure didn't seem

to be kidding. He looked back to Melissa. "How long does it take to build?"

"Depends," she said. "But they're putting those houses up in Rosewood in about four months."

October.

He'd be gone in October, and he frowned. *You might be gone in October*, he amended. He hadn't committed to the tour yet, because Marcy was reluctant for him to go. She wasn't sure why, only that she wanted to wait and see if God had a different plan for them.

Wyatt felt great about the tour, and he didn't need to wait to go to church to know it. But the Sabbath day was tomorrow, and Wyatt figured he'd waited this long, he could wait one more day.

"And if you're really thinking about building," Melissa said, interrupting his thoughts. "A brand new development is coming to Three Rivers, and they'll be estates."

"Estates?" Marcy asked.

"What does 'coming to Three Rivers' mean?" Wyatt asked.

"It means the development has been announced to realtors, but they're not officially on sale yet." She touched her tablet, swiped, typed, and turned it to show them. "They go on sale on Tuesday."

The estates on her screen took Wyatt's breath away. They were huge, sprawling houses, with plenty of land around them. "Animals?" he asked.

"Yes," Melissa said.

"One level?" Marcy asked.

"There will be several models, but yes. There are two or three one-level options. All the upgrades you can think of, even a heated driveway for the one time it snows up here." She smiled and swiped. Swiped and smiled. "Huge master area, with a separate living room. Large, open spaces for family. Big kitchens."

Everything she said manifested itself right there on the screen.

"And let me see...." She turned the table back toward herself. "I think there are options for outdoor buildings too."

Wyatt just wanted to look at the pictures again. He met Marcy's eye, and she was clearly interested in these estates too. He lifted his eyebrows, and she nodded.

"Yep," Melissa said. "It says here that there are options for corrals, barns, sheds, coops, and more." She looked up, her brown eyes bright. "Maybe you'd like to go out there and see those lots too."

"Can we do that today?" Wyatt asked.

"Sure," she said. "We can drive up there."

"Up where?" Marcy asked. "And what will be the name of these estates?" She looked at Wyatt. "The name is important. We have to say to people, 'oh, we live in Monument Garden,' or whatever."

He chuckled and squeezed her hand. "So you're saying the name could break this for us."

"I'm saying it's important." She smiled and looked back at Melissa.

"They're calling this Church Ranches," Melissa said. "It's on Twelve Mile Road, on the northeast side of town."

"Swanky," Marcy said. "Tripp lives out close to there."

"He's not too far north," Wyatt said.

"These are," Melissa said. "And they go up into the hills a little bit—well, as much as we have hills here." She grinned and stood up. "So let's go look at the lots in Rosewood. You can get an idea of what's going on there. And then we can head out to Twelve Mile Road. Sound good?"

"Yes," Marcy said, standing up and shouldering her purse. Wyatt took an extra moment to get to his feet, mostly because he couldn't believe they were going to look at lots today instead of houses.

"There's really nothing for sale right now?" he asked.

Melissa paused at the edge of her desk. "Tell you what. I'll take you by the biggest, most expensive house available right now. Before we look at the lots. And you can decide."

Wyatt nodded, a bit of apprehension threading itself through his bones. Marcy waited until they were seated and buckled in his truck, following Melissa in her car, before she asked, "Why don't you want to build, Wyatt?"

"Because," he said. "It takes a long time." He flipped on his right blinker and started into the turn. "In my head, I thought we'd find something and move before the tour."

"Oh, so this is about the tour."

He glanced at her, her slightly salty tone of voice saying she didn't want to talk about the tour. "Why don't you want me to go on the tour?"

"It's not that I don't want you to go."

"Really? Because that's how it seems." Wyatt had participated in plenty of heated conversations, but somehow, talking to Marcy about something she didn't want to talk about made his stomach clench.

"It's just...I thought you were done with the rodeo."

"I am." Wyatt eased up on the accelerator when he saw Melissa brake. "This has nothing to do with the rodeo." Melissa pulled over in front of a very big house that had a for sale sign in the lawn. He peered at the house as he came to a stop at the curb behind her.

"I don't like this house," Marcy said.

"Why not?" Wyatt couldn't say he particularly did either. "I hate how it's on a street with twelve other houses. There's no room here."

"That," Marcy said, though she lived in a neighborhood like this one. "And where are all the big trees?"

"You think there will be big trees in a development with new homes?"

"There will be at those estates," she said. "They'll leave all the trees there and work around them."

Wyatt had his doubts, but he didn't say anything. Melissa came to Marcy's side of the truck, and Wyatt rolled down the window. "This house is the size you want," she said. "It has a large yard, but no room for horses. It's two levels, and there's no office and no hot tub pad."

"We don't want it," Marcy said. "It's too populated."

"Ah, see that wasn't on your list." Melissa smiled. "But I figured."

"He wants something just like Seven Sons."

Surprise filtered through him while Melissa said, "Let's go to Rosewood," and started back toward her car.

"Do I want something just like Seven Sons?" he asked as he pulled back onto the street.

"I do," Marcy said. "Except not as much land outside. You don't want to run a ranch." She looked at him. "Do you?"

"No," he said quickly. "I don't want a ranch. I just want to be able to keep a few horses and goats if I want to."

"Goats?" She shook her head. "I don't think so, buddy."

"Goats are out? Why?"

"What do you do with a goat?"

"You talk to them."

"You talk to goats." Marcy folded her arms and cocked her head at him. "Are you serious?"

"Dead serious." He followed Melissa out of the neighborhood and back to the highway. "They're good listeners."

Marcy just shook her head. Wyatt liked Rosewood a heck of a lot more than the house in the middle of town. The homes were big, and the lots were too. He could potentially have a couple of acres for the house and the pasture, and it would do. But there weren't many trees, and Marcy seemed stuck on the idea of Church Ranches.

So they drove clear across town and up Twelve Mile Road. The moment the road started inclining, Wyatt knew they were in the right place. "This is it," he said. "There are your trees, Marce."

Melissa turned, and Wyatt followed her. "Oh, they've got lots marked."

"Yeah, they go on sale on Tuesday," Marcy said. "They'll have to be ready."

"We might have to be ready too," Wyatt said. "Do you think these will sell fast?"

"No, Wyatt," Marcy said. "I don't think they'll sell fast."

"Why not?"

She pointed to a sign on her side of the road, and Wyatt slowed to read it. "Oh," he said once he'd gotten to the price tag. "Lots starting at seven-hundred and fifty thousand."

"That's for the *lot*," Marcy said. "We can't live here either."

"Why not?" He stopped beside Melissa, and they got out of the truck.

"Here we are," Melissa said. "There are only fourteen lots up here, and they've all been marked. There won't be a model home, as the builder has a full display in their offices in Three Rivers. We can go there and look at them if you'd like."

Wyatt didn't need to look at the displays. This was the land they wanted. The houses would be high-end here. "How much are we talking for a house, the land, the outbuildings?"

"I thought you said you didn't have a ceiling on your budget."

"We don't," Wyatt said. "But we need to be reasonable." Didn't they?

"It's a gated community," Melissa said. "Everything is private. You wanted that, too."

"Wyatt," Marcy said. "We can't afford this."

He definitely could. He just hadn't told Marcy how much money he had in his bank account yet. She knew he was rich; anyone who'd watched even a couple of his later videos in the rodeo knew. He'd retired as the richest cowboy in the association, for crying out loud. And that was before he counted his inheritance, which was also in the billions.

"Marcy," he said quietly, moving her away from Melissa. "We can afford this. Even if it's ten million dollars."

Her eyes widened, and she searched his face. "Are you serious?"

"Yes," he said. "This is what you want, right?"

"I can't just let you buy—"

"We're married," he said, though they hadn't really

talked about combining their assets yet. They'd been switching off paying her mortgage every month, and the months he did, she paid the utilities. They both bought food with their own money and put gas in their cars with their own money.

Foolishness hit Wyatt. So he'd married Marcy knowing he loved her. She loved him. They'd been living together, sharing a bed, working through her grief. But they hadn't actually combined their lives yet. Why hadn't he done that?

Behind him, Melissa talked on the phone, asking someone for the pricing structure here at Church Ranches.

Wyatt looked at Marcy, unsure of what to say next.

"The base model is roughly one-point-five million," Melissa said, and he turned toward her. "It goes up from there, and Lorenzo, the selling agent I just spoke with, says with every upgrade he could think of, the top price would be about nine million."

"We want one of these," Wyatt said.

Marcy started to protest, but Wyatt gave her a glare that quieted her. "So, which lot would you recommend? I am sort of a celebrity."

Melissa smiled and led him to a corner lot, explaining why she'd pick this one, pointing out the larger backyard, the potential for a back gate right into the woods, and how they could make sure a hot tub pad got poured.

Wyatt let himself begin to fantasize again, and while

the idea of living in a construction zone for the next year didn't enthuse him, owning a private, well-kept house in the woods certainly did.

When they got back in the truck, Marcy wasted no time in saying, "I looked you up online. This says you're worth six-point-seven billion dollars."

He glanced at her, the shock pouring off of her in waves almost comical. "Does it?"

"Wyatt Walker, you tell me the truth right this second. Is that true?"

"Sugar, how many people televise their wedding?"

She sputtered, finally coming up with, "Well, I thought—I mean—your fans...." She exhaled. "I didn't know."

"It's actually a little low," he said coolly. "The western wear line has been going really well." He grinned at her as they left the soon-to-be community of Church Ranches behind. "Now, where should we eat lunch? And nowhere outside; it's *hot* today."

21

"Tripp," Ivory said, waking him. She groaned in the next moment, and that got Tripp's heart beating.

"What?" he asked, sitting up and switching on the lamp beside the bed. "Are you okay?"

"I just had a contraction." She smiled, though her eyes held a wide-eyed fear in them. Tripp felt it tripping through his body.

He jumped to his feet. "I'll get the bag."

"We can't just go right now," she said, scooting to the edge of the bed.

"We can't?"

"We have to time them," she said.

"Time them, right." He practically dove for his phone, swiping so hard the device went flying out of his fingers.

"Calm down, honey," she said, pulling in a long breath.

Calm down? Tripp hadn't been truly calm since Ivory had told him she was pregnant. He was comfortable with his life, and he'd been doing the very best he could with Oliver. But this was going to be a child of his own. A child he'd helped create. And Ivory had to go through labor, and Tripp had never experienced that before.

He remembered the panic on Rhett's face when he'd had his baby, and Tripp hadn't understood it then.

He did now.

He retrieved his phone, wishing it wasn't two-thirty in the morning. "Should I see if someone can come sit with Ollie? Liam said he would. Wyatt. Micah. We can take him to Seven Sons too, and he'll be in heaven."

"Liam," Ivory said. "He said he'd come get him day or night and take him to the ranch."

Tripp woke his phone and called his twin.

"Ivory's in labor or you're dead," his brother said, his voice sounding like he'd swallowed a frog.

"She's in labor," Tripp said. "At least I think she is."

"I am," Ivory said, groaning as another contraction hit her. At least Tripp thought that was what was happening. She held her very pregnant belly with both hands and bent forward, a terrible, painful sound coming from her mouth. It wasn't loud and screechy, and that only made the low sound of pain that much more terrifying for him.

"I'll be there in twenty," Liam said. "Leave if you have to. Ollie won't know the difference."

"He has a bag in his closet," Tripp said. "It's been packed for a few days."

"Got it."

Tripp hung up and circled the bed to kneel in front of his wife. His beautiful, lovely wife who'd been carrying their child for nine months. "How long was that?"

"Not very long," she said.

He reached up and wiped her hair off her forehead. "I'll start timing now." He got the stopwatch on his phone going, and he added, "Do you need a drink?"

"I need to get dressed," she said. "I'm not going to the hospital in an oversized T-shirt with the state of Arkansas printed on it."

He grinned at her. "We're having a baby."

"*I'm* having a baby," she said, though she smiled at him too.

"I love you," Tripp said. And he did. So much. He'd watched her deal with various discomforts over the past nine months, from the nausea and throwing up, to heartburn so bad she'd chew gum until her jaw ached. Then she'd just suck on it. Anything to keep the stomach acid down.

She'd said she'd never had that with Oliver, so she'd been convinced she was having a girl. But the doctor told them they were having another boy, and she'd started calling him Mister Fussy, because she literally got heartburn when she ate cucumbers or something simple like toast.

"Liam said twenty minutes," Tripp said, steadying her as she got to her feet. Those, along with her ankles, had been swollen for three weeks, and Tripp had realized the pure sacrifice women went through when they had children. And he was so, so grateful, because he wanted to be a dad so bad.

Yes, he was Oliver's father, but this was different. This child was *his*, had come from part of him.

Ivory had laid out some clothes to wear to the hospital, and Tripp stayed right by her side as she changed out of her oversized T-shirt. Then he quickly changed out of his basketball shorts and T, just in time to hear Ivory say, "Here comes another one."

He looked at his phone. Five and a half minutes since the last one. He hurried out of the closet to find her in the armchair near the window in their bedroom, her teeth gritted. "How long?" she asked.

"Five minutes and thirty-four seconds," he said. "I'm timing the contraction. Tell me when it's over." He arrived in front of her a moment before she cried out, and everything inside of him wanted to take this pain from her.

Ivory had told him she didn't want him to tell her how awesome she was. Or that she could do this. "I know I can do this," she'd told him. But he wasn't prepared for how much birthing a baby would demand of her.

The pain seemed to roll through her for a long time, and he knew the moment it released. He looked at his phone, suddenly unable to do math. He had an advanced computer science degree, and he couldn't subtract in that moment.

"Thirty-four seconds," he said.

"Getting close," she said.

"We're leaving at four minutes, thirty seconds," he said. "And the moment you hit forty-five seconds."

"Tripp," she said.

"It takes thirteen minutes to get to the hospital," he said, a bit of hysteria entering his voice. "That's three contractions on the way there." He sat on the bed to put on his shoes, then he left her in the recliner to get his wallet, keys, and jacket.

He ran outside to start the truck, and he hurried back inside to grab the bag she'd packed. She had baby clothes, diapers, slippers for herself, as well as clothes for herself to wear home. Tripp was actually glad Ivory had given birth before, because he had no idea what to do.

She'd put peppermints in the bag, and gum, as well as a spare phone charger, her tablet, and a pair of head-phones. She was the most prepared person he knew, and as he tossed the bag in the back seat, his heart filled and filled and filled.

"Thank you, Lord," he said, tipping his head back and looking up. "Please help this delivery to go well. Bless my wife." His throat closed then, and an alarm went off on his phone. Five minutes had passed since the last contraction.

He almost ran back inside. The moment he arrived in the bedroom, Ivory smiled up at him, her chin a little wobbly. "My water just broke."

"Let's go." They didn't have to wait for contractions anymore, and Tripp's heart zig-zagged through his whole body. He took her hand and helped her up, keeping her steady as they walked through their house. He'd known it was a large house, but it felt like a hike to the truck.

He'd just put her in the passenger seat when she groaned and leaned forward. He closed her door and headed around the tailgate just as Liam pulled up. His heart raced, and he was so grateful for his family.

After backing out of the garage, he rolled down his window and Liam leaned in. "Going?"

"Her water broke," Tripp said, and Ivory didn't look over at all. "She's contracting every five minutes. Oliver's asleep."

"I'll pack him up and take good care of him." Liam saluted against his cowboy hat, which was a ridiculous thing to wear at three o'clock in the morning. But Tripp loved his brother with his whole heart as he finished backing out and got the truck headed for the hospital.

Thirteen minutes there.

Then they'd check-in, and someone with more experience than him would be able to take care of Ivory.

"I don't remember it being so painful," she said, panting. "Mister Fussy is not going to be an easy child."

Tripp wanted to laugh, but he was too nervous. "Almost there," he said, though they'd just left. He drove as fast as he dared, actually glad it was the middle of the night, because there was no traffic.

He wanted to call his mother, because she'd want to know, and maybe she'd be able to come help. Ivory's parents lived in Kentucky, and she barely spoke to them. But it was the middle of the night, and Liam would put the news on the family text string at a decent hour.

Ivory had two more contractions on the way to the hospital, and by the time Tripp pulled up to the emergency entrance, his nerves buzzed and frayed.

"Here we go," he said, opening her door and helping her down from the truck. He couldn't remember if he'd taken the keys out of the ignition or not. A quick glance said he hadn't. "Let me get you a wheelchair." He left her leaning against the truck as he ran inside and grabbed the chair.

With her sitting, he gathered his keys and the bag from the back seat, and then he pushed his wife into the hospital to have their baby.

"Tripp," she said as he went past the emergency entrance. They needed to get to labor and delivery, and he knew right where it was, thanks to a hospital tour Ivory had given him a month ago.

But she sounded a touch panicked, and he slowed. "What?"

"I'm bleeding a lot," she said, her voice growing weaker by the word.

He looked down into her lap, which was wet with blood. He swung her around as gently as he could while still doing it quickly and strode into the emergency room. "I need help," he said when he didn't find anyone at the intake desk.

"Tripp," Ivory said again, only a moment before she passed out.

"Ivory!" He darted in front of her and caught her so she wouldn't slump out of the chair. "I need help!" he yelled again, and thankfully, two nurses came out of the nearby door. "She's in labor," he said. "Her water broke, and we came. She's bleeding a lot and she just passed out."

The nurses took over from there, and Tripp had no choice but to back up and let them help Ivory. He followed them through the doors that led to the back, answering the questions one of the nurses threw at him.

Tears filled his eyes, and he had no idea what to do with them. He couldn't remember the last time he'd cried, but as he watched more people gather around Ivory, get her from the chair to the bed, and call for a doctor, Tripp let his tears fall as he prayed.

"Is she okay?" he asked.

"Sir," someone said. "You should wait—"

"That's my wife," he said, new strength entering him. "And she was fine two minutes ago. She's in labor, and I am *not* leaving her." He glared at the woman.

"Who's your OB?" she asked.

"Doctor Linda Tribear."

"We'll call her. Try to stay out of the way." She gave Tripp a quick smile and ducked out of the room. Tripp couldn't look away from Ivory, and he hated how pale her face was and how she still hadn't woken up.

22

Skyler woke when his phone rang, instantly annoyed. It was far too dark for him to be awake, and when he saw Liam's name on the screen, he almost didn't answer the call. Then he realized that it was far too early for his phone to even be ringing, which meant Liam had called three times in the span of ten minutes, deactivating the nighttime silent mode on his phone.

"Liam?" he asked, sitting up and reaching to snap on a light. "What's going on?"

"Ivory is in labor," he said. "And she passed out before they could get to labor and delivery. We're doing a family prayer in five minutes, if you'd like to join in."

"Yeah, sure," Skyler said, though he couldn't remember the last time he'd prayed. Maybe when he'd gone to Three Rivers for Wyatt's wedding, as he needed the extra strength to deal with his large, loud family.

"How's the baby?"

"We don't know anything yet," Liam said. "Tripp called, and he was pretty freaked out. I told him I'd take care of telling everyone."

Skyler nodded, though Liam wasn't there to see. He swung his feet over the edge of the bed, thinking through his day. He'd told his family he wanted to stay in Amarillo for the summer to "get ahead in his classes."

But he hadn't enrolled in any summer classes. He didn't need a job, and Skyler had taken to sleeping late, playing video games for a while when he woke up, walking the city, and hanging out with his friends in the evening.

He didn't particularly enjoy his life, and in truth, he was bored out of his mind. But he hadn't been a good mechanic. And now he wasn't a good student.

No, that wasn't true. When he was in school, he was a good student. He learned the material, did his assignments, and got good grades.

But it was all very boring, and he couldn't imagine himself actually becoming an accountant.

The only reason he hadn't dropped out completely and run for the Pacific coast was because he knew he could return to Seven Sons Ranch and be the accountant there. No suits. No ladder-climbing. Just mindless number pushing while wearing a cowboy hat, eating Jeremiah's food, and riding horses.

"What else can I do?"

"Just pray," Liam said. "We have Oliver, and he's

asleep. We're not telling him anything until there's something to tell."

"Should I come home?"

Home.

What an odd word.

Three Rivers definitely wasn't his home, but his entire family lived there now, and even he could admit that he missed his momma.

"That's up to you," Liam said. "Momma's calling, Sky. Love you, brother. Talk later." The line ended, and Skyler was left with the anxious voice of Liam in his ears.

He knew his brother loved him.

"Love you too, brother," he said, wondering when he'd become the Walker brother clothed in black sheepskin.

The call to go home and be with his brothers filled him, and he got up and got in the shower. Thirty minutes later, he had a bag packed and in the back of his truck. His headlights cut a path through the darkness on the highway, and he was the only vehicle on the lonely road between Amarillo and Three Rivers.

To keep himself awake, he rolled the window halfway down and put the radio on loud. Still, it didn't drown out his thoughts.

He'd taken a giggling girl to Wyatt's wedding, and when Rhett had asked if Skyler was seeing her, he'd just laughed. "No," he said. "We're just friends."

And barely that. He could tolerate Fiona most of the time, and that made her a safe bet to take to his celebrity brother's wedding. He certainly couldn't show up alone. Then he'd be like Micah, wearing a drawn-down face and throwing moon eyes at Simone Foster for the entire wedding.

No, thank you.

Skyler sighed, because he was so tired of thinking about his life, his future. He felt it had a giant crack down the middle of it, and the woman who'd wielded the hammer didn't even know it.

Shayla Davis.

He automatically wondered where she was, and if she'd latched on to another poor sucker with a big bank account. The familiar feelings of foolishness and anger came with thoughts of Shayla, and he shoved everything away.

Not only had Shayla broken his heart into a million pieces and taken it with her when she'd left Dallas, but she'd taken his pride, thousands of his dollars, and his truck.

She claimed he'd bought her the truck, which if someone were to get technical, he had. So he hadn't tried to get it back. The money was cash, and there was no way to prove it was his. The pride and every ounce of love he had to give were gone permanently, and while Skyler had admitted defeat with the mechanic shop, he didn't know how to give up being human.

At the hospital in Three Rivers, he found every one of his brothers, as well as his parents, in the waiting room just outside of labor and delivery. He, of course, was the last to arrive, and he said, "Hey, everyone," as he stepped off the elevator.

"Sky." His mother sounded relieved, and she was already crying when she stepped into him and hugged him tightly.

"Hey, Momma." He clung to her too, because he did love his mother, and he didn't want to disappoint her. And if he didn't want to do that, upsetting or showing his father he wasn't the man he could be was downright devastating to Skyler.

"What's going on?" he asked as his mom released him.

Daddy drew him into a hug too, patting him on the back before just holding him tight. "Thanks for coming. It means a lot to your mother."

Skyler leaned his forehead against his father's for a moment, and then stepped back, feeling more loved than he had in a long time. And he knew that while he wore the black sheepskin, it was just a costume. He wasn't really the black sheep of the Walker brothers. He belonged with them, and they'd be there for him no matter what.

Jeremiah stood with his wife, Whitney, who was also nine months pregnant. She looked scared out of her mind and like she'd been crying, and Skyler's emotions surged.

"Is she...I mean, someone say something." Skyler looked at Liam, who came toward him with the same anxiety on his face that filled every particle of air in the room.

"They stabilized her and moved her up here, but she hasn't woken up. They're doing a C-section right now, and Tripp is with her."

Skyler knew what the words meant, and he knew why everyone was concerned. "She needs to wake up, right?"

"It's concerning that she hasn't," Liam said, drawing Skyler into a hug too. His chest vibrated, and he closed his eyes to keep the burning tears from gathering too deeply. He did not want to cry in this room with all these tough cowboys.

No, Skyler much preferred to weep when he was alone, preferably in the shower so the tears would wash away with the spray.

"They're giving her blood, because apparently she lost a lot, and they think the placenta might have separated prematurely, causing a lot of internal bleeding."

Someone sniffed, and Skyler nearly lost his composure. It didn't help that the moment Liam released him, another brother took his place, until Skyler had hugged them all, even the sisters-in-law.

There were enough places to sit, but only a couple of people actually took a seat. Skyler couldn't contain himself to a chair, and he wandered over to the huge fish tank built into the wall. He felt a lot like the fish—swimming around in a foreign place, wondering what the point of his life was.

He closed his eyes, and did something he hadn't done in such a long time. He prayed.

Honestly, truly prayed for Ivory's health, the well-being of their baby, and for Tripp, who had left a huge hole in their family by not being there to greet Skyler.

It wasn't long before a nurse came out into the waiting room and said, "Walker family?"

"Right here," at least four people said.

"Oh, there are a lot of you." She smiled. "Tripp said there would be." She drew in a deep breath. "We delivered the baby just fine, and he's healthy and crying. Tripp's with him." She looked around at all of them. "We're getting everything finished up with Ivory, and she's got her normal level of blood back."

"Is she awake?" someone asked, and Skyler reached for the hand closest to him. It was Micah's, and his brother squeezed hard.

"I'm sorry," the nurse said. "She hasn't woken yet. We have the best working with her, and I'll make sure you're updated." With that, she turned and went back through a door that led into the maternity ward.

The air seemed to leave the room with her.

Ivory had to wake up. She just had to.

Skyler didn't know her well—he didn't know any of his brother's wives very well. But it was enough that they loved one of his brothers. They belonged to the family, and that meant nothing could happen to them that wouldn't devastate Skyler.

"Now what?" Wyatt asked.

"Now we wait some more," Micah said, dropping

Skyler's hand and moving over to a couch with Simone Foster. They didn't touch or even look at one another, and Skyler's heart bled for his youngest brother too. He knew how much Micah liked Simone, as Micah had confided in Skyler and texted him often.

Another hour passed, and Tripp brought his bundled baby out to the waiting room. He'd clearly been crying, and Skyler stayed at the back of the crowd while everyone took turns meeting the baby and embracing Tripp.

"Skyler," Tripp finally said, pulling him into a hug. "Thanks for coming." They both cried then, and Skyler felt like the whole world was different once again. He'd never seen Tripp cry as an adult, and it was humbling and horrible at the same time.

"Any news on Ivory?" Momma asked.

"She just woke up," Tripp said, taking back his infant son. "Her placenta had ripped away from the womb, and they said it was lucky we were already here, or she may have bled too much before they could save her."

He let the tears run down his face. "Thank you for the prayers. I know God heard them and saved my wife."

Liam put his arm around Tripp, and the sight of the twins leaning on each other was too much for Skyler. He swiped at his eyes and sucked in a tight breath.

"We named him Isaac Luther," Tripp said, smiling through his emotion. "And as soon as they say Ivory can have visitors, I'll let you know."

More hugging. More crying. More cuddling the new

baby. Even Skyler gave the tiny boy a kiss before Tripp went back into the maternity ward.

He felt wrung out and put together backward, and he didn't know what to do about it. His stomach grumbled, and Micah's next to him did the same. "Breakfast?" Micah asked.

"Do we have time?"

"I think we have time." He yawned and stood up. "Momma, we're going to get something to eat. What should we bring back for you and Daddy?"

After that, it turned into a dozen orders, and Skyler's annoyance rose again. His phone chimed, and he pulled it out of his back pocket.

You're not home? I thought we were running this morning.

"Mal," he said under his breath, his thumbs already flying across his screen.

"Who's Mal?"

"No one," he said, not even glancing up at whichever brother had asked.

"You're going running with her? Do you run?"

Skyler sent his message explaining about Tripp's baby in as few words as possible, and looked up. Wyatt stood there, his eyes gleaming.

"Yes," Skyler said. "I run."

"Since when?"

"Since Mal started asking him," Marcy said, smiling. "Right?"

Skyler rolled his eyes. "No, not since Mal started asking me." Though, if he could be honest with the two of them, yes, since Mal started asking him. And he'd gone to her yoga classes and this frou frou smoothie shop she liked.

"We're coming to breakfast with you," Wyatt said, taking Skyler's phone before he could comprehend what had just happened. "So you can tell us all about her."

"Nothing to tell," he said, the chime on his phone making his heart leap.

"Didn't you bring someone else to our wedding?" Marcy asked.

"That's because I'm friends with a lot of people," Skyler said. And maybe—just maybe—he wanted to be more than friends with Mal. He just didn't know how to get there, because he had a reputation that nothing was serious, and he absolutely was not interested in a real relationship.

If he'd known he was digging his own grave, he might have played things differently at the university.

23

Micah kept his head down as he crossed from Seven Sons land to the Shining Star. The path was well-marked, and he'd been walking it for a few months now, since Simone had sat next to him in the rocking chairs on the front porch at the homestead.

Simone had a strict schedule, and if Micah wanted to see her and talk to her, he had to go in the middle of the afternoon, when there was no chance of her sisters showing up in her workshop.

A "she-shed" she called it, and Micah had smiled widely at that. He sometimes went to her cabin in Cowboy Row at night too, but that had ended as summer had dawned, as she liked him to come after darkness had fallen.

And that happened really late at night now, and Micah hadn't been able to keep up with his sleep schedule. Not if she wanted to see him during prime afternoon nap time and then past his bedtime.

In all honesty, he would give up anything to see her. Even sleep.

He knocked on the door to her shed, which she kept locked these days. She'd actually started doing it when Callie had walked in on her and Jarrod making out—Callie's words, not Micah's.

He actually didn't want to think about Simone kissing anyone else, especially the arrogant cowboy who lived only two doors down from her, even now. Micah glanced up, as if he'd see Cowboy Row from here, but Simone's shop sat behind the stables and the chicken coops, sort of tucked into a corner of the ranch. A pasture with several tall trees waited right behind her she-shed, and a sense of peace filled Micah as he waited in the Texas summer heat.

The lock finally jangled, and Simone opened the door a moment later. Blessed air conditioning filtered out of the building, but Micah couldn't move. Her beauty had rendered him mute and immobile once again. How a cowboy in this little Texas town hadn't snatched her up a decade ago, Micah wasn't sure.

"Hey," she said, smiling as he leaned into the door.

He had to step up to enter the she-shed, and when he did, she fell back. He'd held her hand over the months. They'd cuddled on her couch, and a couple of times on a piece of furniture she was working on.

But he hadn't kissed her.

Yet, he thought, his eyes moving to her mouth as he passed her. He still felt like he was walking on thin and cracking ice with her, and it was starting to get old. Would he have to live his whole life on eggshells, because he was worried he'd upset her?

"Wow, look at all of this." He took in the assortment of pottery on a shelf facing the door. She closed the door, locking them inside with all the cool air. "You've been at the wheel forever."

"Just last night and this morning," she said, her voice like music to his ears. She came to stand beside him, and Micah's fingers twitched. It was Simone who slid her fingers into Micah's, and all the unrest in his soul quieted.

"Is one of these for me?" he asked.

"Why would one of those be for you?" she asked, but he heard the teasing quality in her voice. "Oh, wait. It's your birthday next week."

"Another year older," he said, smiling.

"How old?" she asked.

"You haven't guessed right yet."

"Okay, so we're sticking to that."

Yes, Micah was sticking to that.

"Let's see. Last time, I think you were younger than thirty-six and older than thirty-two."

"That's right," he said, though he couldn't actually remember. They hadn't talked about his birthday yesterday, or the day before. He hadn't seen her the day before that, as Tripp and Ivory had finally been released from the hospital, and Micah had gone to their place to help with Oliver while Tripp made sure Ivory was okay at home.

She'd been in the hospital for five days as they monitored her to make sure she didn't have any lingering internal bleeding. She'd recovered quickly once everything had been repaired, but she'd had a Caesarean section, and that didn't heal in a few days. She slept sitting up, her newborn nestled on her chest, and Tripp had been waiting on her hand and foot.

"So I have three choices."

"And one guess for today," he said, grinning at her. He lifted her hand to his lips and watched as Simone's eyes started glittering. A small smile appeared on her mouth, and Micah wanted to kiss it away.

"Thirty-three," she said.

"Older."

She shook her head, smiling in full force now. "Tomorrow I'll get it."

"Friday night," he said. "We could go to Amarillo to that pizza place Skyler told us about." No one would know them in Amarillo, and maybe they wouldn't have to sneak around to see each other anymore.

Simone hadn't actually requested that they keep their relationship a secret, but she hadn't wanted to hold his hand in front of her sisters or his brothers. So her message had come through loud and clear.

In truth, Simone had held him at arm's length for five months, and Micah needed to do something about it.

Kiss her or break up. Those were his two choices.

"I'm totally feeling like pizza," she said.

"Great," he said, actually a little surprised and hoping it didn't show in his voice. "Did you want to come over to the ranch, and we'll go from there? Or do you want me to pick you up here?"

"I'll walk over," she said. "Wait. It's a million degrees outside. You can come pick me up."

"Four-thirty?"

"It's a date."

He got up the courage to look away from the pottery Simone had thrown, and their eyes met. "Tell me what you're thinking," he said. "About me. About us."

Her eyes widened a little, her shock evident. "Oh."

"Weren't expecting that, were you?" He smiled, because while he wanted things to be serious, he didn't want to push her away.

"I'm holding your hand."

"It's been five months," he said.

"And?"

"And I haven't kissed you."

Simone blinked those beautiful, dark eyes that reminded him of a deep, country night. She slid her free hand up his arm and to the back of his neck, her fingernails eliciting a shiver from Micah.

He took that as her way of saying, *You better kiss me*

then, and he took her into his arms and brushed his cowboy hat off into his hand. In the next moment, his lips touched hers, and Micah could've sworn angelic choirs started singing.

It was definitely too hot in the she-shed now, as Simone kissed him back. Everything he'd been imagining this moment to be had come to fruition, and Micah broke the kiss for long enough to take a deep breath, and then he kissed her again.

He lost track of time and space inside the she-shed, and it wasn't until she giggled that he realized he'd backed her into the door he'd knocked on so many times. "Wow," he said, not backing up a single inch.

"Yeah?"

Heat filled Micah's face. "Yeah. Wow."

"I think wow too," she said.

"Yeah?"

She looked at him, and all that flirtatious power between them returned. "Yeah."

"So are we allowed to tell people?"

Simone cradled his face in her hands. "Isn't this more fun?"

Micah didn't know what to say. No, what would be more fun would be holding her hand after Sunday dinner. Cuddling with her on the couch while Jeremiah put a movie on for Whitney, who was due to have their baby any day now.

"I mean, yeah," he said. "This is fun." Kissing her had

been lots of fun. But something deep inside him writhed. Was she embarrassed of him?

"But...." she prompted.

"Yeah, but, I mean. Is this what we are? Why don't you want anyone to know about us?"

Simone sighed, and though she couldn't step back, she slipped away from him all the same. She walked over to the pottery she'd thrown and picked up a piece from the shelf. "I just feel...I don't know. Like, both of my sisters are married to two of your brothers."

"And?" Micah stayed right where he was by the door.

"And, I don't know. It feels a little weird. Like, there are other cowboys out here."

His heart *ba-bumped* painfully in his chest. "So it is me."

Simone didn't answer, and Micah felt the air whoosh right out of his lungs. He'd kissed her, and now he felt like he should break-up with her too. He gave himself a small shake. He didn't want to break-up with her.

His phone went off, the loud ringtone actually startling him. "It's Jeremiah." He fumbled with the lock on the door, got it open, and stepped outside. "Hey," he said, a big, giant sigh accompanying the word.

"Hey," he said, his voice on the outer edge of frantic. "Whitney is having the baby, and I'm headed back to the ranch. Wondering where you are?"

Micah spun in the direction of Seven Sons. He was at least half a mile from the homestead, and he could probably run it in a few minutes. "Five minutes out," he said, already moving. "Where are you? How's she doing? Is she okay?"

"I was out in the corn," Jeremiah said. "So I'm at least ten minutes. If you could get there and see, I'd appreciate it."

"Sure," Micah said, feeling his calf muscle cramping up a bit. He didn't run like Skyler, and while he wasn't overweight, he definitely wasn't in marathon shape. "So you don't know how she is?"

"She called and said she'd had a contraction and could I please come back to the homestead. I called you five seconds later."

"I'll call you back," Micah said, and he gripped his phone tightly and focused on his breathing. True to his word, he reached the homestead only a few minutes later, and he vaulted up the back steps to the deck. All three dogs stood at the door, almost like they could sense a problem inside.

"Look out, guys," he said, reaching over them to open the door. "Whitney?" he called. "It's Micah. Jeremiah called me."

She wasn't in the living room or the kitchen, and he hurried down the hall. "Whitney?"

"I'm in here," she said, and Micah opened the bedroom door. "I was taking a nap, and I woke up and...." Tears streamed down her face. "Where's Jeremiah?"

Micah took in the situation in front of him. The wet

sheets. The way Whitney lay, like she couldn't position herself any differently "He's coming," he said. "I'm calling the paramedics."

"No," she said, but she didn't move. "I'm not having the baby here."

"Yes," Micah said as he dialed 9-1-1. "I think you are."

24

Jeremiah leapt from the back of the truck before Orion had come to a complete stop. Micah had not called him back, and he had no idea what he would find when he went inside the homestead.

He took the steps two or three at a time, his heart racing. "Whit?" he called as soon as he opened the door. Why didn't Micah have her loaded up yet? They should be headed to the hospital, and he'd thought his brother would have his wife ready.

Micah appeared at the mouth of the hallway. "The ambulance is on the way."

"Ambulance?" Jeremiah's vision went white for a moment. "What are you talking about?"

"I'm not a doctor," Micah said. "But she's not making it to the hospital. That baby is coming, fast. And right here."

Right here.

Jeremiah pushed past his brother and sprinted down the hall to the master suite. Whitney lay on her side of the bed, a plethora of pillows stacked behind her. She was crying, and Jeremiah dashed to her side. "Sweetheart," he said.

"I can't stop it," she said, hiccuping. "Micah said we shouldn't move me, and Miah, I couldn't. I tried to get up, and I couldn't. I couldn't."

"Shh, it's fine." He stroked her hair off her forehead, and she seemed sweaty and clammy to him. "I'm going to get a washcloth and a drink. It's okay. It's going to be fine." He hurried into the bathroom and tossed a washcloth into the sink.

He filled a glass with water, turned the water to hot, and went back to his wife's side.

"Yes, she's still in bed," Micah said. "Her husband is here now."

Jeremiah glanced at him as he handed Whitney the water. She drank, and she calmed a little.

"They want you to check her," Micah said. "The ambulance is eleven minutes away."

Whitney screamed, and Micah dropped his phone. Jeremiah spun back to her, with no idea what to do to help her. He'd never had a baby before, and he'd never witnessed a birth. All he could think about was Ivory, and how if she'd had her baby at home, she'd be dead.

And his wife—his wonderful wife that he'd only had for a year now—was screaming like she was about to die.

"Talk to me," he said.

She gripped the sheets and said, "It hurts."

Micah had recovered his phone, and he said, "I'm putting you on speaker."

"Jeremiah?" someone said, and it drew his focus.

"Right here," he said.

"I need you to check her," the man said. "We need to know how far along she is."

"Okay," he said. "How do I do that?"

The paramedic started explaining, and Jeremiah did what he said. Whitney lay back on the pillows, and she put her feet flat on the bed. He checked her, and he said, "Uh, yeah, I can probably fit my whole hand."

"Can you see the baby's head?"

Jeremiah felt like he was having an out-of-body experience, because he wasn't quite sure what he was looking for. "I don't think so."

"Jeremiah," Whitney whimpered, her fingers clenching the sheets again. "Here comes another one."

"She's contracting again."

"Less than two minutes," another man said, and Jeremiah didn't think that was good.

"How close are you?" Micah asked, pure panic in his voice. "What should we do if you don't make it?"

"They have to make it," Whitney said, and Jeremiah's whole world narrowed to her hysteria.

He moved back to her side and looked at her. "Whitney," he said calmly. "Look at me, baby. Look. This is happening. And it's fine. Micah and I have experience with birthing cows and horses."

"Jeremiah," she bit out. "This is not a cow or a horse."

"I'm getting towels," Micah said. "And I'm going to throw a couple in the dryer so they're warm for the baby."

"No!" Whitney cried out. "I am *not* having my baby here. We're not wrapping him in towels!"

"It could be a girl," Jeremiah said calmly. He would not lose his head. He'd spoken true, and he had delivered babies of other species. This was his wife, and he would do whatever he had to do to make sure she was as comfortable as possible. "And we'll wrap her in towels if that's what it takes to keep her warm."

"I can't call anyone," Micah said, returning with half a dozen towels. "Give me your phone."

Jeremiah handed it over at the same time Orion said, "Boss, what can I help with?"

"Can you run out to the birthing shed and get me a clamp?" Jeremiah asked. "And Whitney is going to need some pain meds, Micah. I want her to take those now."

"Jeremiah," she whimpered, and he planted a kiss on her forehead while Micah juggled two phones as he headed into the bathroom to get painkillers.

"I'm right here," he said. "It's going to be okay." He checked her again, and this time, he could definitely see the baby's head. "On the next contraction, you're going to push, Whitney. Okay." He looked past her knees to her face. "You're going to push hard."

She started nodding, little short bursts of her head. Micah helped by having her swallow the pills and then laying a few towels underneath her, and he said, "I called Wyatt. He's calling everyone, and—"

He cut off as Jeremiah pointed to Whitney.

"We can see the head," he said to the paramedics.

"We're six minutes away," they said, and Whitney cried out.

"This baby is coming *now*," Jeremiah said. "Tell me what I need to remember to do."

"Have her push," the man said. "And when the baby comes out, wrap her up in something warm and just leave the umbilical cord. Do *not* cut it or clamp it or anything. We'll do that when we get there."

"I've got my guy getting a cattle clamp," Jeremiah said, disbelieving that he'd just used those words to deliver his baby. His own child.

"You don't need it," the paramedic said. "Leave her on the bed. Newborns are slippery, and that way, she won't fall."

Newborns are slippery.

"Jeremiah," Whitney said through her teeth. "Another contraction."

"Push, baby," he said. "You're going to push now."

She did, a guttural noise coming from her throat. The baby had a shock of black hair that Jeremiah could see as he positioned his hands to catch the infant. "Just like that, hon," he said, his voice growing in intensity. "Push, Whit."

"I am pushing!" she yelled, and in the next moment, the baby's head came out, and the baby turned.

"It's not out all the way," he said.

"I'm going to push again," Whitney said. "Here it comes." She yelled as another contraction overcame her, and the baby's shoulder came out, and just like that, the rest of its tiny body followed.

"Oh, boy," Jeremiah said, staring in awe at this new human in his hands.

"It's a boy?" Whitney asked, but he couldn't answer.

"Micah, I need a towel," he said, and his brother handed him a warm towel. The baby wailed, and it was the sweetest sound in the whole wide world.

Gently, Jeremiah wiped his little face and looked up at Whitney, pure love for her streaming through him. "It's a boy," he said, his voice catching on itself.

"Focus," the paramedic said, and Jeremiah realized he couldn't gaze at his son right now. "Give the baby to Whitney. Keep him covered and warm. They lose a lot of warmth from their heads."

He quickly wrapped the baby and handed him to Micah, who laid him gently on Whitney's chest. She sobbed, and Jeremiah almost lost his focus again.

"Okay," he said. "Now what?"

"Now make sure they're both warm and comfortable, and we'll take care of her when we get there."

"Forty seconds," the second paramedic said.

Jeremiah moved to stand next to Whitney, and they both gazed down at their son. "What are we going to name him?"

He gurgled as if he knew his father was talking about him, and Whitney smiled fondly down at him. "I think Jonah." She put her finger in his tiny hand, and he clutched it. "Jonah Jeremiah."

"That's perfect," he whispered.

"Paramedics," a man called, and Micah rushed over to the door.

"Down here," he said, and a few seconds later two men who looked like they knew what they were doing arrived in his bedroom.

Relief hit Jeremiah, and he moved out of the way so they could take care of Whitney. He'd barely backed away when Liam arrived.

"Oh, Dear God in heaven," he said, his voice awed. "She had the baby right here."

"Jonah Jeremiah," Jeremiah said. "And you better call Momma."

"She's on her way," Liam said. "I came as soon as I got off the phone with Wyatt." He looked at Jeremiah, his eyes wide. "What in the world?"

"It happened really fast," Jeremiah said.

"Freaky fast," Micah added.

"And she's fine," the paramedic said. "Now Whitney, I'm going to need you to push again."

"That's a lot of blood," Liam said. "I'm going to, uh, step out." He faded out of the room, and Micah and Orion went with him.

Jeremiah returned to Whitney's side until the paramedics had everything delivered and deemed her done with labor.

"Okay," one of them said. "Let's get her to the hospital."

She had not given up their son, and Jeremiah took him gingerly from her. "He's okay?"

"Yep, he looked great," one of the paramedics said. "But we'll need to take them both. We have the warmer on in the bus. You should come out with the baby, and we'll bring in the stretcher to get her."

"You're okay?" he asked Whitney, bending down to kiss her forehead.

"Tired," she said, smiling wearily.

"It's almost over," Jeremiah said, and he followed the paramedics out to the ambulance, where they placed his son in the warming unit and then proceeded to get the stretcher out for Whitney. Jeremiah put his finger in his newborn son's hand and let every emotion he had stream through him.

He had not comprehended the vastness of love that he

could feel until that moment, and it was unlike anything he'd ever experienced before.

The sound of a vehicle pulling up met his ears, and he heard Momma's voice say, "The ambulance is here. Praise Jesus."

"Momma," he said, his throat dry and scratchy.

She turned toward him. "Oh, my."

"He's right here. They're bringing Whitney out now."

Momma climbed right into the back of the ambulance and gazed down at her new grandson. "He's a blessing," she said.

"He's fast is what he is," Jeremiah said, chuckling. "I guess he was done being cooped up inside."

"Just like you," Momma said, and Jeremiah smiled up at her.

"Ma'am," one of the paramedics said.

"Tell everyone to come to the hospital," Jeremiah said as Momma climbed down out of the ambulance. Whitney was loaded up, and they had her on oxygen now. "Is she okay?"

"I'm fine," she said. "Feeling lightheaded."

The doors closed, and the one remaining paramedic bustled around in the small space to make sure the two people Jeremiah loved the most were taken care of. "Moving," the driver called from the front, and the man took a seat near Whitney's head.

"Here we go," he said, beaming at Jeremiah. "You did really great in there, Dad."

"Thanks," Jeremiah said, a smidgeon of pride filling him. "I'm definitely going to need a new bed, though, right?"

The man chuckled. "Yes, definitely."

He looked down at Whitney and then Jonah. "It's a small price to pay for such a perfect baby."

25

Wyatt whistled while he went through his email. "Marce, we got the final plans on the house." He pushed away from his computer and looked over to hers. She hummed at him, a signal that meant, *I'm in the middle of this. Give me a minute.*

She fiddled with something on the video she was working on, finally turning toward him a moment later. "What?"

"The final plans for the house," he said. "They came today. We just need to approve them, and they'll start breaking ground."

She blinked, life re-entering her eyes. "Oh. Let's get them approved then."

"We should look at them first," he said, scooting back up to his computer. "Remember how they tried to make that back patio ten-feet by ten-feet?"

And Wyatt had been very clear that he wanted a large patio space. Somewhere big enough to host all the Walkers, their parents, their spouses, their kids. There was no sense in buying a five-million-dollar home and putting in a patio that only he could stand on.

The builder had acted like a bigger patio would break the bank, and Wyatt wanted to make sure he got what he wanted. He clicked to open the new plans, and the blueprints on his twenty-three-inch screen were beautiful.

Marcy came to stand beside him, and together, they looked over the plans. After a few minutes, she said, "You got your patio."

"And the hot tub pad," he said. "I need that."

"Need," she said, shaking her head. "That's a relative term, Wyatt." She moved back over to her computer, and Wyatt let her.

There had been some new distance between them since they'd decided to buy a house together. Wyatt wasn't sure if it was because she didn't want him to pay for everything, if she found the huge lot and house in the hills above Three Rivers too extravagant, or something else entirely.

She'd finally agreed that he could go on his western wear tour, only moments before Jim had called to get the final word. That had definitely put some distance between them, but Wyatt still wasn't sure why she didn't want him to go.

After holding him at arm's length for a year, she suddenly wanted to keep him close. He wasn't complaining about that, not even a little bit. In fact, he had very little to complain about when it came to Marcy, except maybe the fact that she wasn't super forthcoming with her feelings. He wasn't either, and they worked together in the office they shared—*her* office—in silence.

"The plans look good," he said. "Should I sign them and send them back?"

"Yeah, sure," she said, completely disinterested in them.

Wyatt sighed, but Marcy didn't say anything. Her chair didn't squeak to indicate she'd moved at all. "Marcy," he said, unsure of what to say next.

"Hmm?"

"Do you want this house?" They could still get out of it. The lots at Church Ranches hadn't sold quickly, and there were still spaces available. The price tag had kept a lot of people away, but Wyatt had liked the idea of a gated community in the hills, away from town so people couldn't just show up at his doorstep.

More than once in the past six months, he'd seen suspicious cars parked across the street from Marcy's house—*his* house—when he left for work. One of them had followed him all the way out to Three Rivers, where they'd asked him to sign one of his hats.

They weren't dangerous, but Wyatt didn't want them on his front lawn.

"Do I want the house?" she asked.

"Yeah." He swung around, committing to this conversation. He was leaving for his tour in two weeks, and she'd have to handle a lot of things with the building while he was gone. "Do you want the house?"

"Yes," she said, barely glancing at him. "We need a house that belongs to both of us."

"Do we?"

Marcy finally abandoned her video editing. "Wyatt, you're not happy here, and I know it."

"I'm fine here, sugar," he said.

"No, you think this house is mine."

"This house is yours," he said.

"So the new house is needed."

Wyatt looked at her, trying to put the words in the right order. "We've been married for six months now," he said.

Marcy crossed her legs, her eyes never leaving his. "Yeah."

"It's just six more months," he said. "And then I can just...I don't know."

Her eyes widened. "You think you want to be done at a year?"

"I think *you* want to be done at a year."

"Why would you think that? I haven't said that."

"There's something bothering you, and you won't tell me what it is. That's why I think that."

She turned back to her computer, her office chair swiveling easily. He'd bought her a new one when all of the shrieking the old one did had driven him mad.

"See? You're doing it again."

"I'm just getting used to the idea of us being a real couple," she said. "I know you love me, and I love you, but I'm afraid it's not the kind of deep, lasting love we need to survive long-term."

Shock and despair jolted through Wyatt at the same time.

"It's early love," she said. "The kind you have in the beginning of the relationship. The kind you date through, you know? I feel like maybe we're still dating."

Wyatt thought about what they did in the bedroom, and that definitely wasn't dating. That was married life. That was what husbands and wives did.

"So...you're still deciding if you like me," he said.

"No, Wyatt." She sighed. "Of course I like you. And I'm so grateful for what you did for me."

"I don't need your gratitude," he said, an over-whelming flood of foolishness pouring over him. He sputtered and choked, trying to find a lungful of air that wasn't coated with the screaming wail that he was a complete idiot.

She didn't love him. Not the way she needed to in order to stay married to him for longer than it took to make sure Payne's Pest-free was hers.

Marcy looked like he'd thrown ice water in her face. She stood up and closed her laptop. "I'm sorry, Wyatt. I don't know what you want me to say."

"I want you to tell me why you're so opposed to the

tour," he said, following her out of the office and down the hall to the kitchen.

"Because," she said, opening a cupboard only to close it again. "Then I'll be here alone."

"You like being alone," he said. "You're not making sense."

She glared at him and pulled down a box of blueberry pancake mix. "I want you here so we can spend time together."

Wyatt didn't want to argue with her, but they spent plenty of time together. "Okay," he said.

"And I don't want to share you with America for the rest of our lives."

"Ah-ha," he said. "There it is." He searched her face, which was starting to crumple. "Sugar." He took her into his arms, glad when she melted into his embrace as easily as she ever had. "You don't have to share me."

As if God wanted him to prove it, Wyatt's phone rang with Jim's ringtone.

"You should get that," Marcy said, trying to pull away.

But Wyatt only held her tighter. "He can wait."

"He'll have sent you an email," she said. "And he'll just call again." She sniffed as Wyatt finally let her go. He didn't answer the phone though. Fissures ran through his heart, and he didn't know how to stop them.

His phone stopped ringing, and relief filled him. At least until the line rang again.

"Just get it, Wyatt," Marcy said, clearly exasperated.

"Don't go anywhere," he said.

"Where am I going to go?"

Wyatt wasn't sure, only that the woman had access to airplanes she knew how to fly. And he knew where they were, but he couldn't follow her into the sky. "Jim, hi," he said, stepping away from her and out the back door. "What's up? I have maybe two minutes." He looked over his shoulder to find Marcy walking back down the hall.

She'd totally gone somewhere, even if it was still in the house.

"I just wanted you to know I sent over the packing list," he said. "Every item is crucial, Wyatt. I know sometimes you think you don't need some of the items on the list, but you do."

"I didn't need a pink sharpie," he said. "I have a reputation to maintain."

Jim laughed, and that got Wyatt to smile despite the unrest in his gut. "I'm sending a car for you on the fourth. I'll email you the confirmation number for that too."

"Okay," Wyatt said. "Jim, while I have you...."

"Yeah?"

"What if I couldn't do the tour?"

"What?" The snappy quality of his voice wasn't lost on Wyatt.

"I mean, the whole tour," he amended. "Could I skip out on some of the stops? Come back to Three Rivers for a week or so?"

"Why? Is Marcy pregnant?"

The very idea had Wyatt's heart shrinking and expanding much too quickly. "No," he said. "Nothing like that."

"Is it your back?"

"Okay, *Momma*," he said. "I'm hanging up now. I can pack my own bags."

"Wyatt, wait—"

But Wyatt hung up anyway. He'd told Jim two minutes, and he'd given the man that. He shouldn't have said anything about the tour, and he sighed as he went back inside.

He found Marcy feeding her hamster in the third bedroom in the back corner of the house, a room she used for yoga and storage. He leaned in the doorway until she looked at him.

"What did he send you?" she asked.

"Packing list," Wyatt said. "Listen, Marcy, we don't have to get the house. Maybe we should just wait and see if we want to be together after a year." He'd been excited about the house, but maybe she'd just think of it as *his*, not *theirs*. And that was just trading in one problem for another.

"I think I just need more time for this to be more... real."

And that was the biggest, realest thing she'd ever said to him. "So it's still pretend for you."

"Not completely," she said. "And I do love you,

Wyatt." Tears gathered in her eyes. "I don't want you to be upset with me."

"I'm not," he said. "I'd much rather know what you're thinking than try to guess at it."

"That's what I'm thinking," she said. "And I feel guilty for wanting you to stay, and like I shouldn't be jealous, but I *am* jealous, and I feel stupid living in a five-million-dollar home with a man I'm still trying to decide if I want to be with."

Her words formed sharp points and stabbed him. Stabbed him hard, right through the heart.

After all this time. After all they'd been through together. After saying I do, and sleeping together, and building a life for the past six months, she still wasn't sure she wanted to be with him.

Wyatt's breath came in short bursts, just like how he nodded his head. "Okay," he said, because what else was there to say? He'd learned to take a loss with his head held high in the rodeo. He could do the same here.

After all, in the rodeo, the clock was king, and it didn't matter if he thought he'd ridden better than someone else. He had to get to the buzzer, and if he didn't, he didn't win.

Headlines streamed through his mind, and he hated that he was worried about what Jim or the media might say about his divorce after only a year.

And he wasn't sure he could stay another six months as it was. If Marcy wasn't sure about him by now, would she ever be?

"I'm going to go see what my brothers are doing at the ranch," he said. "Maybe I'll get to hold Jonah or Ginger." The babies soothed him, and there was nothing better than a nap on the couch with an infant snuggled up on his chest.

"You don't need to go," she said.

"Yeah, I do," he said. He gave her a watery smile. "I'm not mad. I just need some space to think."

She nodded, and Wyatt turned away from her. He walked faster and faster, stopping only long enough to grab his keys and wallet before escaping her house.

And it was definitely *her* house in that moment. Somewhere he didn't belong. Somewhere he might never belong.

26

Marcy flew over Three Rivers, her destination Shiloh Ridge Ranch, on the southwest side of town, which also boasted some hills. Bear Glover was a good customer, and he and his cousins ran the ranch where the Glovers had been living for generations.

It was one of the few ranches that had a dairy operation, albeit small, and Marcy loved flying over all the black and white dairy cows. They looked like little toys down in the fields, and she smiled to herself.

It seemed odd that something as simple as a cow could make her smile, but these days, she'd take what she could get.

Wyatt had not approved the plans for the house, and in fact, he'd told the builders they needed to put their house on pause for a couple of months while he toured.

He didn't cancel it completely, and Marcy felt like her entire life had been put on pause.

He'd be leaving for his tour in four days, and Marcy couldn't ask him to stay home now. It would be unprofessional and rude, and Wyatt Walker was neither of those things.

She'd never told him this, but the root of her anxiety over their relationship was well, Wyatt himself. He always seemed to get what he wanted. He wanted to go on tour, so he was. He wanted the big house, with the hot tub pad, the locked gates, the sprawling yard and pastures. So he'd gotten it.

What about what she wanted?

And the familiar guilt swept through her like a stiff breeze. Wyatt doted on her constantly. He brought her coffee every morning in her office, and he never complained when she put her cold feet on him in bed. He told her he loved her—though he hadn't since their conversation about the house and the tour and their entire marriage several days ago—and he showed it in a lot of little ways.

He loaded the dishwasher every morning. He stopped by the hangar at least once a week and picked up all the mechanic rags to wash them. She'd never asked him to do those things. He did them, because he knew they needed to be done, and he didn't want her to have to do them.

She *knew* this.

And she *did* love him.

But the doubt was strong within her. Maybe she'd been too enamored with him in the beginning. Living with someone really exposed a person to all the other person's flaws, that was for sure. Because for every dish Wyatt put in the dishwasher, there was at least two pairs of socks left on the bedroom floor. Or the coffee table in the living room. Or under his desk in the office.

The man wore cowboy boots like they were molded to his feet, and by the time she'd found the slew of socks under his desk, she'd been lighting a candle in the office for a week.

So he definitely had flaws—and his bossiness and commanding demeanor that allowed him to get everything he wanted were only two of them.

"Shouldn't you be able to see past the flaws?" she asked the brilliant blue atmosphere in front of her. "Why am I fixated on these things?" It was almost like she was looking for a reason their marriage couldn't work.

"Dear Lord," she prayed as she flew over another picturesque field of cattle. "I know You love me. The cows down in the field prove it. The sun rising each morning proves it. Please help me to know what to do about Wyatt. What is it going to take for me to know we've done the right thing by getting married?"

What proof did she need for that?

Why did she need proof at all?

Marcy wasn't sure, and she felt like she was constantly walking a fine line with her own husband. She did know how to dust a field of corn, and she dipped down in her plane to do exactly that.

Perhaps she just needed more time with Wyatt, and more time on her knees, to know what to do.

"I just don't want to hurt him," she said as she pulled on the controls to swing the plane around for another pass. But she feared she already had.

Maybe this tour would be good for both of them. Maybe then, Marcy would be able to think inside the walls of her own house and learn how she really felt about Wyatt Walker.

———

THAT NIGHT, they loaded up in Wyatt's truck to go to dinner at his mother's. Marcy usually enjoyed the weekly family dinners, because Penny was kind and open, and her sons loved her with all of their hearts.

All the other wives came, and the babies, and the dogs, and Marcy enjoyed Wyatt's big, loud, sometimes obnoxious family.

But she wasn't in the mood to talk to anyone—heck, she was barely speaking to Wyatt as it was.

Momma's made all your favorites, he'd texted earlier that day, while she'd been up in the sky. And if there was one thing Marcy made sure of, it was that she didn't text and fly. She took her phone with her in the airplane, but she never used it.

She'd seen his text when she'd landed, and she understood the code: She couldn't cancel. She could, however, leave the hangar a mess and the plane unattended to, and she'd done just that. She hadn't finished her paperwork or anything, and she'd gone home to take a nap.

So it was that she was freshly rested, perfectly make-upped, and ready for a dinner in her honor. Why she was the one getting all the food made for her when it was Wyatt leaving, she wasn't sure. And she hadn't asked.

Several minutes later, Wyatt pulled up to his parents' house, and they weren't the first truck to arrive. He chuckled as he got out of the truck, Jeremiah's dogs already at his side. Wyatt did have a way with animals, Marcy would give him that. Horses, cows, goats, pigs, dogs, it didn't matter. They all loved him and obeyed him.

She carried a pan of brownies in her hands and went toward the front door, Wyatt falling into step behind her quickly. He guided her inside, his hand warm on her lower back, and Marcy's throat tightened.

Noise filled the house already, spilling out onto the large back deck Micah had added to the house since his parents had bought it. The scent of hamburgers filled the air, along with coffee and popcorn.

Marcy had never been to a meal at Wyatt's mother's without popcorn, and she smiled as she put the pan of brownies on a side counter with the other desserts.

"There they are," Penny announced, a wide smile on her face. "Good to see you, dear." She hugged Marcy, who clung to her for an extra moment. Maybe two. Penny always let her hug her for a long time, and Marcy appreciated it. She'd forgotten what it was like to have a mother figure in her life, and she found she craved it.

Would she lose Penny if she lost Wyatt?

Probably, she thought. She and Wyatt didn't have children, and there would be no reason for Marcy to come visit Penny and Gideon, other than she liked them and wanted to.

Her heart felt like a stone in her chest, struggling to beat against a rigid exterior. She couldn't keep her husband around just because she liked his parents. He deserved a wife who was hopelessly in love with *him*, and while Marcy really wanted to be, she wasn't sure she was.

She stepped away from Penny, gave her a shy look, and went to join Evelyn and Ivory in the living room. "Can I?" She reached for Isaac, and Ivory gave Marcy the baby easily.

He was only a couple of months old, but he held his head up really well, and he had the clearest blue eyes Marcy had ever seen. "Hey, baby," she cooed at the infant. She bounced him lightly and made sure his pacifier was secure in his mouth.

"How's it going?" she asked Ivory, who'd laid back against the couch and closed her eyes.

"Great," she said, with a smile. "I'm just tired."

Marcy nodded and looked back at the precious baby boy. "He's a doll."

"Not at two a.m." Ivory laughed, and Evelyn added something about how Conrad hadn't slept through the night until he was almost six months old. Marcy didn't have any children of her own and couldn't contribute to the conversation.

She watched as Wyatt went outside with Micah and Jeremiah, who was also carrying his two-month-old son in his arms. Wyatt took the baby from his brother, his whole face lighting up like Main Street did at Christmastime. A smile moved across Marcy's face, and she wondered what a child with half of her and half of Wyatt's genes would look like.

"Are you guys going to have kids?" Evelyn asked, and Marcy's gaze flew to hers. She'd obviously seen Marcy watching Wyatt, seen the smile, all of it.

"Eventually," Marcy said, because she and Wyatt hadn't talked about it or planned anything. They weren't talking about much right now at all.

"It's—" Evelyn started.

"Time to eat," Penny yelled, ringing a loud dinner bell in the next moment. The baby in Marcy's arms startled, and she hugged him tight to soothe him. She stood up along with everyone else, and she kept baby Isaac as Ivory got Oliver settled enough for the prayer. Gideon said it, and he had such a powerful, calm, commanding presence.

Marcy liked him a whole lot, and she realized as he asked for health and safety for all of their family and friends, that Wyatt's personality was a lot like his father's.

He was large and in charge, but he possessed a soft side too. A side that had faith and wanted to do what was right.

"I'll take him," Ivory said, and Marcy hadn't even realized the prayer had ended. She gave Isaac to his mother, who put him in a swing in the living room, out of the way. Then she and Oliver joined Tripp in line to get food.

Marcy hung back, because that was what Marcy was good at. Wyatt usually came to her side and waited with her, making everything less awkward. But today, he stayed on the deck, dishing out hamburgers and hot dogs as people came through the line.

She finally reached him, and he grinned at her. "I know what you want." He gave her a hamburger, though it wasn't hard to tell, as she had the appropriate bun on her plate. "Save me a spot by you, would you?"

"Sure." Marcy sure did like the fire in Wyatt's eyes, and she acknowledged that she loved him on some level. She probably always would, because he'd been right where she'd needed him to be at a crucial time of her life.

It was the same reason she was so close with Alyssa and Savannah. They'd been the cousins that had been in town when her mother had died, and she'd relied on them. They'd seen her at her worst and loved her anyway.

Just like Wyatt.

So maybe things between them were okay. Maybe she just needed to get outside of her own mind and not worry so much.

They ate, and the brothers used to stay and chat, play games, or put on a movie. But those with babies had been packing up and going home the moment Penny's delicious desserts were gone. Tonight, she'd made mint chocolate chip ice cream and asked anyone who could to bring brownies.

The twins were turning forty-two on Monday, but Liam and Callie were taking their kids to Bear Creek Lodge for a family vacation and wouldn't be around.

Marcy sang *Happy Birthday* along with everyone else. Snuggled into Wyatt's side as the twins blew candles out on their brownies. Smiled and ate too much chocolate and ice cream.

Before she knew it, everyone had packed up and left, except for her and Wyatt and Micah.

Her phone rang, and she left Micah and Wyatt standing on the deck overlooking the back yard to answer it. "Hey, Bear," she said.

"Marcy," he said, his growl much louder than anything. He liked people to think he was a grizzly, but he was really more of a teddy bear.

"Don't tell me you have a problem," she said. "I flew over everything today, and it looked good."

"No," he said. "No problem."

"Oh, okay."

"I just wanted to know about—well, I wanted to ask you—" He cleared his throat. "Do you know Samantha Benton? Sammy?"

"Sure," Marcy said. "I know Sammy. She runs a great shop in town. Are you having problems with her?"

"No," he said quickly, and Marcy couldn't quite place the emotion in his voice. Was he relieved she knew Sammy? Why was he asking about her?

"My ranch mechanic quit, and I'm looking to hire a new one. But she can't come live out here permanently, because of her nephew and all, and I was wondering if she's really good enough for me to put up with not having her around all the time."

"She's the best car and farm equipment mechanic in the state," Marcy said. "I think she has an award that says so, Bear." She chuckled. "I can see why she wouldn't want to live out there. She has to take Sawyer to school every day."

"Yeah, that's what she said. And he plays soccer too. Practices all the time."

"If you can hire her, she'd do a good job for you," Marcy said. "And you know, you don't have to have a mechanic at your beck and call all the time."

"I know," he said, sighing. "I've just gotten used to it."

"Well, then maybe Sammy's not the one for you," she said. "I think she's had a harder year than me." Sammy's sister and brother-in-law had been killed in a terrible car accident, leaving their six-year-old son behind. Sammy had adopted him and taken on the role of mother, buried two people she loved, and managed to keep her shop open, all within a few weeks.

"She's the one," Bear said. "I just wanted an outside opinion, and I trust you."

"Thanks, Bear," Marcy said. "Maybe work with her, then? Maybe if you pay her well enough, she can pass most of the shop work to her other mechanics."

"I'm not made of money, Marcy," Bear said darkly.

She laughed, because he'd said the same thing to her before when she'd quoted him a price to get rid of a whole herd of grasshoppers. She knew he was, though. *Everyone* in Three Rivers knew the Glover family had money. Old money, and lots of it.

"I'm hanging up now," the grizzly wanna-be said, and Marcy said good-bye.

She turned back to the deck to find Penny had joined Wyatt on the back deck and Micah had disappeared. She clutched her phone in her hand and watched him lean down against the railing, a serious expression on his face.

She moved to the open doorway and leaned into it, trying not to make a noise.

"I don't know, Momma," he was saying. "It's not like our marriage was real to begin with."

"What?" his mom asked. "What does that mean?"

"We've all done it," he said, and Marcy's heart thrashed against all twenty-four of her ribs.

"Done what, exactly?" His mother did not sound pleased, and Marcy willed him to stop talking.

Of course, she knew Rhett and Evelyn's marriage hadn't been real. They'd gotten divorced and then remarried, and everyone in town knew he'd only married her in the beginning to help her with her now defunct match-making business. It had been quite the town scandal, actually, but Marcy thought their story was sweet.

Number one, she'd seen Rhett and Evelyn together, and they were made for each other by God Himself. Number two, she found Rhett's devotion to the woman he loved admirable. He'd loved her so much, he'd married her, even when she wasn't in the same place as him.

"Gotten married without it being real," Wyatt said. "Tripp only married Ivory so she wouldn't lose custody of her son. Liam married Callie so she wouldn't lose the ranch. Jeremiah—"

"Stop it right now," his mother said, almost a hiss. "This is not true."

"It is, Momma," Wyatt said, "And I married Marcy so she could inherit her daddy's crop-dusting business. That's it."

That's it.

A squeak came out of Marcy's throat as his words ripped through her.

Penny and Wyatt turned toward her, but Marcy only had one thought in her mind.

Get out.

Run.

Go!

So she went.

27

Wyatt's heart fell all the way to his cowboy boots.

"You better go after her,' Momma said. "I swear, Wyatt Jeffrey Walker, if you lose that woman, you'll be in big trouble."

"Why will I be in trouble?" Wyatt simultaneously wanted to chase after Marcy and let her go at the same time. He could call Micah to come get him, and he was tired of the tension at Marcy's. He was tired of thinking about the house where he lived as Marcy's.

"Because she's an amazing woman,' Momma said. "Did you really marry her so she could get the business?"

"Yes," he said with a sigh. "And no. I've liked her for a real long time before that." He looked out over the back yard, hearing the engine from his truck roar to life. His heart skipped a couple of beats, but he didn't move to go try to stop Marcy. Let her take his truck. It felt like the right thing to do, because they'd been split for a while now anyway. Even if they'd stayed living in the same house, they hadn't been together.

"You—I don't even know what to say," Momma said. "All of you boys have done this?"

"It starts out that way," Wyatt said. "But obviously, Momma, the others have made it work." He thought of Tripp, though, and how he'd moved back to the ranch after several months of marriage with Ivory. Liam and Callie had split up too, though for a much shorter time. Even Jeremiah and Whitney had experienced a few days there where they weren't sure their relationship would survive.

Momma didn't need to know all the details, and he couldn't believe he'd opened his big mouth. She'd started it by coming out here and saying he didn't seem happy, that she'd noticed he'd been out at the ranch more and more, and without Marcy.

And he'd found that he wanted to talk to someone about the situation. But Jeremiah and Tripp were both busy trying to figure out how to be husbands, new fathers, and keep their lives going. Jeremiah ran the whole ranch. Tripp had an animation job. Liam had two new kids to take care of, and Rhett wasn't around as much as he used to be.

Micah had withdrawn as well—or maybe Wyatt had separated himself from his brothers now that he didn't live at Seven Sons—and Skyler was off in Amarillo. So he hadn't mentioned his recent marital problems to anyone.

"I'm going to go to the ranch." He pulled out his phone as his father came out on the deck.

"Did I hear Marcy leave?"

"Yeah," Wyatt said, glancing at Momma. "I'll see you later." He gave her a hug and moved over to Daddy.

"What's wrong?" his dad asked.

Wyatt felt like crying. He never wanted to disappoint his father. In fact, he couldn't think of anything worse. Enduring all the painful surgeries and recoveries he'd been through was easier than looking into his father's eyes and saying he'd messed up.

But he did, his misery reaching a new low as his desperation shot up.

"I'm sure it's not too bad," Daddy said. "What's goin' on?"

"I'll tell you about it, Gideon," Momma said. "Wyatt, you get on home."

He nodded, because he didn't want to explain the situation to his father. So even though he was thirty-eight-years-old, he left the explaining to his mother.

He called Micah from the front porch and started walking down the road toward the highway. "Can you come get me?" he asked. "I'm at Momma's, and I can't go back to Marcy's."

Home.

He didn't even know where that was.

"Why?" Micah asked.

"Can I tell you later? Like, tomorrow, later? I'm not up to it right now."

"Sure," Micah said. "I'll be there in a few."

————

WYATT HATED the way his brothers tiptoed around him. He felt like he'd been transported back a year, to the time immediately following his back surgery. He'd relied a lot on Micah then too, and Jeremiah.

But this time, it wasn't his back that was broken.

Thankfully, he only had two more days before he needed to be in Dallas to meet Jim and go on the tour. Instead of returning to Marcy's house for his clothes, Wyatt had simply bought new ones. Everything he needed for the tour was replaceable, and though he knew he'd need to eventually show up at her place and get his belongings, it didn't have to be now.

I'll come get my stuff when I get back, he typed out to her, the swing beneath him swaying back and forth. He loved the old oak tree that stood sentinel in front of the homestead, and he'd taken to spending most of the afternoon in it.

He'd already planned to take this time away from Bowman's Breeds, though he'd told Ethan and Squire that he'd come out for a farewell dinner tomorrow after church.

He wasn't looking forward to it, but he could put on his media face and smile through the pain. The Lord knew he'd done that hundreds of times, as he'd once ridden to a championship with a broken rib.

He hadn't talked to Marcy since she'd overheard him at dinner a couple of nights ago. He worried that any contact from him would further injure her, and he certainly didn't want that.

He tapped to send the text anyway. Unless you want it out now. Then I'll send the twins over to get it all.

He knew she wouldn't want to see him, and he didn't blame her.

He looked up, tilting his head back as if he could see through the leaves and into the sky. Marcy might be flying right now, but she probably wasn't. She went up early in the morning and got things done before it became too hot. Then she worked around the hangar, doing paperwork and mechanic duties, before coming home at night.

Wyatt missed her with a fierceness he hadn't anticipated, though he'd felt something akin to it last year after she'd broken up with him in the hospital.

His phone buzzed, and he glanced down at it. *Whatever is fine with me, Wyatt.*

Another buzz.

I'm sorry this didn't work out.

He tapped the phone icon, and let the line ring. "Hey," she said a moment later, and it was clear she wasn't happy.

Wyatt's heart shriveled, and he couldn't get his voice to work.

"Will you please let the marriage stand until February?" she whispered. "After that, I'll pay for the divorce and everything. You'll be free to do whatever you want."

He was already free to do whatever he wanted—and maybe that was part of the problem.

"What did I say?" he asked. "Or do. Or whatever got us so off-track."

"Do you really want to know?"

"Yes," he said. Because if he knew, he could work on changing. And then he could get her back. The thought of not being with her made everything inside him bleed, and he absolutely could not stand it.

"I think...." She started, exhaling heavily. "I don't want to hurt you, Wyatt. Maybe we're just not meant to be."

"I think you're wrong," he said, his voice hoarse. "I think we are meant to be, and I just need to know what I need to do better." The turbulent emotions coursing through him were at such odds with the peaceful atmosphere around him. Blue sky. Green grass. Gentle breeze.

He felt like a hurricane had blown into his soul and taken up permanent residence.

"I think you're not used to sharing your life with some-one," she said slowly. "I think you've always been able to do what you want, because you're the great Wyatt Walker and everyone loves you."

His teeth ground together automatically. He was not "the great Wyatt Walker." That was her first problem—she didn't even see him as just a man. She held him on a pedestal, and she was always going to be disappointed if she continued to do that.

"So it's about the tour," he said.

"That," she said. "Just...everything. You wanted the house in the hills. So we got it. You sort of talk to me like my opinion matters, but it doesn't. Not really. Wyatt still does what Wyatt wants to do."

"I won't go on the tour," he said.

She sighed, and he could just picture her shaking her head, those pretty blonde curls wisping around her face. "You can't do that, Wyatt."

No, he really couldn't. It was far too late to pull out now, as Jim had told him several times.

"And honestly, Wyatt, I might have been able to figure out how to live the Wyatt-lifestyle. Do what Wyatt wants. Because I do love you." Her voice broke, and that broke everything inside him. "But you said 'that's it' about our marriage, even though you told me it wasn't pretend. It was. It *is*. To you, it is."

"No," he said, because he couldn't get his brain to say anything more complicated than that.

"Yes," she said. "I heard you talking to your mom, and Wyatt, if there's one thing I know about you, it's that you can't lie to your momma. And you stood there and said you married me so I could have Payne's. *That's it.*"

Regret heaped on top of his humiliation. He had said that. He hadn't been lying. "But—"

"There's no but, Wyatt. It's fine." She pulled in a breath, and it shook, even through the line. "If you would be kind enough to wait until February, I'd really appreciate it."

He'd known he'd need to be married to Marcy for a year, and he wasn't going to break that promise. Not after he'd broken everything else. "Okay," he said.

"Thank you."

"Marcy—"

"Please, Wyatt," she said, her voice too high now. "Don't make this harder than it has to be. I'm okay. Really."

But *he* wasn't okay. He nodded anyway, pressing his lips together to stop himself from saying something he hadn't censored yet.

"Have fun on your tour," she said, and the call ended.

Wyatt's arm dropped to his lap, his spirit crushed.

That's it.

He'd ruined everything with Marcy with two words.

What an idiot, he chastised himself. And he had two more words streaming through his mind.

Now what?

———

SUNDAY AFTERNOON FOUND him driving to Three Rivers Ranch. He loved the community out here, and he'd miss everyone while he was gone.

A bunch of balloons had been tied to the sign on the highway announcing the turn-off to Three Rivers, along with a sign that said, *We'll miss you Wyatt.*

A smile filled his soul, and Wyatt sure was glad for it. He hadn't had much to smile about these last few days. His chest pinched at the childish handwriting, because he knew Josiah and Will had made it. Garth's kids might have helped too.

When he rounded the last corner, he dang near burst into tears. All of the animals he'd worked with at Bowman's Breeds had been brought out and tethered to the fence, with several cowboys lingering with them.

He pulled to a stop when he saw Ethan and Brynn, his heart so, so full. "Here we go," he whispered to himself. "Keep it together." He hadn't cried over Marcy, and he wasn't going to lose his composure over a few good-byes either. Heaven knew he'd said plenty of them in his life.

"Look at this," he said, his smile stretching across his whole face. "You brought out my friends." He patted Jalopy's neck. "Hey, buddy." He petted cows like they were dogs, touched each horse and spoke to them, and smiled as he finally reached Ethan and Brynn.

He engulfed them both into a hug at the same time, and the three of them laughed together.

"We tried to get Maleficent," Brynn said, swiping at

her eyes. "But she's being used in the rodeo in Lexington this weekend."

"I know," Wyatt said. "I saw her online. She's winning a lot."

"She was trained by the best," Ethan said, grinning. "Now, come on. All the kids have been workin' on something real special for you."

"Oh, boy," Wyatt said. "I can't wait."

"We're eating at Pete's today," Brynn said. "They've got the tables and everything set up, and he's been smoking brisket for days."

"I can smell it," Wyatt said, thinking all these good people had spent their precious time, money, and energy on him, and he didn't deserve it.

Brynn led him across the dirt road and parking lot to the big glass building that functioned as the corporate offices of Courage Reins, the equine therapy unit here at the ranch that Pete had founded and still ran.

Inside, a great, loud shout of "Surprise!" filled the air, and Wyatt saw more balloons, streamers, and a room full of people.

"Oh, my," he said, his emotions not allowing more than that to be said. The cowboys that had been tending to his animals had followed him, and they crowded in behind him, quickly taking spots on the sides.

He saw Squire Ackerman and his wife, Kelly. They had four kids now, and Wyatt experienced a moment of jealousy at all the other cowboy had that he didn't. Pete stood next to him, along with Chelsea and their three boys, who each held a sign wishing Wyatt luck on his tour.

Garth, the foreman, smiled at him, along with his wife and kids. Bennett and Beau grinned at him mischievously, and Cal and Trina, Kenny and Taryn, Lawrence and Andi, Tanner and Summer had all gathered. Even Squire's parents were there, and Wyatt barely knew them. Of course, everyone in Three Rivers knew Heidi Ackerman because of her bakery, and Wyatt hoped she'd brought some of her chocolate soufflés.

"Ready?" Bennett called, and Wyatt looked at him. "One...two...three!"

Everyone reached up with their right hand and took off their cowboy hats, if they were wearing one. Those that weren't waited a beat, and then they were all waving to him, their wrists going up and down as hands and hats flapped.

Good-bye.

Thank you.

We love you.

Wyatt had known Three Rivers Ranch was a special place. He'd loved driving out here every day, even if he did complain about the distance sometimes. He'd known he was supposed to be in Three Rivers. He'd known he belonged here, with his brothers at the family ranch, and with all of the friends he had out here at this ranch.

He just hadn't known how much he loved them until

that moment. How much he loved them and how much *they* loved *him*.

Not bothering to pull back on the reins of his emotions, he reached up and took off his own cowboy hat and waved it at all of them, laughing through his tears as a cheer filled the building, the sky, his entire soul.

28

Marcy woke on Monday morning and stayed in bed for a minute. Somehow, she knew Wyatt had left Three Rivers.

It was Labor Day, and she'd scheduled a day off. Why, she wasn't sure. She had nothing to do around the house, and she'd known Wyatt would be gone. Now that he was really gone from her life—she looked to her left, where he used to sleep in the bed with her—she felt a bit lost.

She got up and got herself in the shower. She went through her morning routine, because it brought her comfort. She could get things done if she just focused on her daily tasks and completed them one at a time.

Shower. Get dressed.

Get coffee going.

Feed the hamster.

Check her email.

She ate a piece of toast with her coffee, realizing she didn't want to spend the day alone. It was still plenty warm this first weekend of September, and she quickly picked up her phone and texted Alyssa. *What are you doing today? Could I tag along with you and Dale?*

Her cousin and Dale both loved getting outside with their kids. Savannah would be busy with her long-time boyfriend, but Marcy had a hunch she'd text Savannah too, if Alyssa wasn't available.

She didn't get a text back right away though. She'd just finished her toast when her doorbell rang, and then a child knocked on the door. Her heart leapt, because she knew exactly who it was.

"Remmy," she said upon opening the door. She scooped Alyssa's daughter into her arms and hugged her. "How are you? I haven't seen in you forever."

"I bwought you dis." She handed Marcy a piece of paper that had coloring and some semblance of letters on it.

"Oh, it's so pretty," she said, setting the five-year-old on the ground. "What is it?"

"A pawty," the little girl said. "Momma said I could invite you."

"Of course I'll come." Marcy couldn't decipher the writing though, and she looked at Alyssa, who carried her baby on her hip.

"It's tonight," she said, handing Marcy a white pastry bag from Heidi Ackerman's bakery. "I didn't think you'd have anything going on, what with Wyatt leaving this morning." She hooked her thumb over her shoulder. "But his truck is still in the driveway. Is he not going on the tour?" Her eyes held hope, but Marcy shook her head.

"No, he went," she said. "Come in. Y'all are letting out the cold."

Alyssa and Remmy came all the way inside while Alyssa said, "Savannah is on her way over. We thought you might need some shopping therapy."

"I totally do," Marcy said, sighing as she sank onto her sofa. She looked at the invitation again, seeing candles where she hadn't before. "Oh, my goodness," she said to Remmy as her cousin put the baby on the floor with a couple of toys. "It's your birthday tomorrow."

"Yep." The little girl climbed right into her lap, and Marcy squeezed her tight. "Daddy's gonna be gone."

She glanced at Alyssa, who stood in the kitchen, pouring herself a cup of coffee. "Dale's doing ten days on, five off," she said. "So it's going to be brutal for the next ten days."

"I'm around," Marcy said. "And alone now."

Alyssa turned, her eyes sharpening. "Alone now? Wyatt's just going to be gone for a few weeks."

"Until Thanksgiving, Liss." She shook her head. "And it doesn't matter. We broke up."

"You broke up?" Alyssa hurried into the living room. "Honey, you're *married* to him. You don't break up. You get divorced."

Marcy shook her head, because it was all semantics anyway. "I don't want to talk about it." She looked down at Remmy and LJ, chewing happily on something from her spot on the floor. "Tell me what you want for your birthday. Can you believe I don't have a gift yet?"

That got the little girl talking, and though Alyssa didn't say anything, Marcy knew she hadn't stopped thinking about Marcy "breaking up" with Wyatt. Sure enough, when Savannah finally arrived about ten minutes later, she jumped to her feet and said, "Did you know Marcy and Wyatt broke up?"

"What?" Savannah closed the front door behind her. "I thought we were okay with him going on the tour."

"We were," Marcy said, sighing.

Remmy climbed down from her lap and said, "Mawcy, can I play with Robot?"

"Sure, sweetie. I already fed him, though, so no more food, okay?'

"Okay." The little girl skipped down the hall to Marcy's yoga studio and pet sanctuary, leaving her alone with both of her cousins and their undivided attention despite the baby on the floor.

"I'm not talking about Wyatt," she said. "We just...it might not work out. That's all. It happens."

"She said 'might,'" Alyssa said.

"I heard it," Savannah said.

"Guys, really." Marcy got up and hung the invitation on her fridge. "And I wasn't lying when I said I didn't have a present for Remmy. So we really do need to go shopping."

"Maybe if you told us what happened this time with Wyatt, we could help you." Savannah got up and set her purse on the kitchen counter.

A glinting caught Marcy's eye, and she sucked in a breath. "Savvy. Are you wearing a diamond ring?" She made a grab for her cousin's hand, and sure enough, she had a brand-new rock on her left ring finger. "Liss, get over here."

A shriek filled the kitchen, and the sound was filled with delight and joy. "It happened last night," Savannah said. "And I wanted to surprise you. I haven't told anyone yet, not even my mom."

Alyssa grabbed her hand from Marcy, who could only beam at her cousin. "Congrats," she said, hugging her tightly. "I'm so happy for you."

And she was. She honestly was. Savannah had been by her side for years now, and Marcy only wanted the best for her. Gabe was a good man, and he'd take amazing care of Savannah.

She just couldn't help thinking about Wyatt. He was a good man too, and he could take amazing care of Marcy. She knew, because she'd experienced it.

How could there not be more to their marriage than just her getting Payne's? Did he really feel that way?

When she'd spoken to him a few days ago, he hadn't tried to explain. She had cut him off once, but she didn't need to hear him say, *But that* was *why we got married, Marce.*

Her nickname in his voice haunted her as she drifted to sleep as it was, thanks. She'd asked him to wait until February, and he'd agreed. She'd asked him not to make this harder than it had to be, and he'd agreed.

And then he'd left.

Not for the first time in her life, Marcy wished she could leave Three Rivers as easily as everyone else seemed to be able to.

First, her brother. Then Momma. Then Daddy.

Now Wyatt.

"Let's get this show on the road," Savannah said. "I want to hit the boutique first, because Andi sent an email about a new shipment of skirts, and they'll sell out."

No one argued with that, not even Marcy, though she wasn't really a boutique type of woman. She could browse and be happy with wherever they were. And at the boutique, she wouldn't be able to see anything that would remind her of Wyatt.

They had to park clear down the block from the cute little boutique, and it certainly seemed to be busy this Labor Day. They had to go up the steps single-file, and Marcy went last.

When she looked at the display in the window, she froze, dumb-struck.

Now carrying Wyatt Walker cowboy hats for that man in your life! boasted the sign in the window, at least six of

Wyatt's hats above it. Not only that, but a huge replica of his signature adorned the top of the window, and Marcy prayed the ground would open up and swallow her whole.

———

A COUPLE OF WEEKS LATER, Marcy sat at her laptop, her day's work done. She hadn't gone through her personal emails for a while, and Nick Marlow had called to ask her if she'd gotten the emails he'd sent.

She hadn't, because she hadn't checked. She was now, and sure enough, she had three emails from the estate planner that she needed to respond to. No, she hadn't sold the house yet, and it suddenly became a weight around her neck she didn't know how to elimi-nate. Bryan hadn't said anything about it either, and Marcy knew she should be thankful they hadn't gotten in an argument about how the estate should be handled. She knew some families had bitter fights after parents died.

Yes, she was still married to Wyatt.

Yes, she had the financial information for the second quarter of the year for Payne's Pest-free. She handled everything for Mr. Marlow, and scanned the rest of her email. It was mostly junk, stuff she signed up for to get discounts and coupons.

An email from Church Ranches caught her eye, and she clicked it open. Her heart didn't quite fit in her chest when she saw the majestic pictures of the homes they were building up in the hills just outside Three Rivers.

Mr. and Mrs. Walker, the email read. *No one has bought the lot you were previously interested in, and I'm wondering if you have any continued interest in it? I can take $10,000 off the purchase price if so.*

The reason they'd backed out of the house wasn't because of money, a fact that Marcy felt all too keenly as she stared at the message. Had Wyatt gotten this too? She checked to see who the email had been sent to, and yes his email was listed.

She wasn't sure why, but her chest felt hollow and cold. He'd wanted a house that was theirs, and Marcy had too.

Now, there was no *they.*

Now, everything was *his* and *hers.*

Everything in her life had gone cold without Wyatt, and she hated it.

Then do something about it, she thought. She wanted a home she could build with a good man like Wyatt.

Maybe she just needed to go get it. Get him back. Get it all back.

She hit reply on the email and started typing, feeling irrational and out of control. And maybe like she was the sanest she'd ever been at the same time.

SEPTEMBER BECAME OCTOBER, and one day, she left the hangar by lunchtime to be able to get to the offices for Church Ranches at her appointed time. To get there, she had to pass her father's house, and she took a moment to pull into the driveway.

She'd grown up here, in this house. She'd loved her childhood, loved her parents, loved Three Rivers.

She got out and went inside the house, which was stale and way too hot. There was no spirit here anymore, despite the family photos still lining the mantel. She'd never been able to take them and box them up.

"Maybe it's time," she said, as she'd been living her life with a lot of maybe's lately. She had emailed about the house, and she was signing intent-to-purchase papers today. There was no maybe about that.

She hadn't spoken with Wyatt in over a month, and she'd often thought that *maybe* she should just call him.

She looked around the house from her spot just inside the front door. She should sell it, but it didn't quite feel like the right time.

"Soon, though," she said to herself, taking a deep breath. She'd been feeling better with each passing day, and she knew she was strong enough to sell her parents' home now. She pulled her phone and dialed her brother.

"Marcy," he said, surprise in his voice. "What's going on?"

"Nothing," she said. "I'm just wondering how you feel about Dad's house."

"When you're ready to sell, I am," he said. "It's fine. I know you have some attachment to it, and I don't need the money."

"I think I'll talk to a realtor about it," she said. "I still have some things I need to clean out."

"All right," he said. "And listen, while you're here, I wanted to let you know that I've been seeing someone, and we're going to her folks' for Thanksgiving."

"Oh," Marcy said, a smile touching her mouth. "That's great. What's her name?"

"Diane Littleton," he said. "She's a doctor at the downtown hospital."

"Wow," Marcy said. "A doctor. So your kids will be like, geniuses."

Bryan laughed, but he sobered quickly. "Will you be okay for Thanksgiving? I know Wyatt's family is huge, and I figured it would be okay."

The breath left Marcy's lungs. "Yeah," she said, her voice a shell of what it usually was. "I'll be fine."

"Great." Bryan went on to tell her a little bit about Diane and where she was from, but Marcy's mind raced past everything he said. Her focus was on the fact that she'd lost all of Wyatt's family too. She hadn't seen or spoken to any of them since that last family dinner at his parents' house.

She wondered if she could call Penny and go to lunch with her. The idea sprouted and grew, and she waited for Bryan to stop talking.

"This is all so great," she said.

"I have to go," he said. "But I can't wait for you to meet her."

"I can't wait either."

The call ended, and Marcy acted, the way she had when she'd emailed back about the house.

She dialed Penny, a prayer cascading through her whole being. "Please," she whispered. "Please, please, please."

29

Mallery Viera held the phone to her ear, but she couldn't speak. She'd stopped listening to the mechanic when he'd said, "Seven hundred."

There was more to the amount she'd need to come up with to get her car running again, but it didn't matter what numbers came after the seven hundred. She didn't even have *one* hundred dollars to spare on her car.

"All right," she said, utterly defeated. She'd already dropped one class this semester so she could work more, and she was barely at half-time status with the university. At this rate, she'd be lucky to be forty before she graduated from college.

"All right, you want me to start?"

"No," she said. "I can't pay for it. I'll come pick it up." Her mind raced through her options. Maybe she could put the car repairs on a credit card. *But then how will you pay that?* she asked herself.

No, it was better to live off what she made. She'd added another yoga class at the fitness center where she'd worked for a few years now. She had three new clients for personal training. And she was working at the soda shop that night.

Her fingers ached already, because she had arthritis in her hands that made gripping the small scoops, straws, and cups difficult after the same repeated motions. But she needed the money, and she could walk to the soda shop from her modest apartment.

Skyler could come pick her up, so she didn't have to walk home in the dark, and she reminded herself to text him once the numbness wore off.

"Mal," someone said, and she jolted out of her own mind.

"Yeah?" She looked up to find Grant Bellerion standing there. "Another tour?" She tightened her ponytail and put on her game face. She hated that she'd chosen to work at the fitness center instead of going to school fifteen years ago. But, now that she'd been here for so long, she did get a lot of clients, simply because she got first pick of who she tried to sell on a gym membership.

A lot of the guys were jealous of her, because she sold more memberships than them. It wasn't her fault she had curves and *luscious Latina flair*—their words, not hers.

And her boss was happy as long as memberships kept going up and up.

"Yeah," he said. "And someone dropped off dinner for you. I put it in the workroom."

"Who?" she asked, following him out of the back room where she'd escaped to take her phone call.

"Guess," Grant said. "Same tall, dark, buffed out bull rider who's always coming by." He grinned at her. "When are you going to give in and go out with the guy?"

"Okay, first off," she said. "He's not a bull rider. Second, he's never asked me out. We're just friends."

"Oh, it's cute how you think so." Grant laughed and held the door for her. The noise from the gym assaulted her on first contact, and Mal worked to put a smile on her face. "Trust me when I say he's interested."

"What makes you think so?" She spied the people waiting for a tour. An elderly couple. Perfect. Her curves and tight muscles wouldn't matter, and she could almost guarantee a sale. Older people loved her, and she sent a prayer of thanks up to her deceased Nana for spending so much time with her as a child and then a teenager.

"No guy brings by food and drinks and cookies just because," he said. "He wants something from you." He waggled his eyebrows, but Mal was much too old for sexual innuendo. She forgot that she worked with a lot of people that were a decade younger than her.

"Hello," she said, reaching the elderly couple. "I'm Mal. I understand you want a tour of the facilities."

"Yes," the woman said. "My husband recently had hip surgery, and the doctor said he needs to do something."

"Do you have bikes here?" the gentleman asked, yelling above the music.

Mal smiled at him, his brash nature so much like Pops. "We do," she said. "And we have a quiet room. Should we start there?"

"Oh, my, yes," the woman said.

"What are your names?" Mal said, gesturing for them to go to their right.

"Ethel and Luke," she said.

"Well, Luke, we have bikes here, which would probably be good for your hip. But we also have a dedicated therapy pool, with classes taught by physical therapists who specialize in rehabilitation after injuries."

"Wow," Ethel said.

"It is part of our diamond membership," Mal said. "So that's a couple of tiers up, and we'll get there in a few minutes....." She continued the tour, unsurprised when Ethel and Luke bought two diamond memberships only thirty minutes later.

She pulled out her phone and texted Skyler. *Thanks for the food.* She sent the message and quickly tapped out another one. *And I get off at eleven-thirty. Too late for a ride home?*

Not too late, he said. And anytime. Class is boring without you.

She smiled at the screen, Grant's words swirling

through her mind. She'd known Skyler for over a year now, and she'd never known him to be serious about anything. He was an eternal optimist, in her eyes, and his life was one of luxury and ease. She wasn't sure why he didn't have a job or who paid his bills. She knew he was from Austin, but that his family now lived in Three Rivers. She knew he had six brothers and a bunch of sisters-in-law, some nieces and nephews, and a good sense of humor.

She knew he made her feel safe, and she knew he was an older student like her, though they'd never talked about age. She knew she liked to run with him, because he was fast, almost like he had phantoms chasing him, and she liked a challenge. She knew he was intelligent but didn't want anyone to know.

He hadn't gone out with anyone seriously in all the time he'd been at college, and she wondered if he was as lonely as she was.

Most of all, she knew he was hiding something from everyone, including her. She knew the mere thought of him made her pulse increase, and she started typing another text.

Grant says a guy doesn't bring a woman as many dinners as you have for me unless he wants something. So... what do you want?

Could she ask him that?

"Mal."

She flinched, her thumb dropping onto the send button before she could decide.

"Yeah." She shoved her phone in the side pocket on her leggings.

"I need an override on a monthly charge," the front desk attendant, John, said.

"Coming." She ignored her phone as it buzzed against her leg, because she wouldn't like it if John had his focus on his device when he should be working. She'd check it later.

She refunded the charge, apologized profusely, met with a client, and wiped down all of the treadmills in the theater room before the next big feature showing. Skyler never left her mind, and she finally locked herself in a bathroom stall to see what he'd said.

Haha, he'd texted. I don't want anything from you Mal. I just like being your friend.

The last word sharpened and stabbed her right through the heart. "Friends."

Of course.

Skyler wasn't serious about anything or anyone. Why she thought she'd be different, she wasn't sure.

————

LATER THAT DAY, before her shift at the soda shop, Mal picked up the mail from the front stoop of the apartment she rented. There were actually three converted apartments in the house, and she sorted the mail into two piles and left them for the other tenants.

A white envelope with green stripes caught her eye, and she knew exactly what it was. Her green card application. She'd seen a dozen envelopes like this in the past, and they still made her heart push out the wrong kind of beat.

She didn't open the envelope right away, choosing to get inside and lock the door first. There shouldn't be a problem. She was going to school, she had a job, and she'd finally applied for her conditional green card to become permanent. She'd lived in the US for fifteen years. Everything else in the pile was junk, leaving Mal with just the green card envelope.

She finally opened it, shocked by the bright yellow paper. She'd heard stories of papers like this, and her eyes scanned quickly.

Tears came. "No," she said, the breath leaving her body.

They'd denied her conditional green card upgrade status. Her two years were up.

She had to attend a hearing before an immigration judge, and she might have to leave the country. It was that horror that rendered her mind blank and her emotions spiraling.

She slid to the floor, the bright yellow paper with black, all-capital letters on it fluttering to her side.

She could appeal, but she didn't know what she'd done wrong. She'd thought she'd put in all the supporting paperwork. Why had they denied her? She had a job. She was going to school.

She needed an immigration attorney—but they cost money. Money she didn't have.

What a terrible ending to a stupid day—and she still had another full shift to work. Exhaustion filled her, and she felt like she'd never get ahead. Wasn't that why she'd come to America in the first place? To find a different life than the one her parents and siblings had in Mexico?

And what had she been doing with her precious time? Selling gym memberships.

Shame filled her, and she felt even more ridiculous as she tilted her head toward the ceiling and said, "Dear Lord, help me."

She hadn't prayed out loud in years, and most of the time, God wasn't anywhere near her heart or mind. So why she'd thought to pray tonight, she wasn't sure. But she needed help, and she had no one to turn to.

She wasn't sure how long she sat on the floor in her rundown kitchen.

"Mal?"

She perked up with the addition of Skyler's voice to her life. He appeared at the corner, concern on his face. Relief crossed his fine features, but Mal couldn't speak. The appearance of him in her apartment—somewhere he'd only stood outside of—felt like a direct answer to her earlier plea.

"There you are." He knelt in front of her. "What's going on? Are you hurt? Why didn't you go to work?"

She just shook her head, her face cracking from all the

dried tears. She didn't want to tell him. Didn't want him to see the yellow paper.

"Mal." He put his hand on her shoulder. "You're scaring me."

With numb fingers, she picked up the yellow paper and handed it to him. He kept his eyes on hers for an extra beat, and then he looked down at it.

"Oh." He exhaled the same way she had earlier, and he balled up the paper in one fist. "Come on. Let's get you up. This calls for ice cream."

She protested when he put his hands on her body, though she'd dreamed of holding his hand. Kissing him. Spending time with him that extended beyond the careful box of friendship he'd put her in.

"I don't want ice cream," she said, finally getting her voice to work. Her foot slipped on another piece of mail that had fallen to the floor when she had, and Skyler steadied her, pressing her into the counter behind them.

Time froze, and Mal looked up into those dark eyes that had sparked attraction at her before. Maybe he didn't feel it too. Maybe he was just better at hiding his feelings. Maybe she should just kiss him and get it out of the way.

She did that, practically lunging at him and matching her mouth to his. A strangled sound came from his throat, but Mal slid her hands up his arms to his face, and his surprise softened into acceptance.

And then he was kissing her back. *Really* kissing her

back, one hand burning into her hip and the other burying itself into her hair as he kissed her, and kissed her, and kissed her.

30

Skyler had lost his blasted mind. And now he was on a runaway train called Kissing Mal Felt Great, and he couldn't stop.

She was the one who finally got control of herself and broke the kiss she'd started. "Sorry," she said. "I'm sorry. I don't know what that was. I'm just all over the place today." She squirmed away from him, and Skyler stood panting at the counter, unable to move.

"I missed my shift. Did I lose my job?" She gave a startled cry, swiped up her purse, and headed for the front door. "I have to call Hillstone."

"Mal," he said, finally gaining some reason to his brain. "Wait."

"I can't wait. I'm an hour late for work."

"Hillstone called me," he said. "When you didn't show up. He said he hoped you were okay, and not to worry about coming in." Why couldn't he look anywhere but at her mouth? Why did he want to kiss her again?

And not just kiss her but take her down that short hall to her bedroom and show her he could make this day better for her. His mother would be so disappointed he had thoughts like that, not that he'd ever acted on them.

But he still felt like there was something wrong with him for wanting Mal as much as he did.

"Hillstone called you?" She seemed frantic, looking from him to her phone and back.

"Yeah," he said. "And you're a lot more than an hour late. More like three hours. He's really worried about you."

"I'll call him." She lifted the phone to her ear and looked somewhere past Skyler. Foolishness filled him, when only a few minutes ago he'd been worried about Mal too. It wasn't like her not to be exactly where she said she'd be, exactly when she said she'd be there.

He knew she worked too hard, but he also knew she had to. She had no financial support from her family back in Mexico, and she'd been working to support herself, pay her tuition, keep her car running, and pay her bills by herself. She'd recently gotten the job at Sips, and he hated watching her work herself into the ground.

He looked around her apartment, where she'd never invited him, and he wanted to buy the house and bulldoze it. People shouldn't live like this, with peeling walls and threadbare carpet. Especially Mal.

He wasn't exactly sure when Mal had gone from friend

to love interest, but it had definitely happened. And before she'd thrown herself at him and kissed him. The inferno that had started in his core and spiraled out of control after only one stroke of her mouth against his still burned in his gut.

"Okay, thanks," she said, and Skyler looked at her. She lowered the phone, and the general panic that hung in the air seeped away. "I don't need to go in." Her voice sounded like a melody to Skyler, and he fisted his fingers.

That was his physical response to trying to keep his feelings contained. He'd been dealing with them for months, and most of the time, he was in complete control.

Mal looked at him now, though, and Skyler skidded. Every muscle tensed again, but he had no idea what to say.

She sighed and set her purse down. "So, this is my place." She put a smile on her face, and it could've lit up Time Square at Christmas. "Should we sit and talk for a minute?"

"All right." He stepped around the couch separating them and sat. Mal took her time coming over, and she sat on the other end of the sofa. "What are—?"

"About that kiss—oh."

"You go ahead," he said, because he wanted to talk about the kiss too.

"No, you go."

There were too many things to talk about, and he couldn't just blurt out the things revolving in his mind. Could he?

"I was just going to ask you what you were going to do about the green card thing." He gestured in the vague direction of the kitchen. "I mean, it says there's a hearing. Are you going to go?"

"You have to go," she said. "If you don't, it's bad."

"You've been before?"

She nodded, her eyes on her hands now as her fingers twined around each other in her lap.

"So we'll go," he said. "Tell them how you're working two jobs and going to school."

"I told them all that." She shrugged and sniffed. "Well, I only had the one job at the time."

Skyler knew nothing about immigration laws, and he suddenly wished he'd been studying law instead of accounting and business. "Mal," he said. "Tell me what you need."

She lifted her eyes to his, and Skyler felt the heavens open. "Please," he said. "Tell me what you need, and I'll help you."

"Why?" she whispered.

There were so many reasons why, and Skyler struggled to find one that wouldn't give away too much.

You already kissed her like your life depended on it, he thought.

"Because, I like you, and I want to help you." He hoped she understood what he really meant. "Because what just happened in the kitchen, I want to do again."

Heat filled his face, and his heart beat terribly fast in his chest, a betrayal beat against his mind.

He honestly wasn't sure which one was leading right now.

"I need money," she said. "I need to get my car fixed, and I need to hire an attorney." She exhaled and reached up to brush her hair out of her face. Skyler remembered what it was like to fist his fingers in all that glorious, dark hair, and his blood heated again.

"I have a lot of money," he said, very quietly, focusing on the carpet in front of him. And he used it, sure. More than any of his brothers, he knew that. But he still had nine figures in his bank account, and if he couldn't use it to help a friend, what was it all for?

"Okay," Mal said, and his gaze shot to hers.

"Okay? I was expecting you to argue with me." Like she had before. In fact, she'd never let him pay for one thing, not even a soda out of a machine after class.

She lifted both hands in a *what do you expect?* gesture. "I'm desperate." Her voice broke. "I might be deported, and I'll need a car to get back to Mexico."

"I don't want you to be deported."

"That makes two of us."

His mind whirred. He needed an hour in front of his computer. "What can we do?"

"I will meet with an immigration attorney," she said. "If you'll pay for it, I'll be in your eternal debt."

Skyler smiled, because while Mal was certainly in

turmoil, she knew how much he liked saying things like "I'll be in your eternal debt."

"Let's go to dinner," he said. "And talk some more."

He once again expected her to decline, but she stood up and said, "Thank you, Skyler. I'm starving, and I don't have anything to eat here."

His heart twisted in his chest, and the male, overprotective side of him wanted to shield her from everything bad in her life. He put his arm around her and drew her into his side. "You should've told me sooner."

"Told you what?"

"That you needed money. That you were living somewhere like this." Embarrassment filled him. What had she thought of his apartment—somewhere she'd been countless times before as they studied for tests, hung out, watched movies, or had coffee after they'd run six miles?

What a fool he'd been. Though he knew poverty existed around him, he hadn't known *she* was living in it.

She didn't answer, and Skyler took her hand in his as he led her to his truck. Maybe a denied green card was the answer to his prayers, though he hadn't really been saying a whole lot of those lately.

He had been wondering how to transition from friends to more-than-friends with Mal for months now, and he'd done a terrible job at it. He knew better than most that repressing his feelings resulted in an explosion.

And if you get close to her, he thought as he started his

truck and backed out of her driveway. You'll have to tell her all about those bombs in your life.

————

THE NEXT AFTERNOON, Skyler leaned back in his desk chair. The heat blew in his luxury apartment, and he had plenty to eat. His bed probably cost more than Mal's car, and nothing in the world seemed quite right.

He'd been reading about immigration laws, student visas, conditional green cards, permanent green cards, and immigration hearings for the past couple of hours. His mind was full, and his heart beat in a strong rhythm.

And he had an idea.

He'd always said he wouldn't get involved with another woman again, and this was actually the perfect way to make sure that didn't happen.

He needed to marry Mal. They were great friends. He could keep things platonic now that he'd released the sexual tension that had been building inside him for a while.

Then his family wouldn't ask questions. His mother wouldn't look at him with sad eyes. And Mal would get to stay in the US.

He picked up his phone, wondering if she was working that afternoon. He dialed her, a yawn pulling through his chest. They'd been out late the night before, as neither one of them seemed like they wanted to leave the other.

He hadn't kissed her again, and it was fine. He was okay. He could do this.

"Hey," she said when she picked up. "I'm on break and have about six minutes."

"Oh, I only need sixty seconds," he said. "Hear me out."

"Okay," she said, plenty of doubt in her voice.

"I think we should get married," he said. After that, his words rushed in a stream as he explained why and what they could show the immigration judge. "At the very least, they'll give you a twelve-month extension while they look into the legalities of the marriage."

"Skyler," she said, frustration heavy in both syllables. "Those types of marriages rarely work. They see through them."

"Ours will," he said. "They don't know how long we've been dating. They won't know when I proposed. We could've been planning to get married for weeks now."

"I don't know," she said.

"Everyone knows we're friends. Even my brothers know I go running with you. No one will be surprised."

Except him.

Oh, and his whole family. His vision turned white as he thought about showing up with Mal out of the blue and saying, *Hey, everyone, meet my wife.*

Silence poured through the line, but Skyler had said his sixty seconds' worth of stuff. Now it was up to her.

"You know what?" she asked. "I'm feeling crazy today. Let's give it a shot."

Skyler thought about all the things he'd read with just a few quick searches. He knew there were consequences that went all the way to fraud if someone determined their marriage wasn't real.

"Okay," he said. "But it's going to need to happen quickly. Your hearing is the second week of January, and we need to be married and living blissfully together by then."

"Okay," she said.

"It takes three days to get a marriage license in the state of Texas." He took a deep breath. "So, what are you doing after class on Thursday?"

31

Wyatt groaned as his alarm went off. He'd been getting up early, staying up late, traveling, smiling, waving his hat, and signing autographs for two months now. He was in the last leg of his tour, and he'd arrived in Philadelphia last night. Late, late last night.

Really this morning, and he had a set time of five-thirty a.m.

He'd slept for three hours, and all he could do now was pray that the makeup artists at the Digital Shopping Channel could make him look good. He showered, dressed in the most popular shirt of his western wear line, carefully perched his signature cowboy hat on his head, and left his room.

Jim waited in the living room of the suite they shared, and he nodded to the mug on the small dining table there.

"Bless you," Wyatt said as he picked up the mug. He

found a few pills next to the coffee, and he swallowed them with his first swig of the brew.

"It's two hours this morning," he said. "Then we're done for the day. So a nap is in your future. We don't leave for Helena until tomorrow morning."

Wyatt nodded, though he'd read through his itinerary. That had changed about him in the time since he'd left the rodeo. And maybe some things Marcy had said had prompted that change.

He needed to listen more. He could do that.

He needed to sacrifice what he wanted for her. Or others. He could do that.

This early morning call to the set proved it.

No, he told himself. This tour was about him, and him alone. If he'd have demanded a different film time, they would've given it to him. He didn't want to be that person, that beast who "did what he wanted to do," no matter what.

While he rode the circuit, he relied on Jim to tell him where to be and when. And he usually showed up. The keyword there was *usually*, and this time, Wyatt was determined to show himself and his manager that he could well, manage his own affairs.

So he knew what time he needed to get up. He knew where he was supposed to be, and when, and in fact, he'd already checked in for his flight tomorrow morning.

"You should go home for the weekend," Wyatt said. "I can get myself to Helena, and we don't have an event until

Monday night. You could have two nights in your own bed." Wyatt glanced at his manager, and really the only friend he felt like he had at the moment. Even Momma's texts had slowed, and Wyatt wondered if Texas had floated away from the rest of the country.

It felt like it.

"Bertie would like it," Wyatt said as Jim looked at his phone.

"She would," Jim said.

"Then I'll buy you a ticket," he said. "Let me grab my laptop."

"I can buy my own ticket."

"I know." Wyatt got up, a twinge of pain shooting down to his knee. Winter was definitely coming in Philadelphia, which was much farther north than Texas, and Wyatt wished it was him returning home to spend a couple of nights in his own bed.

The problem was, he didn't know which bed that was.

Yes, you do, he told himself. He wouldn't be returning to Marcy's for anything except his clothes and toiletries. His desktop computer in her office. He had just enough time to buy a ticket for Jim, and then they went downstairs to the car waiting to whisk them off to the set.

A woman dressed in an expensive skirt suit met them at the door, all smiles and handshakes. She offered food, coffee, tea, anything Wyatt wanted. She seemed flushed by the time she led him onto the set where they'd film his segment.

"Oh, wow," he said, pausing to take in the display. They'd decked out one of their studios in everything cowboy. And not just cowboy. Texas cowboy—and yes, to Wyatt, there was a difference.

"It's perfect," he said, smiling at Georgia. "Just beautiful." His hats lined the back wall, and the shirts were stacked just-so on the counter. His WW—Wyatt Walker—brand sat in the center of the back wall, and Georgia went on to explain that it would be on the screen the whole time too.

"So you'll do the shirts first," she said. "Then the hats, and we have children coming as well. And then, we'll reveal the belts."

"Do you have them?" Wyatt asked. The DSC had signed a contract with Wyatt to be the first to reveal the new item in his western wear line—belts. They came in black and brown, and the buckle could easily be changed for anything else, including championship buckles from the rodeo.

"They're right over here." Georgia stepped onto the set, and Wyatt followed her. The sight from this side of the camera was much different, as there were no wires or cords, no chairs, no people bustling about.

And boy, were the lights hot, and he hadn't even started performing yet.

Georgia pulled out a box that looked like it had been made with wood, which of course, it was. "That's nice," he said.

"Yes, each belt comes in a signature storage box," she said. "Which you'll sign on camera at least three times."

"Right," he said. "And when will I meet Shelley?"

"She's in makeup right now," she said. "Which is where you should be." She lifted the lid on the box, revealing a black leather belt that Wyatt would've bought for himself whether it was from a celebrity or not.

He whistled, and took the belt out. "And they come in six adjustable sizes," he said, reciting what he'd memorized from the product sheets he'd been given to study.

"That one's your size," she said. "So you'll replace your belt with that one on-air, and we'd love to have you show viewers how to exchange the buckles." She dropped her gaze to the huge championship belt buckle Wyatt currently wore, and when she met his eyes again, he nodded.

"Yeah, I'm prepared for that." Wyatt felt as prepared as he could be, and he followed Georgia to makeup, where he met a blonde named Shelley who would help him through the segment.

An hour later, he stepped onto the set in front of at least thirty people, most of whom wore headsets, carried clipboards, and wore professional clothes. He felt under-dressed in his jeans and long-sleeved shirt, despite his jeweled belt buckle.

"Ready?" Shelley asked, immediately pressing her lips together one last time.

"Absolutely," he said.

"Try to smile," she said, and Wyatt just blinked at her. She may have been in front of a camera for a while, but he'd been playing live crowds for two decades. He didn't need to be told to smile. He knew he appeared to be stand-offish, even a bit tired of the whole show, before it started.

But once it did...Wyatt flipped a switch and his charm and charisma flowed from him. He didn't know how he did it. It just happened.

"And we're on in thirty," someone said. Wyatt looked down at the screens embedded in the counter in front of him. A shelf just below that held a bottle of water, and he reached for it and took a drink.

"Ten," someone said. "Nine, eight, seven, six, five, four...."

Wyatt had been on television before, and when the director's fist balled up, it was ground zero, and he flipped the switch.

"Hello, y'all," Shelley said, almost pouring it on a little too much. "Welcome to this special edition of the Digital Shopping Channel, where we have so many surprises for you today. Many of you know this tall drink of water standing next to me." She giggled, and Wyatt played his part perfectly and chuckled too. "As Wyatt Walker, the winningest cowboy in rodeo history. Is that right, Wyatt. Winningest?"

"That's what they tell me," he said, shooting a grin at her and then the camera. "And we're going to be going through my affordable line of western wear for the cowboys and cowgirls in your life today, as well as revealing a brand new item that isn't available anywhere else."

"That's right," Shelley said seamlessly, and it was a thrill to work with someone with experience and know-how. "But we'll tell more about that later." She gestured to his body. "You're wearing your clothes. Tell us what you have on."

And just like that, his products were front and center. He did all the things he was supposed to do—he signed cowboy hats while Shelley spoke to buyers live on the air, personalizing the inside of the hat bands for their loved ones for Christmas. He smiled and laughed and cracked jokes.

He mentioned the maker of the clothes and hats, two companies that were owned by the same parent company and had a reputation for high-quality items. "So you'll be getting something of value," he said. "Which is important to me. I'm still a working cowboy, and I don't want my hat to let me down while I'm out training with the horses."

He spoke to callers, and when it was time to reveal the belts, he was the one to lift the lid. He changed out his belt and added the new buckle to it.

The two hours passed in a blink of an eye, and with twenty seconds left, he looked right into the camera, thinking of his father, his momma, and Marcy.

"Thanks for bein' here with us," he said, making sure he didn't say "today" or "this morning," as DSC would show this special several times over the next two months as they went into prime shopping season.

"And just before we go, I want to tell you a little about why I wave my hat the way I do after every ride." His throat tightened. He'd never revealed this to anyone before, and now he was doing it in front of thousands. "I started waving like this as a tribute to my father, who gave me everything I have today. It meant *thank you. I love you, Dad.* I knew he was watching, because he watched all of my rodeo runs."

He took a moment to breathe and center himself. "And over the years, it became a wave to my mother, letting her know I was alive and happy and okay. It meant *thank you. I love you, Momma.*"

He swept his hat off his head and held it at his chest. "And then, it started being about the fans, the people who showed up and cheered for me, gave me a piece of themselves by sharing their energy with me as I rode. And so now, when you wave your Wyatt Walker hat, you too can say, *Thank you. I love you.*"

Wyatt lifted his hat up in his signature wave. He moved his wrist in his signature up-and-down move, the hat flapping at the camera. "And now I add my wife to the sentiment, because she supports me in everything, and I couldn't be here without my sweet Marcy. So thank you, Marce. I love you."

His throat felt extremely dry. He continued to wave

his hat, and it seemed to go on for several seconds before someone said, "And we're out."

He lowered his arm and looked at Shelley. "That was a joy," he said, taking her into a hug. "Thank you."

"Oh." She patted him on his upper shoulders. "Well, you're very welcome."

Jim appeared on set, and he ushered Wyatt down out of the spotlights. The switch got flipped off, and Wyatt took the towel and cold bottle of water his manager offered. He wiped his face, and drank, and utter exhaustion overcame him. This was always how his body reacted after such a high for so long.

Outside, two cars waited at the curb, and Wyatt realized he'd be going back to the hotel alone. He grabbed onto Jim, and said, "Thanks for everything, Jim."

"I didn't know that about your hat," he said, pounding Wyatt on the back. "You're such a good man, Wyatt."

Wyatt stepped back, his smile a bit shaky now. "Thank you. I really appreciate that."

"I thought your hat wave was a brilliant piece of marketing to bind you to fans. It means so much more now that I know it was something else."

"It was both," Wyatt said. "The message is always the same."

"Two important messages," Jim said, putting his hand on the door handle. He paused and turned back to Wyatt. He removed his own cowboy hat—one of Wyatt's, of course—and waved it at him.

Thank you, Wyatt.

I love you.

He nodded and allowed his driver to open his door so he could slide in the back seat. Wyatt sighed and pulled his phone out, wanting to call Marcy and say those two messages he'd just given to the world.

He did appreciate her, as she'd given her permission for him to come on this tour, even when she wasn't happy about it. And he did love her.

He flipped his phone over and over, only looking up when the driver said, "It's a pleasure to meet you, sir."

"Thank you," he said. "It's nice meeting you too."

He understood what Marcy meant about sharing him with America, but he had no idea how to fix that.

32

M arcy rushed out of the hangar, well-aware that she had grease under her fingernails still. The hangar was a mess besides, and she vowed to come back after lunch and clean it up.

But it was Tuesday, and she had lunch with Penny every Tuesday. She tapped her phone a couple of times after she got behind the wheel. "On my way," she said into her phone. "Sorry, I'll be a few minutes late."

She didn't bother to check to make sure the voice-to-text feature worked. She sent the text and threw the car into reverse. Penny was used to Marcy running late, but she still didn't want to disappoint Wyatt's mother.

She was aware how odd it was to be sneaking off to lunch with her estranged husband's mother. But she'd called Penny weeks ago, and the woman had agreed to meet her for lunch. The truth was, they got along splendidly, and Marcy felt her mother's spirit when she spent time with Penny.

They'd talked about Wyatt at length, and Penny didn't push Marcy in either direction. She was a good listener, and Marcy felt comfortable telling her almost anything. Her phone chimed several times on the drive to town, and she took a moment in the car to check the messages.

Only one had come from Penny—No problem. I'll get us a table when I get there.

The others were from Bryan, and he once again wanted to know if Marcy needed help getting the house on the market. She decided to call him quickly, and he picked up on the first ring.

"I'm sorry to keep bothering you about it," he said. "I just want you to be able to move on."

"It's okay," Marcy said. "I know I need to do it. I didn't think I was ready, but I am now."

"I can come for the weekend and help with whatever you need."

"That would be great," she said. "This weekend?"

"Yes," he said. "Hey, real quick, did you happen to record Wyatt on the Digital Shopping Channel? I heard he was amazing, and I missed it."

Marcy opened her mouth to respond, but she found she didn't know what to say. No one besides Penny knew she and Wyatt weren't in the best of places. Well, his brothers probably knew, as he'd stayed at Seven Sons for the few days before he'd left on tour.

"I didn't," she finally said. "But they replay stuff all the time. I could probably find it and record it for you." And she needed to watch it for the first time.

Or maybe she shouldn't. She felt like someone had taken a surgical knife and pulled it right down the middle of her heart. And a heart divided against itself couldn't beat for long.

"That would be great," he said. "I'll get a flight and let you know when to expect me."

"Okay," Marcy said, excited to see her brother again. "There's not much left in the house."

"Could you call a realtor and have them meet us at the house on Saturday?"

"Sure," she said.

"I can if you don't want to."

"I can do it," Marcy said, watching as Penny walked into the restaurant. At least she hadn't kept her waiting—yet. "I have to go, Bryan. I'll see you soon."

"Love you, Marce."

Marce.

Her voice caught. "Love you too." She hung up quickly, drawing a long breath. She could do this. She'd met Penny for lunch a handful of times now, and she wasn't someone Marcy feared.

It was the advice she wanted that she didn't know if she could handle or not.

She got out of the car and went into the restaurant,

catching Penny just as the hostess started to take her to a table. "I'm here," she said.

"Oh, here she is." Penny's face lit up, and she pulled Marcy into a hug. "It's good to see you, dear."

"Good to see you too." They followed the woman to a table and waved away the menus. They'd been to this restaurant several times before, and Marcy got the chicken barbecue ranch tacos every time, with the tortilla soup.

Penny got cheese enchiladas, with extra Spanish rice and refried beans. They both got sweet tea, though Penny sometimes ordered strawberry lemonade.

"What's got you shook today?" Penny asked, spreading her napkin over her lap.

"I was just talking to my brother," she said. "He's coming this weekend, and we're going to get my father's house on the market."

Penny's expression softened, and she reached across the table to cover Marcy's hand. "That's got to be hard. I remember when we moved my mother out of her house of fifty-seven years. Boy, I knew then why God had given me seven sons." A smile crossed her mouth, but it didn't stay long as it wasn't meant to be jovial.

"The house is mostly cleaned out," she said. "Wyatt and I did it last winter."

"That's good."

"I just haven't been able to let go of it yet," she said. "It's time. I know it's time." She looked up and into Penny's soft, brown eyes. Eyes that would accept whatever

Marcy said. "I couldn't take down the family photos on the mantel."

"You will," Penny said.

The waitress arrived, and they put in their orders. Once alone again, Penny said, "I wanted to talk to you about Wyatt's birthday."

Marcy's heart bumped painfully for a moment. "It's tomorrow."

"I want to tell him about our lunches."

Marcy opened her mouth, but nothing came out.

"He'll be home in two weeks, Marcy, and you should...." She shook her head. "I'm going to tell him, and I want your blessing. He should know we're getting together. He should know you haven't given up on him."

"Is that what I've done?"

"Yes," Penny said. "That's what you've done. Or rather, what you haven't done."

Marcy needed something to drink, as it would provide a pause for her that she needed to align her thoughts. But their waitress was nowhere to be found. "I want to," she said. "Talk to him. I just don't know how."

"Come to Thanksgiving," Penny said. It wasn't the first time she'd invited Marcy to come for the holidays, and Marcy had initially balked at the idea. She still did, and she shook her head.

"I'm going to my cousin's," she said. "I won't be alone, but I don't want to have a public thing with Wyatt." She shook her head. "I'll figure out how to talk to him."

"Birthdays are a great time," she said. "That's all I'm saying."

Their drinks arrived, and Marcy reached for hers quickly. "I agree," she said. She just didn't know if she had the courage she needed to call her husband and wish him happy birthday.

———

THE NEXT DAY, Marcy woke while it was still dark. Now that it was mid-November, it did stay dark later in the morning, but it was early by any standards. She didn't know where Wyatt was right now, though she could've looked up his itinerary on her phone. He'd shared it with her back when they were still on good terms.

She knew he was ending his tour in Montana, and it would be even earlier there. "Even better," she thought, because she wanted him to start his birthday with a message from her. She wasn't going to steal Penny's thunder and tell him about their lunches, and she tapped out just two words.

Happy birthday.

There were so many more short phrases she could've used. *I miss you. I love you. I'm sorry.*

Her fingers hovered above the screen as her mind whirred. What to send, what to send....

She hit send and let her phone drop to her chest. What would Wyatt do with that text? Maybe he'd call.

Maybe she should offer to call. Maybe she should send all the other phrases.

I miss you.

I love you.

I'm sorry.

Can you call me later?

Can you forgive me?

Can we figure out how to be together and share our lives with the world?

I would love to talk to you.

She felt flattened, as if the world had collapsed on her, pushing all the air out of her lungs. She closed her eyes and focused on breathing.

Just one more breath. Just one more.

Before she knew it, her phone was ringing, startling her out of slumber. Surprise and adrenaline combined in her chest, and she felt new life enter her body.

And when the screen read Wyatt, all of her cells rioted.

"Hello?" she answered.

"Marcy," he said, and nothing more.

She hadn't sent any of her thoughts, but Wyatt had somehow gotten the messages anyway.

"I sure do miss you," he said.

"I miss you too."

He sniffed, but Marcy couldn't imagine the tough, tall cowboy crying. "I'd love to see you when I get home."

"When will you be home?"

"The day before Thanksgiving," he said.

"I'm eating with Savannah and her family. I know your mother is doing something at her house."

"You're not...of course not." He exhaled. "Maybe Friday?"

"Yes," Marcy said. "Let's get together Friday."

"Do you do that Black Friday thing?"

She gave a light laugh. "I think you've forgotten who you're talking to."

He chuckled too, and the sound had been something Marcy had sorely missed in her life. "So no shopping. Lunch?"

"Make it dinner," she said. "I have to fly in the morning, same as usual."

"Dinner it is," he said, sobering. "Thank you for the birthday wishes, Marce. That text meant the world to me."

She nodded, her words stuck in her throat. "Be safe," she managed to say, and the call ended.

She got out of bed and went into the living room. After turning on the TV and searching for Wyatt Walker on the guide, she found a replay of Wyatt's special on the DSC. She pushed the record button, and satisfied that maybe she'd taken another step down the path that would bring her and Wyatt back together, she went to shower.

Then she was going to check her email and see if there were any updates with the construction she'd restarted in Church Ranches.

And she had a phone call to make to a realtor to make

sure she and Bryan could get their father's house on the market that weekend.

Marcy felt like the pieces of her life were finally coming together, and a slip of happiness moved through her. It had been such a long time since she'd truly been happy that she barely recognized it.

But it was there, and as she showered, dressed, and got herself up into the sky to begin her day's work, she reflected on the times she'd been the happiest over the past few years.

They all had Wyatt Walker in them, and she knew then that she needed to get him back.

33

Micah sat at the counter in the homestead, the lights brightening the night. With Wyatt on tour, and Jeremiah and Whitney new parents, Micah often had the homestead to himself after nine p.m.

And he cherished those times, because he had a glimpse of what his life could be if he moved out of the homestead. He'd never wanted to do that before, but he'd just broken up with Simone, after another four months where she didn't want anyone to know they were seeing each other.

And frankly, he'd had enough. He didn't understand why she didn't want her sisters to know—both of them were married to Walkers!

The only thing Micah could come up with, but Simone would not admit to, was that she was embarrassed to be with him. And he didn't need that in his life, thank you very much.

He'd spent a couple of years with a woman who wanted him to be more than he already was, do more, make more money. Stephanie had really only warmed to him once he'd inherited his money from his father, and Micah had immediately started distancing himself from her then.

It had taken a while, because he'd loved Stephanie, and if she hadn't been so concerned with his status in Temple, he'd probably have married her long before the inheritance.

His phone chimed, but it only added to his surliness. Thanksgiving was next week, and he couldn't wait for Wyatt to return. He needed someone to talk to face-to-face, as Wyatt was busy, Skyler had basically disappeared, and Micah's older brothers now had wives and families occupying their time.

They'd come to his rescue should he need them. He knew that. They loved him; he loved them.

But he needed someone to hash things out with that wasn't distracted by a wailing baby, a pregnant mare, or texts from his wife. Micah didn't blame Jeremiah or Liam for those things. Life changed. Things shifted. He knew that. Being the youngest, he'd seen it over and over throughout his life.

Just when he'd arrive at a station, Rhett, Jeremiah, and

the twins would leave it. He understood it, but he sure did miss Wyatt keenly in moments like this.

The text bore his mother's label, and Micah swiped it open to read it. *Dinner at three next Thursday. Food assignments are as follows:*

Micah scanned the list, knowing his mother could easily make everything on the list. She simply liked it when everyone had something to bring. The wives asked anyway, and they wanted to be useful. Micah was perfectly happy to eat whatever was there.

He'd been assigned to bring a pumpkin pie, which he could buy from the bakery. No problem.

His eyes caught on Simone's name, and he wanted to take the phone outside and throw it as far as he could. He couldn't get away from the woman, as he'd run into her just that morning as she unloaded her newest acquisition into her shop. He'd been helping Callie with building out a balcony on her and Liam's bedroom.

He'd seen her yesterday at lunch, which Jeremiah had served at the homestead. And in a cruel act of God—Micah was sure—he'd seen Simone at the grocery store. He'd only stopped as a favor to Jeremiah and had literally never been to Wilde & Organic before.

And there was Simone, picking out sweet potatoes while he needed Russets.

He'd ducked back around the end of the aisle and pretended to be completely absorbed in the gourmet coffees until he could be sure Simone wouldn't be in the produce section anymore.

Now he'd have to spend Thanksgiving with Simone. And she'd probably be at the homestead after church in a couple of days too.

Thoughts of leaving Seven Sons and Three Rivers entered his mind, as they'd done before. Just as quickly, he pushed them away. He was done running. He'd left Temple over a woman, and he wasn't going to let another female drive him out from where he wanted to be.

Confirmed, he sent back to his mother, the first one to respond. He usually was, just another reminder that his life had been reduced to odd carpentry jobs around two ranches, and he missed his shop in Temple fiercely.

He folded his arms on the counter and laid his head on them, his cowboy hat pushed to the side. "What should I do?" he asked. "Lord, I could start a shop here. Should I? And what about Simone? Is she embarrassed of me? What do I need to do differently?"

In that moment, he realized that he hadn't given up on Simone. And that only made him angrier.

"Is that the answer?" he asked, his words angry as they filled the cavernous kitchen. "Really?"

He didn't want to pray anymore, not if the answer was going to be, *Change yourself so Simone isn't embarrassed of you.*

He wasn't sure why she would be. He showered, he kept his hair trimmed and neat. He worked out. He had an employable skill which he didn't need to use, because he literally had billions of dollars in the bank. He took care of his responsibilities around the ranch, and he loved his family, the nieces and nephews, all of them.

What wasn't to like?

He got up and went down the hall to his bedroom, ready to stop thinking for the day. But Simone would not go as easily, just like he couldn't seem to physically remove her from his life either.

He finally fell asleep sometime close to midnight, after another bout of prayer, begging the Lord to please let his mind rest for just a moment.

———

THE FOLLOWING DAY, Micah left the ranch in the morning and headed to the bakery in downtown Three Rivers. It was the last weekend before Thanksgiving, and the two grocery stores in town looked incredibly busy. Cars filled the lot, and Micah was glad he didn't have to go there.

He drove past the downtown park, which had holiday banners stretching from tree to tree. At night, all the tree trunks had been wrapped in brightly colored lights to create a festive atmosphere.

White and blue snowflakes stuck out from every lamp-post along Main Street, and Micah actually smiled at them. The brothers had a tradition at Seven Sons to get all the decorations up the weekend after Thanksgiving, and Micah was looking forward to it.

The street became more and more crowded, and soldiers got added to the snowflakes on the streetlights.

He had to park a couple of blocks from the bakery, and he realized what he'd thought would be a quick trip to get a pumpkin pie was easily going to take him an hour. Thinking quickly, he pulled out his phone and called the bakery as he walked toward it.

"Bakery on Main," a woman chirped.

"Yes," he said. "I'd like to order a pumpkin pie for pick up. Two. Two pumpkin pies." He had a lot of people to satisfy with the dessert, and though it wasn't the only one that would be at dinner, it was the most traditional.

"We can have those ready in thirty minutes," the girl said. "Can I get your name?"

He gave it to her, along with his phone number, and he detoured toward a bagel shop. It too was busy, but he only had to stand in line for ten minutes before ordering a bacon, egg, and cheese bagel.

He enjoyed his breakfast, continued down the street, bypassed the line, and picked up his pumpkin pies from the to-go line. Feeling proud of himself for avoiding the holiday chaos, he grinned at the girl there and turned to go.

A brunette stood there, and for a moment, Micah thought it was Simone. He almost dropped the pair of pies he'd just paid for.

But it wasn't Simone.

"Oh," the woman said. "I'm sorry." She giggled and reached out to steady the boxed pastries that bobbled in Micah's hands. She looked at them and then back to Micah. "Pumpkin pie. That's what I'm getting too."

"I can barely stand the stuff," Micah said, smiling at her. She had dark eyes like Simone, and she might be a little too young for Micah, who had moved into his thirties a few years ago. "But my mother gave me an assignment, and I'd rather not show up at all than show up without the pie."

She laughed and said, "You must have a mother like mine."

"I'm Micah Walker."

"Of course you are," she said.

He had no idea what that meant, and the chatter and noise in the shop was overwhelming for him, who spent most of his time in the quiet of the country.

"Excuse me," she said, stepping around him as the line behind him inched forward.

"I can't get your name?" he asked.

"Kayla Wharf." She stepped up to the counter, and Micah couldn't seem to look away from her.

"You're Wyatt's brother, right?" a man said, and Micah looked at the cowboy in the line next to the to-go counter.

"That's right."

"I'm Bennett, and I work with him out at Three Rivers

Ranch." He grinned and extended his hand for Micah to shake.

Juggling the pies, Micah managed to get the job done.

Bennett leaned toward Micah. "And you don't want to get involved with Kayla," he almost whispered. "She's still got a boyfriend, and I'm pretty sure her last name is Walters, not Wharf."

Micah looked back at the brunette still at the counter, foolishness flowing through him. "Thanks for the heads-up," he said.

"Anytime," he said. "Tell Wyatt I said hello."

"I will," Micah said, and he got out of the bakery before he could make a bigger idiot of himself.

———

THANKSGIVING ARRIVED, because Micah couldn't slow down time. He showed up with his pumpkin pies and Jeremiah and Whitney, immediately being overshadowed by the baby as Momma reached for Jonah.

Rhett and Evelyn had already arrived too, and Micah put his pies on the counter where the desserts went.

Tripp and Ivory arrived next, and Momma now had two babies in her arms. She could still direct people to do what she wanted, and she didn't give up the baby boys until Callie and Liam arrived with their family—and Simone.

Momma was finally forced to admit she had to work in

the kitchen, though Jeremiah and Gramma Lucy were there too. Jeremiah laughed with their grandmother, and Micah wished he'd liked to cook. Gramma had tried to teach everyone, but Jeremiah was really the only one who'd been truly interested. It helped that Momma and Daddy had lived with them when Jeremiah was thirteen—the perfect age to be able to learn to cook.

Micah had been five years old at the time, and there wasn't much a five-year-old could do in the kitchen. So he stayed out of the way now, watching those around him.

Wyatt finally entered, but Marcy wasn't with him. Micah alone knew why, and he instantly moved over to his brother's side. "Hey." He gave him a healthy pat on the back as he hugged him. "I've missed you so much around the homestead."

"I've missed everyone," Wyatt said, and just like that, a sort of cheer went up from the rest of the family. Everyone loved Wyatt, and Micah moved out of the way so Rhett could say hello, then Liam, Tripp, and Jeremiah.

"Where's Sky?" Wyatt asked.

"Not here yet," Micah said, sticking close to his brother and lowering his voice. "Anything with Marcy?"

"Seeing her tomorrow," Wyatt said without looking at Micah.

"I hope it works out," Micah said.

"I do too," Wyatt said. He finally looked at Micah, and he saw the despair mixed with hope there. "And Simone?"

"She arrived with Callie," Micah said, his throat closing.

"And the two of you?"

"Nothing to tell," Micah said, still respecting Simone's wishes to keep their relationship a secret. He didn't normally do that, especially with Wyatt or Skyler, but his humiliation was strong enough to keep the secret for now.

The door opened at the same time someone knocked on it, and Skyler came in. "Hey," he said, a wide smile on his face.

Relief filled Micah, at least until he saw the gorgeous woman enter behind Skyler. He looked from Skyler to her, his interest shooting toward the sky.

"This is Mal," he said.

"Oh, the one you run with," Wyatt said, his eyebrows up under his hat band.

"Yeah," Skyler said, glancing at the dark-haired woman. She had big, brown eyes and full lips. Flawless skin, and she definitely looked like she ran a lot. Skyler hadn't been serious about anyone in a while, but he tucked Mal against his side as if they were together.

Were they together?

Micah wanted to ask, but Momma had caught sight of the last son to arrive, and things exploded from there. Skyler introduced Mal around, never using the word girlfriend. He never said anything but, "This is Mal. Mal. This is Mal."

Mal was charming and sociable, and she fit in just fine with the other women there.

"I feel like a black sheep," Wyatt muttered.

"I don't have anyone here either," Micah said.

"Yeah, right," Wyatt said as Simone turned and looked right at Micah.

He froze as if he'd been caught by a police helicopter, and all the chaos of his family fell away.

And he knew then that he didn't want anyone else's name or number. He wanted Simone Foster, and his heart wailed, wondering why she didn't want him too.

34

Momma loved watching Jeremiah work with her mother-in-law in the kitchen. The two had enjoyed a special relationship for three decades now, and they put out some delicious food, if Momma did say so herself.

And she did.

"All right," she said loudly, above the din of her seven sons, their wives, babies, and children. She'd shaken the hand of Mal, the woman Skyler had brought with him from Amarillo, just tickled that he'd come.

He hadn't committed to the meal until the week before, and he hadn't mentioned bringing someone.

"We're ready. Gideon."

Her husband stepped to her side, and a flash of love for him filled her. He's always been right beside her, and she beside him. They'd been together now for almost fifty years, and pure gratitude for the life they'd built together flowed over her.

No, things had not always been easy. They'd lost homes, businesses, and friends. They'd lived with his parents for a year. And they'd had amazingly good times too, with the birth of seven healthy children, a business that had finally taken off, and their years on the beach she loved so much.

"We're thrilled to be here with you this year," he said. "We love Three Rivers, and we're grateful for each of you, your relationships with each other, and that you love and forgive us." He swiped at his eyes, the gruff cowboy getting soft in his old age. "I'll say a prayer, and then Momma and Gramma have instructions for us." He looked at her, but she nodded to Jeremiah.

"Jeremiah does," Daddy said, and he reached up to remove his hat. The other boys did too, and he gave a beautiful prayer for family, friends, and any who needed help.

"Amen," she said when he finished.

Jeremiah gave instructions for the food, and Momma edged over to Ivory, who held five-month-old Isaac on her hip. "I'll take him," she said, because she wanted life to be as easy as possible for her sons and their wives.

Ivory smiled at her and passed over the baby before moving to pick up her plate and start to help her son get turkey and mashed potatoes.

Momma watched Micah, who wore a general air of

unhappiness about him. Her heart ached for him, as he'd always felt slightly left out of the family. With the boys spread out over twelve years, they naturally formed friendships with those closest to their ages. But Skyler had almost removed himself from the family, and she watched him next.

He leaned close to Mal, and the woman smiled in such a way that said she'd definitely kissed Skyler. So there was something going on there, whether Skyler had used the labels and terms or not.

Bless him, God, she prayed. He needs the extra help, and I love him so much.

She usually tread carefully when it came to Skyler, choosing selectively what she sent to him. She only wanted him to feel love from her, never judgment or disappointment, as he'd always put those things on himself without any help from her.

But she felt him moving farther and farther away, and she couldn't help but want to pull him back to her. Hug him close and make sure he knew how much she loved him. How much God loved him.

She watched Daddy give Skyler a tight hug, and she swallowed and pushed back tears. He loved the boys as much as she did, and they often prayed over their sons for quite a long time each evening.

A loud laugh drew her attention, and she looked at Wyatt. Wyatt, who'd shown up to Thanksgiving dinner without his wife.

Of course, Momma knew where Marcy was, but she hadn't stopped hoping and praying Marcy would come to dinner anyway.

"Bless them all," she prayed while pressing her lips to baby Isaac's head. "And help Wyatt work things out with Marcy."

She'd texted him on his birthday that she and Marcy had been having lunch together, and Wyatt had called instantly. He hadn't been upset, but rather...resigned. At least that was what Momma thought. Her most charismatic son seemed a bit dull without the woman he loved, and she desperately wanted him to be able to work things out with her.

She knew they were seeing each other tomorrow, and she didn't need to say anything to either of them. She'd learned over the years of parenting adult children that sometimes she just needed to stay out of their business.

Micah, Wyatt, and Skyler stuck close to one another, and she wondered if anyone else noticed. She certainly did, and her heart ached for the three of them. She'd done the best she'd known how with the boys, and she loved all of them. She was proud of all of them.

"Momma," Wyatt said, noticing her standing there. "Give me the baby and come eat." He effortlessly took Isaac from her, but instead of her going to get something to eat, she latched onto him and hugged him tight.

"I love you, son."

"I know, Momma." He clutched her too, his muscles

much bigger than hers. His personality much brighter. Of all the boys, he reminded her of Gideon the most. He was willing to take the biggest risks. He was the one who put himself out there for the world to love.

"I love you too. Thanks for cooking for us."

"Oh, that was Gramma Lucy and Jeremiah," she said, stepping back. She wiped her tears, because she was so blessed to have such good sons.

She met Skyler's eye and moved over to sit beside him. "Save me this seat?"

"Sure thing, Momma," he said, smiling at her. She knew that smile, though, and it hid a lot of pain.

Help Wyatt, she prayed as she put a slice of turkey on her plate.

Bless Skyler, she added as she ladled gravy over her meat and potatoes.

She glanced up and caught Micah watching Simone. And open the eyes of Micah and Simone so they can find true happiness.

With her plate full, she returned to the table. "I sure do love you boys," she said to Skyler, putting her arm around his shoulders. "Thank you so much for coming."

"I wouldn't miss it, Momma," he said, and she actually believed him.

"Oh!" A cry went up from the table as four-year-old Denise had reached for something and had knocked over her apple cider.

"I've got it," Momma said, jumping up from the table.

"It's fine. Just fine." After all, there was nothing she wanted more than to help those she loved, and as she wetted a washcloth at the kitchen sink, she thanked God once more for her greatest blessings—her husband, her children, and her grandchildren.

35

Marcy flew over Three Rivers, the rest of the town still in a stupor of turkey, no doubt. She herself had eaten plenty of poultry the day before, but she'd still managed to get up before the sun, get to the hangar, and get her fields done for the day.

So thank you, Marce. I love you.

She'd watched Wyatt's special on the DSC, and wow. The man was made to be in front of crowds. She hadn't known why he waved his hat like that, but she did now.

And he summed up everything he felt for the people in his life so easy.

Thank you.

I love you.

As she taxied to a stop and drove the airplane into the hangar, her nerves bubbled beneath the surface. She'd be seeing him in the flesh that day. And she couldn't wait.

She'd neglected some chores around the hangar over the past week or two as she'd finished up preparations on her father's house so she and Bryan could list it for sale. They'd met with a realtor, who'd given her a list of things to do. They'd been easy, but Marcy had taken days to get them done, and the house had finally gone on the market on Monday.

Since it was empty, she didn't need to know every time there was a showing. She'd asked Charles, the realtor she'd hired, to let her know if feedback came in she needed to know about. Otherwise, she just wanted him to sell the house. Earn that commission she'd be paying him.

She walked around the hangar and picked up the blue mechanic rags and put them in the washing machine. As she started it, she thought of Wyatt. He'd often done this chore for her, and she missed him more powerfully in that moment than she had before.

She'd known she wanted him back for a couple of weeks now. They'd texted a little bit since then, but it seemed neither of them wanted to have their serious conversation over the phone. Especially not through texts.

She finished her paperwork, changed the rags to the dryer, and drove home.

Wyatt's big, black truck sat in her driveway, with the man himself behind the wheel.

Her heart flipped and flopped, and she was glad she'd prepared her surprise for him before she'd left to fly. She'd also brought in the holiday decorations from the garage, and she was grateful she wouldn't have to put them up herself.

She pulled into the garage, got out of the car, and turned toward Wyatt. He too slid from his truck, approaching her slowly.

"Hi," she said, tucking her hands in the pockets of her hoodie.

"Hey." He ducked his head and then lifted it to look at her. A smile touched his mouth, and Marcy wanted to run to him and hold him close.

So she did.

He laughed as he caught her around the waist.

"I know it's not fair," she said as she balanced herself against his shoulders. "I've never felt stupider than I have since you left. I'm sorry." She buried her face in his neck, the scent of that cologne and aftershave like coming home. "I'm sorry."

"I am too," he said, gently setting her on the ground. He didn't back up though and kept his strong arms around her. "I've missed you so much."

She held him as tight as he held her, realizing that now that they were together, she wasn't as nervous. He soothed her anxiety, and that was priceless to her.

"Come inside," she said. "I have a surprise for you."

"You do?" He stepped back and gazed down at her.

"And just so you know, I'm so sick of doing the laundry at the hangar. So I need you to come back and do that for me."

He chuckled, and Marcy laughed with him. They went inside, and Marcy glanced at the boxes of decorations, as well as the folder and ring on her kitchen counter. Wyatt almost always settled there at some point, and she hoped he would today too.

She moved into the kitchen, and sure enough, Wyatt sat at the counter, right in front of the ring and the folder. "Marce, what's this?"

"That's my wedding ring," she said, turning to face him. Her pulse bobbed in her neck, but she looked right at him. "I watched your DSC special, and you're an amazing man. I had no idea your hat waving meant those things."

He swallowed, his eyes bright.

"I want to wear that ring again," she said. "I'm in love with you, Wyatt Walker. And I don't know how to share you with millions around the world, but I'm willing to figure it out if you're willing to help me figure it out."

He picked up the ring and twirled it in his fingers. "I'm willing to do that."

Marcy smiled and moved around the counter. "Open the folder."

He met her eyes for a moment, and then did as she'd instructed. Only a few seconds passed while he studied the papers inside, and then he sucked in a breath.

Time for speech number two.

"I want to build a life with you, Wyatt," she said, her voice catching on itself. "And we should build a home together. Not just a physical home, but a home between the two of us. So no matter where we are, if we're together, we're home."

He looked up at her. "You bought the house at Church Ranches."

"Yes," she said. "And they're already building it, so we can't back out."

Dear Lord, she prayed. Please help me build a home and a life with this man.

He looked back at the folder for several long seconds. Then in one fluid movement, he got to his feet, took her face in his hands, and kissed her.

Joy dawned in her soul, and as she kissed him back—this tough, tender rodeo champion. Her husband. The man she loved—Marcy got all of her prayers answered.

"I love you," he murmured. "I love you so much."

"I love you too." She laced her fingers behind his neck and kissed him again.

———

"WE'LL DO the tree in the front window," Wyatt said the next morning. His family got together the Friday and Saturday after Thanksgiving and decorated the ranch and homestead. The twins had already called dibs on the huge oak tree out front, and it was almost done. They'd been out at the ranch for most of the afternoon yesterday, because the oak was such a big job.

Rhett's family had loaded up all the boxes they needed

to spruce up the front fence with Christmas ornaments, garland, and wreaths.

He looked at Marcy. "It's fifteen feet tall."

"So you'll be setting it up," she said. "I'll decorate the bottom half."

He grinned at her as Jeremiah said he and Whitney would do the tree there in the living room. Marcy had never had two trees in her house before, but the homestead could probably hold half a dozen Christmas trees.

Whitney cooed and grinned at her son from a spot on the living room couch, and Micah was just finishing his cup of coffee.

Their momma stood at the stove, humming. She broke her tune to say, "I'll have the wassail ready in an hour, and the mac and cheese will be done then too."

Marcy walked over to her while Wyatt recruited Micah to come work on the front window display. "We have to do the porch too," he said. "And you can get up on the ladder for me. My back can't handle that."

She glanced over at her husband, slightly worried about his back. He'd probably over-exerted himself on tour, and she'd have to ask him about it later.

"Hey, Momma." Marcy put her arm around Wyatt's mother and leaned into her.

"Morning, dear." She squeezed her back and looked over to Wyatt, Micah, and Jeremiah as they walked out the back door. "So you and Wyatt made up?"

Marcy couldn't help smiling. "Yes," she said. "I just told him I wanted him, and I wanted to build a life with him, and I was really sorry." She breathed in the scent of cinnamon, cloves, and hot apple cider. "And it seemed to work."

"That boy has a heart of marshmallow," Momma said with a chuckle. "But he would've taken you back no matter what. He's loved you for a long time."

Marcy knew that, but she'd never get tired of hearing it. Wyatt had said he loved her yesterday, probably a dozen times. In the kitchen. As he took her down the hall to their bedroom and made love to her. When he took her to Musgraves for dinner.

"I need—can someone take Jonah?" Whitney asked, her voice on the heavy side of panic.

Marcy spun toward her and hurried over to her. "I've got him. Are you okay?"

But Whitney rushed away before she answered, making a mad dash toward the bathroom in the hallway behind the office. She retched, and Marcy's concern spiked. Jonah fussed on her hip, and she bounced him. "It's okay, baby," she said. "Mommy just doesn't feel good."

"She's pregnant," Momma said. "She just hasn't told Jeremiah yet."

"And she told you?" Marcy's eyebrows went up, and she glanced toward the front door, toward where the bathroom sat.

"She hasn't told anyone," Momma said. "But she was sick at lunch yesterday too."

"Maybe she has a flu bug."

Whitney came out of the bathroom, and her usually pale skin was a deathly gray color. She gave Marcy a weak smile and said, "Thank you. I'll take him."

Marcy handed the little boy back to his mother and watched as Whitney curled up into the corner of the couch and laid her son over her shoulder, patting his back. Within a couple of minutes, they were both asleep.

"Yep," Momma said. "She's pregnant."

"Jonah is only five months old."

"Jeremiah wanted a lot of kids," she said, smiling. "Guess he's gonna get them."

Marcy saw the men returning, each of them carrying boxes. "They're coming back."

"Okay, don't say anything. It's not our news to tell." Momma lifted a frying pan off the stove and moved over to the sink to wash it.

"Honey, you should see how many decorations these boys have," Gideon said, holding the door for his sons. "We don't need to buy any."

"I'm buying all new stuff, Gideon," Momma said. "In fact, it's time to go. The store will be open by now."

Gideon sure didn't look enthused about going Christmas ornament shopping with his wife, but he closed the door behind Micah and walked over to where she stood at the sink, drying her hands on a tea towel.

Momma gave Marcy one more hug, and then they left. Wyatt had taken the tree down the hall to the front room in the house, which apparently used to be an office that Tripp and Liam had once shared. Now that they both had their own homes, the room acted a bit like a library, and Jeremiah had put a comfortable couch in the room, with a recliner and a tall lamp that shone light down on whoever might sit in the room to read.

"It's a huge window," she said, admiring it. "I think our place will have big windows like this in the front." She turned to Wyatt, who was wrestling with the pre-lit Christmas tree—and losing. "Can we put wreaths on all of our windows?"

"What?" he asked, looking up at her, his cowboy hat askew.

Marcy giggled and stepped over to him to push the box down. The boughs of the tree scraped against the cardboard and popped out. Wyatt went stumbling backward a step or two, a grunt coming from his mouth.

He wore a dark look as he settled his hat straightly on his head. "You're saying we'll have to do this at our house too?" He shook his head. "Can we hire someone?"

Marcy tipped her head back and laughed. "Yes, cowboy billionaire. You can hire someone to hang wreaths on our house."

"Good," he said with a smile. "Now, let's get this tree set up so we can move on with our lives."

"You don't like decorating for Christmas?"

"Not particularly."

"Why's that?"

"I like it when it's done," he said. "I think it's pretty. But I think I might be allergic to this fake pine stuff." He looked down at his arms, already scratching at the little red dots.

"I think you are," Marcy said, surprised. "Well, at least we know you're not immortal."

He looked at her, shock in his eyes. They softened quickly, and he reached for her before she could dart out of the way. "Come here, Mrs. Walker," he said.

She squealed, but she didn't put up a real fight against him. She wouldn't win anyway, as he outweighed her two to one. He kissed her, and Marcy kissed him right back.

"I'm not helping if you're going to make out in front of me."

Marcy broke the kiss and snuggled into Wyatt's chest to hide her face. Embarrassment funneled through her.

"Sorry, Mike," Wyatt said, stepping back. "We won't." He gave Marcy a look that said they'd pick up that kiss later, when they were alone, and she ducked her head again to hide her smile.

"Sorry, Micah," she said. She hadn't been around Seven Sons or the Walker brothers much over the course of the last few months, but she knew there was something bothering Micah.

Wyatt got the tree set up while Micah kept bringing in

boxes of ornaments. Marcy had never seen so many balls and baubles, tinsel and picks, flowers and bows.

"I'll get the lights up outside," Micah said, taking a box out there.

Marcy worked with Wyatt, and an hour later, the tree glittered with hope, brotherly love, and peace. "It's really pretty," she said.

"Let's go see it through the window." Wyatt took her outside, where Micah was looping long pine tree garlands through the porch railing. She followed Wyatt down the steps and to the front yard, and sure enough, looking back at the house, with the lights on the gutters now, the garland in the railing, the wreath on the front door—and the Christmas tree visible in the window—the homestead looked like a lodge right off a Hallmark movie poster.

Wyatt put his arm around her, and she leaned into him. "I love Christmas," she said.

"Me too, sweetheart," he said. "And I can't wait for us to celebrate our first Christmas together."

Marcy couldn't wait for that either. She couldn't wait to start building a new version of home with him, and a thread of happiness pulled through her.

Thank you, Lord, she thought. Thank you for forgiving me. For helping me get out of my own way. For allowing me the opportunity to say I'm sorry.

Thank you.

I love you.

36

On Christmas morning, Wyatt woke next to his wife. That fact made him so very happy, and he took a moment to study Marcy and admire her beauty.

There was so much more to her than a pretty face, that was for sure. He reached over and ran his fingertips down the side of her face. She stirred, and Wyatt watched her wake up, pure peace streaming through him.

"Merry Christmas, my wife," he whispered when her eyes opened all the way.

A soft smile touched that mouth he loved so much. "Merry Christmas, my husband."

"Do you want to make the coffee, and I'll see if Santa came?"

"I want to make the coffee, because you're not great at it," she said.

Wyatt chuckled, touched his lips to hers and kissed

her sweetly. "I want to leave in time to go by the house in the Ranches before we go to Seven Sons."

"Okay." She rolled away from him and sat up on her side of the bed. She pulled a robe over her nightgown and walked out of the bedroom while Wyatt was still in bed. He groaned as he sat up too, knowing he needed to tell her about his back. He feared going to the doctor, because he was worried he needed another surgery.

He stretched toward the wall, going as far as he could. First to the left, then the right. He leaned forward, working out the kink in his back one inch at a time.

"What are you doing?" Marcy called. "I see presents out here, and one of them is huge!"

Wyatt stood up with a smile and pulled a shirt over his head. Down the hall, he saw that Santa had indeed found the Christmas tree at Marcy's house. "Would you look at that?"

Marcy crouched in front of the tree. "It has my name on it." She turned and looked at him, her bright blue eyes dancing with merriment.

"Open it," he said, the faint scent of coffee starting to waft through the house.

"I got you a much smaller present," she said, straightening. "You're a *very* hard man to buy for."

He took her into his arms, enjoying the softness of her body next to his. "You're all I need, sugar."

She smiled up at him, turned back to the tree, and

plucked an envelope from its boughs. "Remember, it's the thought that counts."

Wyatt grinned at her and opened the envelope. It had a fancy certificate in it for a bacon of the month club. He laughed and drew her into a hug. "I love bacon so much."

"Every month for a year," she said. "I'll even fry it up for you."

"I love it. Thanks." He picked up the big present and handed it to her. "Same stipulation. It's the thought that counts."

Marcy smiled while she ripped off the paper. "We never had big Christmases," she said. "I think my parents had money, but my dad didn't believe in a lot of presents."

Wyatt thought of the boxes and bags he'd loaded into the house up in the Ranches. She was definitely going to get a big Christmas this year. He hadn't gone back to work at Bowman's Breeds in the month since he'd been home, and he'd basically spent his time shopping for Marcy.

She squealed as the box became visible. "It's one of those Kurigs!" She danced around the box. "Thank you, Wyatt. Thank you so much."

"There's another one in your hangar," he said. "Then you can have coffee or tea or hot chocolate any time you want."

She looked at him, her smile so beautiful. "When did you have time to take a present to the hangar?"

"Last night," he said. "I may have taken a few things up to the house too."

She laughed, her blonde hair spilling down her back. "I can't wait to see everything."

"It's a big Christmas," he said. "I don't really believe in small holidays."

"You don't believe in small anything."

"Nope." He drew in a deep breath and added, "And not to ruin Christmas, but I think I need to go to the doctor once the New Year hits." He lifted his right shoulder, feeling something pull in his lower back. "There's something not right with my back."

As he suspected, concern and worry crossed Marcy's face, and she came closer to him. "Are you okay right now?"

"I need some pills already," he admitted.

"I'll get them." She headed into the kitchen, and Wyatt let her go. He liked her taking care of him, and he enjoyed their morning together, with coffee and pumpkin bread she'd bought at the bakery a week ago just to make French toast out of on Christmas morning.

With both of them showered and ready, he drove them up to the Ranches, his eye picking out every new detail since the last time they'd come. "That lot next to ours sold," he said, nodding toward the sign.

"Our roof is on," Marcy said. "And look at all that cement."

They came every week to look at the house, talk to the builder, and dream. It was the dreaming Wyatt liked best, as he'd always had a mind that took him into the stratosphere. He'd spent a lot of his life reaching for those dreams, and he'd gotten them too.

But the best thing of all was being married to a good woman and spoiling her rotten, so he really liked watching her open the gifts he'd left for her inside the house. The fireplace was in at least, and he'd piled all the bags and packages there.

"You should've told me," she said. "I would've gotten you more."

"I don't need more," he said.

"Neither do I." She paused, her eyes widening. "Wyatt, did you get me all of this because you think I need more?" She gestured to the soft pillows and downy throws he'd bought her. The necklace and the earrings and the new walking shoes she'd admired a couple of weeks ago when they'd gone to the mall together.

"No," he said simply.

"Are you sure?" She didn't move to open another gift. "Because I don't need more, Wyatt. I really don't."

"I got them, because I like watching you open them," he said. "And seeing you smile. And knowing that you're happy." He nodded to the last bag. "I think you're going to like that one."

She smiled as she reached into the bag and took out the red and green tissue paper. She pulled out the gift, a gasp filling her throat. "Wyatt." She left the professional video camera that would mount to her airplane on the hearth and melted into his arms. "I love you." She kissed him, and this was no sweet Christmas morning kiss.

"There's no bed here, sweetheart," he said.

"Doesn't matter," she murmured against his lips before claiming them again. Wyatt sure did like kissing her—or rather, being kissed by her.

"We'll be late for dinner," he said.

"Skyler will be later."

Wyatt couldn't argue with that, and he kept on kissing his wife.

———

THEY WERE late by the time they showed up at Seven Sons. Even Skyler had beaten them, and he had the same woman with him that he'd brought to Thanksgiving at Momma's.

"Hey, Momma," Wyatt said, giving her a hug first. After he'd gotten home, he'd tried to go to lunch with her and Marcy, quickly realizing the two women needed that time alone together. He couldn't say he wasn't jealous, but he was working on it, the same way Marcy was working on figuring out how to share him with America.

His western wear line had done really well for the holidays, and more than one article about the true meaning behind his hat waving had been published. Wyatt didn't regret revealing what that gesture had really meant, because he believed it was good to spread more love and more gratitude throughout the world.

The house smelled like sugar and salt, chocolate and coffee, and Wyatt smiled at Jeremiah before giving him a big hug too. "Thank you for cooking for all of us."

"Keeps me relevant," Jeremiah said with a smile. "And you barely made it." He lifted his eyebrows as if he knew Wyatt and Marcy had been late because they'd been making love in their new home.

"Slept late," Wyatt said. "My back's been bothering me again."

That got Jeremiah's eyebrows to go down, and he shook his head. "I'm sorry, Wyatt. What are you going to do?"

"About what?" Tripp asked, joining them.

Wyatt took his baby boy from him and said, "I'll go to the doctor in January."

"What's going on?" Tripp looked from Jeremiah to Wyatt.

"His back hurts."

"Just a little," Wyatt amended.

"Are we ready?" Rhett called.

A baby cried somewhere, and Jeremiah turned and searched the house. Other people talked, and laughed, with Oliver chasing Denise as she squealed and ran toward the front office.

Wyatt watched the craziness, and his heart felt like July—warm and sunny and bright. He loved his family. He loved how Marcy had seamlessly integrated herself into the group, and she stood over by the back door with Jeremiah's dogs, Evelyn, Callie, and Simone. They smiled and laughed about something, and Marcy tucked her hair behind her ear.

Mal, Skyler's girlfriend, stepped over to their group, and they immediately made room for her.

Skyler sat on the couch with Daddy, and Wyatt stepped that way. If they weren't going to be eating for a while, he might as well sit down. He'd just sat when Jeremiah said, "Okay, we're ready. Let me grab Whitney, and we'll get started."

He hurried down the hall, returning a moment later with his wife and son. He nodded to Rhett, who got up on the chair as if his voice wouldn't be loud enough to be heard. "We always do announcements at Christmastime. If you have an announcement you want to make, you just step up and say it."

"Do we have to stand on the chair?" Liam asked, grinning at Rhett.

"No," he said, laughing. "And I don't have any announcements, so I'm gonna get on down from here."

Wyatt knew the announcements were generally good news, but he wondered if he should tell everyone about his back. He could sure use their prayers. So he cleared his throat, somewhat surprised the noise hadn't ratcheted right back up once Rhett had gotten off the chair.

"My back hurts again," he said. "If you have some extra time during your prayers, I'd appreciate them."

"Oh, Wyatt," Momma said, coming over and giving him a hug.

"I'm fine," he said. "I am. I don't need to be babied."

"I wasn't babying you." She swatted his chest, and Wyatt smiled down at her, and then shot a grin to Marcy too.

Jeremiah raised his hand and looked at Whitney. "We're pregnant again."

Cheers and "Congratulations!" lifted into the air, and Wyatt loved that his family was expanding.

No one else stepped forward, and Wyatt wished Micah had some news of him and Simone. But they weren't even standing next to each other, and he made a mental note to add the two of them to his prayers.

"That's it?" Rhett asked, pausing. "Okay." He looked at Jeremiah. "We'll let—"

"I have something," Skyler said, standing up from where he'd been sitting on the couch with Daddy and Wyatt. He cut a look to Mal, who came to his side, and then he looked at Momma. He swallowed and shoved his hands in his pockets.

"Mal and I are married." He cleared his throat. "She's my wife."

No one moved, and Wyatt assumed they were experiencing the same numbing shock that he was.

Wyatt

"What?" Momma finally asked, the word made mostly of air.

Mal took Skyler's hand, and they looked at each other. A certain level of anxiety streamed from them, but she smiled, and that softened Skyler instantly.

Ah, so he definitely liked this woman.

Neither of them said anything, which was so like Skyler. He'd said it once; he didn't need to say Mal was his wife again.

His *wife*.

Married without anyone in the family there to see it.

The calm before the storm passed, and then everyone started talking at once.

Wyatt couldn't help laughing, because he knew that Skyler had just been the sixth brother to enter into a fake marriage, and he couldn't wait to find out why.

Marcy joined him on the couch. "Why are you laughing? Your mother is *crying*."

He put his arm around her and put his lips right next to her ear. "Just because we got married in front of a crowd with Momma in the front row doesn't mean it was real—at first. Remember? That's what's going on here. It's not real."

"You don't think?"

Wyatt looked at Skyler, who smiled at Daddy, who shook his hand. Wyatt had had twenty years of experience in front of crowds, faking his way through pain, exhaustion, and annoyance with a smile on his face.

And Skyler could use a few lessons, because Wyatt could see his nerves.

"But hey," he said to Marcy while Tripp and Liam approached Skyler and Mal. "It turned out well for us, right? Maybe he and Mal will make it work."

"Your other brothers have done it too," Marcy whispered. "Right?"

"Right," Wyatt said, pressing a kiss to her temple. "It'll be a good story, though. I can't wait to talk to Skyler." But he wasn't going to do it here, not with Jeremiah trying to get in there and say congratulations.

"I do love you, Wyatt," Marcy said, as if he needed to be reassured right then. "We're not pretending anymore."

He looked at her. "I know, sugar. I love you too." He kissed her quickly and scooted to the edge of the couch to get up. "Now I'm going to go see when I can take my brother to lunch so I can find out what's going on."

As he waited his turn to grab Skyler in a hug and tell him how happy for him he was, he took a moment to send a prayer of thanks to the Lord that he and Marcy had graduated from pretend to absolutely real in their relationship.

———

Keep reading to find out if another Walker brother can get his happily-ever-after in Three Rivers! Can Skyler really settle down with Mal? Or will this fake marriage turn into

Wyatt

disaster? Chapter one and two of **SKYLER** are next!
Keep reading!

Sneak Peek! Skyler - Chapter One

Mallery Viera woke the morning after Christmas, the fact that she had a live, breathing man in bed with her still foreign and strange.

Number one, she and Skyler didn't sleep in the same room in his huge, posh, luxury apartment in Amarillo.

Number two, her feelings for Skyler had her wanting to slide closer to him under the sheets and go back to sleep within the warm safety of his arms.

And that absolutely couldn't happen.

He was doing her a favor, that scorching kiss in her kitchen from weeks ago notwithstanding.

She wasn't going to make a bigger fool of herself.

She and Skyler weren't supposed to be in Three Rivers, but after his announcement at lunch yesterday, they hadn't been able to leave.

His momma was a Southern giant through and through, and Skyler hadn't been able to deny his mother the opportunity to take them to breakfast and "get to know Mal."

Mal had held Penny's gaze, but she'd probably have wilted had Skyler not warned her about the intensity his momma possessed.

And Mal was certain all of their secrets would be exposed at breakfast. Penny was like an FBI agent, and there were as many words spoken in the times of silence as there was when she was speaking.

On the other side of the bed, Skyler shifted, a groan coming out of his mouth. He lifted his head, and their eyes met.

Pure anxiety flashed inside her, but she managed to smile.

"This bed is terrible," he complained.

"It's not great," she agreed. Everything Skyler owned was the finest and most expensive. He hadn't told her how he'd come to be so wealthy without a college degree and within the first thirty-five years of his life.

She hadn't asked.

But the evidence of his money was everywhere, from the huge, brand-new pickup truck he drove to the four-bedroom apartment on the top floor of a downtown high-rise in Amarillo.

Mal hadn't stepped over such luxurious carpet in all

her life. And her bed was like sleeping on clouds and cotton candy and the exhalations of unicorns.

The first couple of nights had been hard for her, but she had a door that locked. She wasn't truly afraid of Skyler. She just couldn't believe the situation she'd gotten herself into.

"So," he said. "What did you think of my parents?"

Mal found the conversation while they lay in bed intimate and sweet. Living with Skyler had been quite different than running with him or being friends with him or laughing while he tried to fold his body into yoga positions while she taught.

He was more reserved. Serious in a way she'd never seen from him before. He seemed to have two sides—the public Skyler he wanted others to see.

And the real Skyler, who didn't really know who he was. The real Skyler didn't show himself to very many people, but Mal had seen him, especially around his family.

"I actually liked them," she said. "And you weren't kidding when you said your brothers are loud."

He smiled at her and propped his head on his hand. Did he find it odd they were lying in the same bed? Just because they had a piece of paper that said they were married didn't mean they really were.

They'd kissed the one time in her kitchen, and then a quick peck four days later when they'd met at the courthouse for their wedding.

"Yeah, we're all loud," he said with a smile. The same smile she'd seen him flash to others during parties, lunches, or other social occasions. "You have to be when you're growing up with six brothers. If you weren't loud, you didn't eat."

Mal giggled and looked up at the ceiling. "Do you think we'll go back to Amarillo today?"

She was very careful not to say home. She wasn't even sure where her home was right now. She needed to get her courage up though, and she needed to start thinking and acting like Skyler's wife.

Her hearing with an immigration judge was only sixteen days away now, and she'd need to be convincing enough to get an extension on her green card.

Skyler had dived into the issue, and he told her some new fact he'd read that day almost everyday. He'd said that the judge would likely set another hearing in the future until the immigration agents could determine whether or not their marriage was real.

"It's usually a year," he'd said.

"But I can't work," she'd said.

"You don't need to work," he said. "I have plenty of money." And that was the closest he'd come to saying anything about the finances.

Mal didn't know what to do with herself if she didn't have school and work. She'd petitioned the judge to be able to continue her classes and her jobs, but she wouldn't know until the hearing happened.

She was slowly going insane, she knew that.

"We have no clothes," Skyler said. "So yes, I'll tell Momma we're going home today."

Mal didn't mind sleeping in her clothes—in fact, she slept in her clothes every night. Skyler had borrowed a pair of basketball shorts from his brother, Micah, and a T-shirt with a horseshoe printed on it.

He was as sexy as ever, and Mal rolled away from him and sat up, hoping he hadn't been able to see her attraction to him.

She wasn't sure why she was trying to hide it. He'd been the one to kiss her, as she reflected on every day. Every single day.

He'd said he wanted to kiss her again, the one and only time they'd talked about the episode, only minutes after it had happened. But he hadn't.

She hadn't known how to bring it up. How to put her hand in his. How to cuddle into him on the couch while they watched movies and studied and went running.

Their lives had simply gone on, but she was now on his lease, and she'd filed all kinds of papers to get her new name on all her legal documents.

"Mal," Skyler said, his voice that quiet, contemplative one she'd only heard a few times now. This was the real Skyler Walker talking, and she wanted to hear what he had to say.

"Yeah?"

"Would you go out with me tonight?"

For some reason, his vulnerable question struck her as funny. She tried to hold back her laughter, but that only made it burst from her mouth in more of an explosion.

He got up and came around the bed, sitting next to her and taking her hand in his. That got Mal's laughter to dry up, because now her heart raced like a champion horse.

He wore a playful smile on his face, and when their eyes met, showers of sparks cascaded down her back. "What's so funny about that?"

"We're married," she said. "What am I going to say? No?"

"You could," he said. "Do you want to say no?"

Mal swallowed, the dark depths of his eyes searching hers. She shook her head. "No."

"Great." His eyes dropped to her mouth, rebounding back to hers quickly. "That Japanese place? Sushi?"

Mal didn't get sushi and vegetable tempura as often as she'd like, because it was expensive. But Skyler didn't worry about that.

"Sure," she said. "I haven't been there in forever."

Skyler nodded. "Awesome. And uh...never mind."

"No, say it," Mal said.

"It's just...we've been married for five weeks now."

"Yeah."

"And I'm fine. I am. I just...." He hung his head. "I'd like to try that kiss again."

Mal's pulse rippled, and an icy excitement spread through her. "You would?"

"Yeah." Skyler looked up and met her eyes. Mal didn't know what to say. She didn't know what to do.

So she commanded her mind to stop trying to figure everything out, and she just acted.

She leaned toward him, and he leaned toward her. In the next moment, Skyler Walker kissed her, and Mal pulled a breath in through her nose.

This kiss wasn't as wild, or as uninhibited, as the one they'd shared in her kitchen weeks ago.

It was just as passionate, and Skyler once again threaded the fingers on one hand through her hair as he kissed her. Mal sure did like that. She liked kissing him.

She simply liked him.

———

"Morning, Momma," Skyler said an hour later, releasing Mal's hand as he stepped over to his mother and embraced her. He dwarfed her, just like all of his brothers did too.

Mal honestly wasn't sure how Penny Walker had carried any of the Walker men to term, especially twins. She was probably five-foot-four at the most, and Skyler could likely lift her up and throw her as far as he wanted.

Of course, he did spend a lot of time in the gym on the bottom floor of his apartment building, as he didn't have a job like most students. He only had four classes, and two of them were throwaways—like floral arrangement and bowling.

His mother laughed as she hugged her son, and Mal wasn't surprised when the woman embraced her next. She'd hugged Mal yesterday too, though her shock had kept her at bay for a few minutes.

"I've got pancakes in the oven," she said, stepping back. She wore a wide smile that didn't seem fake at all, and she put off a warmth Mal basked in.

A keen sense of missing her own mother hit her, and she hurried to put a smile on her face too. She was a lot like Skyler in that she put on a mask to hide how she really felt.

"Smells like bacon," Skyler said. "Oh, and sausage."

"Daddy likes the bacon," his mother said. "It's not my favorite."

"I'm with you, Momma." Skyler smiled easily at her and turned as his father came down the hall. "Mornin', Daddy."

They also embraced, and Mal got a hug from the freshly showered Gideon Walker too.

"What are you two up to for the rest of the holidays?" Momma asked as she gripped a pair of tongs and started pulling the strips of bacon from the pan.

Mal's mouth watered, because out of sausage and bacon, she definitely preferred bacon.

"Just going back to Amarillo," Skyler said, his voice a touch too casual.

"You don't have family, Mal?" Penny asked, glancing over her shoulder.

Mal suddenly realized how hard it was to lie to the woman, and she didn't want to fib anyway. So she said, "My family is all down in Mexico, ma'am."

"We'll go see them in a couple of months," Skyler said.

Penny didn't ask any more questions about that, thankfully, but she did say, "How many siblings do you have, Mal?"

Mal could easily talk about her two sisters and two brothers, and that got them through the setting up of breakfast, the prayer, and getting their food.

The four of them sat down at the kitchen table, and Mal felt a sense of peace she hadn't in a long time. She'd always been comfortable with Skyler, and they'd had a good time together in the two years since she'd known him.

She laughed and smiled, contributed to the conversation by talking about the beaches in Mexico. Penny's face lit up then, as she loved the beach.

By the time she and Skyler left the house, Mal almost wished they could stay longer.

Not really, but almost.

She threaded her fingers through Skyler's, let him open the door and help her into the truck, and then while he walked around the front of the vehicle, she slid over on the bench seat so she'd be sitting right next to him.

He looked at her when he got in beside her, and Mal decided if she was going to be married to this man for at least the next year, she should get to kiss the devilishly handsome cowboy whenever she wanted.

So she did.

And while she knew she was his wanna-be wife, he sure did kiss her like maybe, just maybe, they could have a real relationship...someday.

Sneak Peek! Skyler - Chapter Two

Skyler Walker used to have thirty-five-hundred square feet to himself. Somewhere he could escape the façade he carefully crafted. But within the walls of his own home, he was able to be himself.

Except Mal lived in the apartment now too. And he wanted her there. It just meant he needed a few minutes to himself in his own bedroom as he tried to figure out how to be the Skyler Walker she'd known and the Real Skyler Walker.

Honestly, playing both parts was utterly exhausting. Only a few people knew who he really was, and two of them—Micah and Wyatt—had been texting him all morning.

During breakfast, during the drive home. He'd muted their conversations after telling them he'd be driving for an hour as he and Mal made their way back to Amarillo.

That hadn't stopped his brothers from continuing their conversation without him. Normally, he'd be annoyed at the slew of messages he had to wade through. But he needed their support in this moment, and he sat down on the edge of his bed to read through the string.

Breakfast on Saturday? Wyatt had asked.

Yes, Micah had said. I'm in. I'm going to lose my mind over Simone.

And Skyler can tell us about Mal, Wyatt had said. Sorry about Simone, Mike. What's going on with that?

They continued to go back and forth, and Micah had finally admitted that he'd been the one to break up with Simone Foster, because she didn't want anyone to know about their relationship.

And I'm just not sure why she's embarrassed of me, Micah had ended with.

Wyatt, who had literally been well-liked by everyone for his entire life, went on to tell Micah there was nothing about him she could possibly not like.

Skyler smiled at that. When he wanted to feel good about himself, he could go to Wyatt. His older brother definitely didn't have a confidence problem.

"And why should he?" Skyler asked himself. Wyatt had been a cowboy billionaire even before he'd inherited part of Daddy's money. Everyone in the rodeo scene adored him, and even more-so now that he had his own line of western wear.

He hadn't had a failed business. He hadn't had a

girlfriend steal from him and cause the federal authorities to come asking questions about fraud and embezzlement.

He sighed as his thoughts always seemed to come back to that situation in Dallas. He wondered if there'd ever be a time when he didn't think about all that had happened there and end up angry.

Or if he could possibly ever truly feel happy. He'd experienced some of it at the homestead at Seven Sons, he knew that. The ranch there seemed to have a dome around it that kept negative things out. And Skyler really liked going there.

He thought he was the brother wearing the black sheepskin, but at Seven Sons Ranch, everyone just accepted him. After his announcement yesterday before lunch, every single person had come over to hug him and Mal.

Yes, they'd been shocked. There were definite questions in Jeremiah's eyes, and Momma's, and out of all of them, Micah had seemed the most leery.

But he'd still said congratulations, hugged him and Mal, and not demanded to know the truth.

He'd have to tell them on Saturday, and the thought didn't terrify him. Someone should know. Someone who could help him know what to do.

At school here in Amarillo, Skyler felt like he knew what to do to be liked, to get someone to laugh at something he'd said, to get a woman's number.

But with a marriage to Mal...he had no idea what he was doing.

Saturday breakfast is fine, he said. *Here? Or are you going to make me drive to Three Rivers?*

Three Rivers, Wyatt said. *You're not doing anything anyway.*

Ditto Wyatt, Micah responded. *Amarillo doesn't have anything good for breakfast.*

Skyler scoffed, because that was so false. But he smiled, didn't argue, and said, *Fine. Breakfast at ten on Saturday. No women.*

No women, Micah said.

Wyatt took slightly longer to confirm the female-free breakfast date, but he did a few minutes later.

Skyler showered and changed his clothes, as he'd been wearing the same set for over twenty-four hours now. When he finally opened his bedroom door and went down the hall to the kitchen, he felt like he could face Mal again.

He sure did like kissing her, and seeing her sitting on the couch in the living room, lifting a mug to her lips, actually made his heart lighten and start tap-dancing.

"Hey, pretty girl," he said, bending over the back of the couch and placing a kiss on Mal's cheek.

"Hey." She sounded surprised, and Skyler wanted to kick himself in the teeth. She looked at him, but he turned and went into the kitchen too.

"Why do you do that?" she asked.

"Do what?"

"Pretend."

"I'm not pretending." But he kept his face turned away from her as heat rushed into it. Embarrassed heat. He poured himself a cup of coffee, stirred in sugar and cream, aware that Mal had gotten up from the couch and approached him.

"You've literally never said, 'Hey, pretty girl,' to me," she said, frowning.

"You didn't like it." He nodded and stirred his coffee. "Got it."

"It's not that I didn't like it," Mal said, sighing. "Okay, look, we've got to talk."

Talking. One of Skyler's least favorite things to do.

"Okay," he said anyway.

"I think we rushed into this marriage thing, because of my court hearing." She groaned as she sat on the barstool at the kitchen peninsula. "I've got a charley horse."

"Want me to rub it out?"

"Would you?" She looked at him with a hopeful look on her face, and Skyler smiled. A real smile. One that brought true happiness to his soul.

"Sure, get that lotion you like." He held up one hand. "Wait. I'll get it. Can you get back to the couch?"

"Yeah."

Skyler went into the bathroom she used and found the lotion labeled *Energy*. Skyler could admit he enjoyed the citrus smell of it, with a hint of lavender.

Fine, maybe that was what the bottle said. But it smelled good.

He sat on the ottoman in front of Mal, and she lifted her foot into his lap. He'd rubbed out her charley horses in the past, but there was something sensual about the action this time. He kept his eyes down as he put lotion in his hand and started massaging it into her calf.

"Can I keep talking?" she asked.

"Sure," he said.

"So I know we had a hurry-up marriage. But we've been living together for five weeks, and I feel like I know you less than I did when we were just friends."

Skyler didn't know what to say. She was probably right, because he'd retreated inside his tortoise shell the moment they'd said, "I do."

There had been no honeymoon. They'd been married on a Thursday, and he'd helped her pack and move everything she owned on Saturday.

He'd put her name on the lease. He'd printed all the forms she needed to fill out to get a new driver's license and the forms she should've filed but didn't. He'd done anything he could to make it look like he and Mal had started to merge their lives. That their marriage was real.

He'd read a lot online, and it seemed like everything would be examined, from all angles, and he wanted to leave no stone untouched.

Why?

He'd asked himself that question a million times. And

the truth was, he didn't know, other than helping Mal felt like the right thing to do.

"So I think we should establish a few rules," Mal said.

"Okay," Skyler said.

"Inside these walls, we are who we are. We're honest with each other in all things. Anything we're worried about, we get to say. Anything we don't like about the other, we can talk about."

She flicked her foot, and Skyler looked up. "Skyler, you don't have to pretend with me."

Being real was something he longed for, and all he could do was nod.

"We're messy, and sometimes we stink." She smiled at him. "I mean, I can only imagine what your running shoes smell like, and it's not good. And that's okay."

"Okay," he said.

"You don't have to go hide in your bedroom."

Skyler's heart jumped over itself. "Sometimes I need some time to myself after something stressful."

"Fair enough." She gave him another soft smile, and she really was beautiful with her big, brown eyes, all that dark hair, and her olive skin. "But you don't have to then come out and be fake with me."

"What if I think you're pretty?" Skyler kept his hands moving along her calf, up and down and around. Mal *was* pretty—more than pretty. Beautiful.

"Do you?"

"Yes." He looked at her. "I might be out of my mind

here, Mal. But I really like you. I fought against a relationship with you for a long time, because well, just because."

"You're thirty-five," she said. "You've had girlfriends before."

"Yeah." He cleared his throat. "And I'm not really interested in love and marriage." In fact, he pretty much thought they were both fake. Unattainable.

"Oh."

"I mean, I wasn't," he said. "So I never asked you out. I never let myself do more than think you were beautiful and run with you and text you."

"Do you think you could change how you feel about love and marriage?"

Skyler wanted to. His whole soul ached to be able to feel normally about women again. Maybe with Mal....

He could only nod.

"Okay," she said. "For full disclosure, I've had a crush on you for months now, even before you offered to solve my problems and support me through this." She ducked her head and tucked her hair, and a powerful satisfaction moved through Skyler.

"Thanks for telling me," he said. "I like you too, in case you haven't figured that out."

"I figured." She grinned at him. "When you asked me out while we were lying in bed this morning."

He chuckled. "There's so much about this that's awkward, isn't there?"

"Not if we don't want it to be." She leaned forward. "And Sky, I don't want it to be."

"Me either," he said, still massaging her calf. "I'm going to breakfast with my brothers on Saturday."

"Oh? What are you going to tell them?"

"The truth," he said. "I think they could help me."

A panicked look marched across her face. "Skyler, I don't think that's wise. You said the immigration agents would interview family and friends."

His morals began to battle. He didn't want his brothers to have to lie for him. He didn't want to lie to them.

"I think we need all the love and support we can get," he said, trying to search for the right thing to do. Maybe his gut would tell him. But Skyler knew it wasn't his gut that talked to him. His momma would be downright mortified if she knew he'd given God's glory to his gut.

Skyler was mortified at that too.

He dropped his eyes back to her slender leg, trying to work through how he felt. It was impossible. Not something he could do in a few minutes.

"I don't think that's wise," she said, gently pulling her foot back. "My leg feels much better. Thank you, Sky."

He lifted his eyes to hers. "I like it when you call me Sky."

Mal slid forward and touched her lips to his in a sweet kiss. "Just think about Saturday, okay? You're smart, and I trust you."

Skyler nodded. "Thank you, Mal." He hadn't felt very

trustworthy since Shayla had stolen from him, skipped town, and left him to deal with the authorities on his own.

Bumbling, and shocked, and unsure of what to say, Skyler had narrowly escaped getting arrested. He'd been questioned multiple times, and the FBI agent he'd spoken to the most had given him a card and said, "Answer if I call, Mister Walker."

Theron Oaks hadn't called, thank the Lord above. In that moment, Skyler realized he needed to do a lot more thanking of the Lord above. And talking to Him. Pleading with Him. Finding out what God wanted him to do. Because if God wanted him to do something, Skyler knew the Lord would provide a way.

And he should enlist Mal in his endeavors.

"So," he said. "Let's talk about religion."

"Religion?" she asked.

"Yeah," he said. "Because I have a feeling we're going to need all the help we can get."

———

Read **Skyler** today, which is available in paperback! Get it here by scanning this QR code with the camera on your phone.

Liz Isaacson

Seven Sons Ranch in Three Rivers Romance™ Series

Rhett (Book 1): To save her business, she'll have to risk her heart. She needs a husband to be credible as a matchmaker. He wants to help a neighbor. **Will their fake marriage take them out of the friend zone?**

Tripp (Book 2): She needs a husband to keep her son. He's wanted to take their relationship to the next level, but she's always pushing him away. Will their trivial tie take them all the way to happily-ever-after?

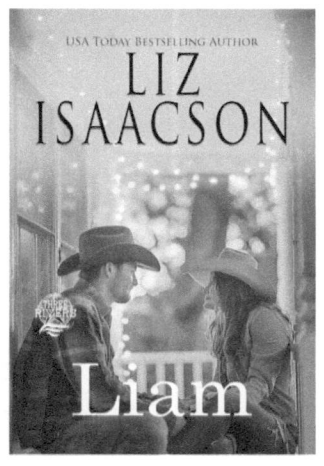

Liam (Book 3): She's desperate to save her ranch. He wants to help her any way he can. Will their invented I-Do open doors that have previously been closed and lead to a happily-ever-after for both of them?

Jeremiah (Book 4): He wants to prove to his brothers that he's not broken. She just wants him. Will a fake marriage heal him or push her further away?

Wyatt (Book 5): To get her inheritance, she needs a husband. He's wanted to fly with her for ages. Can their pretend pledge turn into something real?

Skyler (Book 6): She needs a new last name to stay in school. He's willing to help a fellow student. Can this wanna-be wife show the playboy that some things should be taken seriously?

Micah (Book 7): They were just actors auditioning for a play. The marriage was just for the audition – until a clerical error results in a legal marriage. Can these two ex-lovers negotiate this new ground between them and achieve new roles in each other's lives?

Gideon (Book 8): It's 1971, and Gideon Walker is on the cutting edge of all the technology coming out of Texas. He has big dreams and wants to make something of himself. Then he meets Penny Aarons, and everything changes. He only has eyes for her, but she's got plans and dreams of her own...

Read this origin romance for Momma and Daddy from the Seven Sons series today!

Last Chance Ranch Romance Series

Journey to Last Chance Ranch and meet curvy, mature women looking for love later in life. Experience sisterhood, goat yoga, and a fake marriage against a stunning, inspirational ranch background—and some sexy cowboys too!

Last Chance Ranch (Book 1): A cowgirl down on her luck hires a man who's good with horses and under the hood of a car. Can Hudson fine tune Scarlett's heart as they work together? Or will things back-fire and make everything worse at Last Chance Ranch?

Coral Canyon Cowboys Romance Series

Visit stunning Wyoming for another family of cowboys... The Youngs! The series includes second chance romance, friends to lovers, family saga, Christian values, clean and sweet romance, single dads, equine therapy themes, police dog training, brotherly relationships, return to hometown, fish out of water, and country music stars!

Tex (Book 1): He's back in town after a successful country music career. She owns a bordering farm to the family land he wants to buy...and she outbids him at the auction. **Can Tex and Abigail rekindle their old flame, or will the issue of land ownership come between them?**

Steeple Ridge Romance Series

Get cowboy brothers working together at a horse farm in beautiful Vermont in the Steeple Ridge Farm romance series! With sweet, clean, and faith-filled western romance in a complete series, you'll get a cowboy billionaire, friends to lovers romance, holiday romance, and second chance romance with fun and unique plots (aquaponics, anyone?).

Her Billionaire Cowboy (Book 1): Tucker Jenkins has had enough of tall buildings, traffic, and has traded in his technology firm in New York City for Steeple Ridge Horse Farm in rural Vermont. Missy Marino has worked at the farm since she was a teen, and she's always dreamed of owning it. But her ex-husband left her with a truckload of debt, making her fantasies of owning the farm unfulfilled. Tucker didn't come to the country to find a new wife, but he supposes a woman could help him start over in Steeple Ridge. Will Tucker and Missy be able to navigate the shaky ground between them to find a new beginning?

About Liz

Liz Isaacson writes inspirational romance, usually set in Texas, or Wyoming, or anywhere else horses and cowboys exist. She lives in Utah, where she writes full-time, takes her two dogs to the park everyday, and eats a lot of veggies while writing. Find her on her website, along with all of her pen names, at authorelanajohnson.com